Shakespeare's Twin Sister

Richard Seltzer

Shakespeare's Twin Sister

ISBN 13: 978-1-7367318-7-1
Library of Congress Control Number: 2021944311

Cover Photos: Daniil-kuzelev-Unsplash
Cover design © by All Things That Matter Press
Published in 2021 by All Things That Matter Press

To Princess Mary Orbeliani, who I met in her nursing home in Penticton, British Columbia when she was 98 and I was researching an historical novel about her brother (*The Name of Hero*, Tarcher/Houghton Mifflin, 1981). Simma Holt wrote an article about her entitled "The Princess on Welfare" published in the *Vancouver Sun* in 1972.

Acknowledgments

I want to thank the following people:

Rex Sexton, his widow Rochelle Cohen, Rennie McKinney, and Nancy Felson for their frequent helpful feedback and encouragement

Ardelle Cowie, whose dissertation on Robert Greene's *Menaphon* prompted me to start this novel

My son Tim for his expertise in fencing and fighting in general. He was a great help in making the sword fight in Paris realistic.

Diane Motowidlo

The beta readers at The Spun Yarn (thespunyarn.com)

Gabi Coatsworth for her monthly Writers' Rendezvous meetup sessions and her advice which led me to find my terrific publisher, All Things That Matter Press

Phil and Deb Harris at All Things That Matter Press for their excellent editing

And my son Bob for his continuing support

I'd also like to thank the following books for their facts and inspiration:

All of Shakespeare, which I reread twice in the Pelican edition.

All of Marlowe.

William Shakespeare, A Documentary Life by S. Schoenbaum

Shakespeare: The Biography by Peter Ackroyd

Will in the World by Stephen Greenblatt

A Year in the Life of William Shakespeare: 1599 by James Shapiro

The Year of Lear: Shakespeare in 1606 by James Shapiro

Contested Will: Who Wrote Shakespeare? by James Shapiro

The Reckoning: The Murder of Christopher Marlowe by Charles Nicholl

Shakespeare's England: Life in Elizabethan and Jacobean Times by R. E. Pritchard

Life in Renaissance France by Lucien Febvre

Prologue: The Princess on Welfare

Thursday, January 15, 1987

It was Thursday, the best day of the week, Kathy's day to play therapist. Her pace was light and brisk as she maneuvered through the winding corridors, past elderly in wheelchairs and others with walkers, and those strong enough to walk gripping the railing to keep their balance. One old lady in particular, the oldest of the old, caught Kathy's eye and raised her spirits. Lettie, short for Leticia, meaning "happiness" or "joy," was ninety-nine years young. She was one of Kathy's patients, the one who above all the rest made her feel her work had meaning.

Lettie refused to use either wheelchair or walker, despite severe arthritic pain in all her joints. She held onto the rail with both hands and shuffled along, steady and determined. Not that she had anywhere to go. Twice a day, she ventured forth into the corridors, for the exercise, in hopes of living another day and then another and another, to discover what continued life might bring of experience and memory, to squeeze the last drop from the still-moist cloth of life. She wasn't done yet. She'd keep going. It was her duty, her God-given chore, and she wouldn't let up regardless of the pain of movement. "Fuck the pain," she would say in Russian, which even after forty years in America was still the language she thought in, her English being an awkward translation of her native thoughts.

Her name was Mrs. McNamee, but she didn't have a drop of Irish blood. McNamee was her married name.

To Kathy, who never knew her mother, much less a grandmother, Lettie was like a great-grandmother. Kathy was fascinated by Lettie as an example of how long and varied a life could be.

Leticia Orlov had been her birth name. Her grandfather, a nephew of one of Catherine the Great's lovers, rose to the rank of general and was made a prince by Alexander II. Hence Lettie, only child of only child, inherited the title of *princess*.

She was a princess by marriage as well. At eighteen, her parents married her to a general who was both wealthy and well-connected. He was a widower twenty years older than she, with half a dozen children from his first marriage, the oldest of whom was older than she was. He was a hereditary prince of Georgia, a cousin of a lady-in-waiting to Czarina Alexandra. Lettie should have been proud to have been chosen by such an important man.

When he died eight years later in the Battle of Tannenberg at the beginning of World War I, she moved from Petersburg to his family estate in Sochi on the Caucasian Riviera, near the beach on the Black Sea. She was twenty-six, independently wealthy, and as long as she remained unmarried, she was free to do as she pleased. It pleased her to swim, to read, and to paint watercolors of the countryside.

After the October Revolution, when a Red army was approaching, she fled by boat to Istanbul and then to Dubrovnik on the Adriatic coast of Yugoslavia. Having left her fortune behind, she taught French at a secondary school, and in her free time painted one landscape watercolor after another, until twenty-three years later, at the age of fifty-three, she met and married Sean McNamee, an American of Irish descent.

Sean was ten years younger than Lettie. He spoke no Russian. She spoke no English. When they needed words, they used French. But they didn't need words very often. They understood one another at a glance. A sailor, he had jumped ship in Dubrovnik, charmed by the beauty of the place and by the beauty of the older woman he saw painting watercolors on the beach. He found work repairing cars. They were married three months later. Then three months after that, he was shot as a spy by invading Italian troops. He was no spy. The fact that he was American made him suspect. When the war ended, that false charge and her marriage certificate enabled her to get a visa to go to America.

Even though she was only married to Sean for three months and had only known him for six, she went by his name for the rest of her long life. Instead of Princess Orlov or Princess Bubnov, she was known as Mrs. McNamee, and forty-six years later, her eyes still sparkled when she heard that name—a reminder of the man who had been the love of her life.

Kathy knew that much from Lettie's roommate, a distant cousin of hers, ten years younger than her—a mere eighty-nine—the path of whose life was equally haphazard and intriguing, but who had no title and no talents.

Even at ninety-nine, Lettie continued to paint, largely scenes of the Adriatic coast from memory. And she could play much of Chopin on the piano also from memory, with accuracy and feeling, despite arthritis that was so severe she could hardly unwrap a piece of candy. Her fingers remembered the music and became young again once they touched the keyboard.

And regardless of her talents and her exotic past, Lettie was special. She could look at you in a way that said she cared about you and every word you said, even the words and phrases that she didn't understand, having never fully mastered English.

Seeing Lettie in the hall—her frailty, her feisty determination— Kathy wanted to do something special for her, to honor her as she deserved to be honored. For months, she had considered calling the *Transcript*, the local newspaper, to ask them to send a reporter to interview "the Princess on Welfare." Now she dared not procrastinate any longer, for Lettie, despite her grit and guts, couldn't have much longer to live.

Bill Greene was the reporter she wanted. She had read several articles with his byline. She had asked a friend who worked at the paper and found out that he was a grad student in English, who was taking a break to decide on a topic for his dissertation. That reminded her of herself, with a Master's in psychology and mulling what she might focus on for a doctorate. And, she had to admit to herself, the photo they published next to Bill's byline was also a factor in her choice. He reminded her of a young Robert Redford.

She reached for the phone to call the paper, but it rang before she could pick up the receiver. It was Maggie, who filled in for Kathy's caregiver duties on Thursdays.

"Come quick!" Maggie said. "Lettie's room. Something's wrong. Very wrong. I can't explain on the phone. You'll have to see it to believe it."

PART ONE: Lettie

1 ~ I am Shakespeare

Lettie's room was at the far end of the facility, in the Arden Wing, and the corridors, as usual, were crowded with walkers and wheelchairs. Kathy proceeded quickly, but carefully, reminding herself that if this were a medical emergency, Maggie would have simply said so.

The overall structure, known as *The Stratford*, consisted of one new building and five Victorian houses linked by enclosed corridors. The lobby, the assisted-living apartments, and Kathy's office were in Avon, the new building. The Victorian buildings all had Shakespeare-related names: Arden, The Globe, Shrewsbury, Verona, and Midsummer. The rooms were designated with letters instead of numbers. Lettie was in Arden C.

The Shakespearean theme was evident everywhere. The lobby, the corridors, the common rooms, and the dining rooms were decorated with pictures from Shakespeare's time or from his plays.

At first, Kathy had doubted that it was a good idea for a nursing home to have a theme like that. But she had learned that it boosted the public image of the facility and helped promote rentals of assisted living units, and it didn't matter to the residents, most of whom knew little about Shakespeare.

In the nursing-home buildings, nearly all the residents had qualified as *destitute* and hence were paid for by Massachusetts Health. Over ninety percent of the residents were women. Men didn't live that long. Lettie had been here for fifteen years. She was now the oldest resident. If she survived to a hundred, they'd hold a ceremony in her honor. There had been only two others in the facility's thirty-year history. That would be an opportunity for another article in the local paper.

Each of the original Victorian houses had a common room with a fireplace, mahogany paneling, high ceilings, and bay windows that looked out on the surrounding woods and gardens. Residents rarely looked out the windows. They focused their attention on the television at the other end of the room.

The bedrooms were packed as tightly as possible, with six feet between beds. Depending on the size and shape of a room, it might hold from two to five residents. Lettie was in a double, which she shared with her cousin.

As Kathy entered the Arden Wing, Lilly, one of the caregivers, was leading Madame Albrand, Lettie's cousin and roommate, in the opposite direction. Madame Albrand was shaking and crying, confused and distressed.

Maggie was waiting anxiously outside Lettie's shut door. She hastened to explain, "Lettie had just returned from her morning constitutional. She had laid down for a nap. I had changed the beds and was bundling the dirty laundry, when I realized Lettie wasn't moving, not at all. She didn't seem to be breathing. You know how there's always a hoarseness, a roughness to her breathing. I thought she might be dead. She looked dead. I spoke to her. I squeezed her hand. No response. Took hold of her wrist to feel for a pulse. Couldn't feel a pulse. I raised an eyelid. The pupil was dilated. Still no response. Then, suddenly, the eye was staring at me, very much alive, surprised, shocked. Then she started flailing at me, with strength I couldn't imagine her having. I'm probably bruised all over from trying to hold her down and calm her. She was mumbling gibberish. Not a word of sense. And she didn't react to my words. I yelled for help. Lilly and Francine came running. Together, we held her down—it took all of us. We restrained her, arms and legs, with plastic ties to the bed rails. Madame Albrand was terrified. She insisted on being moved. She doesn't care if she has to sleep on the floor somewhere, anywhere, so long as she isn't in the same room as this mad woman—her cousin, her best friend."

Kathy opened the door.

Lettie's watercolors were taped to the walls, from floor to ceiling, unframed colorful pieces of paper. As always, there was an easel, with watercolor paints, near the window, with a work in progress.

Lettie, flat on her back on her bed, was mumbling, unintelligibly, looking at the ceiling, pulling at the plastic ties.

"What's she been saying?" asked Kathy

"I don't know. I can't make out the accent. When she freaked out, I held a pocket mirror to her face, thinking it might help calm her to remind her who she is. That's when she started saying whatever it is she's saying. She's been making the same sounds over and over again, like she's trying to scream, but it comes out as a whisper."

"And you can't understand her? You've never had trouble understanding her or any of the other Russians."

"It doesn't sound like Russian. I don't know what it sounds like."

Kathy brought her ear close to Lettie's mouth, with a hand at the ready to defend herself if necessary.

Then she quickly pulled her head back.

"Did she bite you?" asked Maggie with concern.

"No. I think I understood her."

"Yes. Yes. What's she saying?"

"She's saying, 'That's not me. I'm not me.'"

"What the hell could that mean?" asked Maggie. "You're the psychologist. Have you ever heard of such a thing?"

Kathy turned back to Lettie, and loudly, but with sincere concern, asked her, "Who are you?"

Lettie struggled, strained the muscles of her neck, trying to speak loudly, but she only made a faint whisper.

Kathy leaned close to listen, then pulled back with a puzzled look.

"What did she say?" asked Maggie.

"She said her name is Shake something."

"Shakespeare?" asked Maggie.

Lettie nodded and smiled.

Maggie laughed with relief. "Yes, Shakespeare. That must be it. Then she's another suggestible, like Ophelia."

"Ophelia?"

"That happened a few years before you got here. One of our oldest residents started calling herself Ophelia, Hamlet's Ophelia, the one who killed herself. We worried at first that she might be a suicide risk. But she was sweet and calm. Her daughter said she had played that role when she was in high school. We guessed that with all the Shakespeare in the naming and the decoration here, she flipped to the delusion that she was Ophelia. It was harmless. It made her happy. We on the staff and her roommates, as well, played along with it. We all had fun playacting with her. She died peacefully in her sleep not long after that. If Lettie's a suggestible like that, we can deal with it. No need to alert the administration or the relatives. Maybe she'll snap out of it as fast as she snapped into it. But even if she doesn't, we can handle that. No big deal."

Kathy was skeptical, but she, too, wanted to avoid making an issue of this. Lettie's only known living relative was her cousin roommate, who was just as destitute as she was. If Lettie were deemed to have a mental health issue, the State would have her transferred to a mental health facility, where, in all likelihood, she'd be sedated and warehoused. Her life as a conscious caring human being would be over. Kathy wanted to do everything she could to help Lettie come back to herself.

2 ~ Will's Twin Sister

Kathy removed the restraints and spent the rest of the day, her therapy day, with Lettie, talking calmly, reassuring her like you might a dog who was spooked by the sound of thunder. Lettie stared at her silently, then fell asleep, then woke up again, frightened and confused.

Trying to trigger associations that might help Lettie flip back to her old self, Kathy pointed to and talked about the watercolors on the walls around them. And she brought in the cousin and other friends who always sat with Lettie in the dining room and spoke Russian with her. But Lettie showed no sign of recognizing them or of understanding anything they said.

Apparently, Lettie had the same arthritic pain in all her joints. But she seemed to have forgotten the tricks and workarounds that had enabled her to do simple tasks in the past. She made no effort to sit up, much less to stand.

When Lettie spoke, her faint voice sounded different than it had before. It was as if she were relearning to use her vocal cords. She knew the words she wanted to say and the associated sounds, but she needed to learn how to manipulate her tongue and throat and breath to make those sounds. And she had lost her Russian accent. She sounded British, with an antique flavor. Kathy struggled to get used to Lettie's new speech pattern, to get a feel for the rhythm, to recognize when one word or phrase ended, and another began. Lettie seemed to appreciate that Kathy was making a special effort and sought to speak as clearly as she could.

Kathy was puzzled. Normally, the memory problems of the elderly came on gradually, not overnight. And Lettie, even at her advanced age, had shown no symptoms before.

Now, suddenly, Lettie seemed fascinated with her sheets and her nightgown. She stroked them with a look of surprise and wonder.

Seeing that, Kathy put her hands on Lettie's hands and asked, "What's so different? What's so special? These are like all the other sheets you've had for the last fifteen years. Why do you look so surprised?"

"How? How is this possible? What hand could ever weave this?"

"Hand? This isn't handmade. It's just a sheet like any other."

"Not by human hand," Lettie affirmed. "Like so much around me here. Magic."

Kathy laughed. "If we had magic powers, the last thing we would do would be to make sheets."

Then Lettie pointed to the lights on the ceiling and walls, "And light without fire, that, too, must be magic."

"Just plain old electricity." Kathy guided Lettie's hand to a switch on a bedside table. Click and a light went off. Click and it went on again. Another switch. Push and the head of the bed went up. Push again and it went down. Push another button and the foot of the bed went up and down.

Lettie smiled, not as if she understood, but rather that she appreciated the value of such wonders

At lunchtime, Kathy fetched soup and crackers from the dining room. With a spoon in one hand and with the other hand holding Lettie's hands, tenderly but forcefully, she fed Lettie in bed. Kathy kept up a monologue of small talk. Lettie would answer direct questions, in her new faint voice, but didn't volunteer any information about herself, any thoughts or memories.

Slowly, sliding her questions in as if part of a conversation rather than performing tests and interrogation, Kathy discovered that Lettie had no idea of the date, the year, even the century, and couldn't answer any questions about current affairs or history. She didn't know her own name or life history and didn't recognize anyone. But she could count backward by threes or by any other number, and she could remember sequences of five words reliably and sometimes as many as ten words. She could repeat long strings of random letters and numbers. Her short-term memory, which for most people was the first to go, was flawless. Her mind was mature, but not aged. She was extremely quick and alert.

Kathy hadn't tested Lettie before. There was no need for it. But these results were even more puzzling than the failure of Lettie's memory. Old people forget. Their abilities degrade. Sooner or later it comes, inevitably. But old people don't suddenly become as mentally agile as the young. That was counter to the unwritten but obvious law of mental entropy— with advancing age, mental ability always gets worse. But Lettie now consistently performed better on cognitive tests than Kathy could. She was extremely sharp, unbelievably sharp. Despite the frailty of her body, she was a brilliant woman.

At dinnertime, Kathy helped Lettie into a power-driven wheelchair and started pushing her down the corridor to the dining room. Lettie noticed the buttons on the handle, like the buttons on the bedside table, and pushed now one and now another, delighted when the chair went forward and backward, as if she had never encountered such a marvel before. Then Lettie controlled the propulsion and if Kathy hadn't steered her straight, she would've repeatedly bumped into the walls as well as people in wheelchairs and with walkers, not so much by mistake as on purpose, like a kid on the bumper cars at an amusement park.

Kathy guided her to her assigned table, where Madame Albrand and six other friends were already seated. Each of them got up, walked over to her, hugged her, and kissed her on the cheeks, delighted that she was apparently cured of whatever malady had triggered her bizarre behavior that morning. Lettie hugged and kissed back, smiling with a look of wonderment, not giving any sign that she knew who these people were, and not understanding when they addressed her in Russian.

Afterwards, on the way back to their room, Madame Albrand tried to keep her wheelchair even with Lettie's, but they kept getting tangled, to Madame Albrand's annoyance and Lettie's delight. And Lettie stopped abruptly in front of one picture after another—the Globe Theater, the Tower of London, and a black-and-white picture of William Shakespeare. She pointed at each with glee. Fortunately, Kathy was there to minimize collisions, to let other residents by, and keep Lettie on course.

Thinking that perhaps Lettie's trouble understanding might be due to a hearing problem, Kathy cleaned her ears and borrowed a hearing aid from the medical office. But that didn't seem to make any difference.

Madame Albrand shook her head, as a mother might at a naughty son, thinking, "Boys will be boys." She stretched out on her bed with the reading light on and focused on *War and Peace*, in Russian. She had been reading a couple pages of that each night for the last few years.

Maggie stopped by to check on Lettie before going home and found Kathy at the bedside, coaching Lettie, repeating her real name and facts about her real life, hoping to trigger memories, hoping that Lettie had not fallen into the deep dark pit of dementia.

Lettie smiled. She now seemed amused rather than scared, as if she wondered what this nice lady might do next, and what new magical devices she would reveal.

Kathy repeated dozens of times, "You are Lettie. You are Lettie McNamee, Mrs. McNamee. You were born Leticia Orlov, Princess Orlov."

Then she asked Lettie again, directly, like a teacher trying to make progress with an autistic child, "What's your name? Please tell me your name."

Finally, Lettie replied. Kathy leaned closer to hear better, and Lettie repeated, "Kate."

"Kate," Kathy exclaimed with delight. "You remember my name! Yes, I am Katharine and everyone calls me Kathy."

"No," Lettie insisted. "Kate."

"That, too. That could be a nickname for me. You can call me Kate if you want."

"No. Not you. Me. My name is Kate."

"Kate?"

"Kate Shakespeare."

"Shakespeare? You think you are the playwright?"

"Yes. I write plays. I wrote plays. Many plays. Would that I could write again."

Kathy stared, at a loss for words. Lettie's voice was faint and rough, but her words were clear. With communication, there was hope. But how could she deal with this delusion? Maybe she should play along, like the staff had with *Ophelia*, get her to talk more, get a clearer idea of what she believed and then coax her from that fantasy back to reality.

13

Kathy stated rather than asked, "You are William Shakespeare," trying to say that with a straight face.

"Nonsense," Lettie replied. "I'm not Will. I'm Kate."

"Kate Shakespeare?"

"Yes. Will's sister. Will's twin sister."

Kathy put her arms around Lettie and hugged her tight and wept compulsively. She was stumped. This wonderful and creative old lady who she felt so close to was lost in a fantasy world. Lettie's Shakespeare obsession wasn't just triggered by the theme of the nursing home. It was totally bizarre. Lettie wasn't imagining that she was William Shakespeare or any other historical figure or character from fiction. Rather, she thought she was someone who had never existed, not even in a novel, someone who probably no one else had ever imagined. This was unheard of. How could she possibly bring Lettie back from that? And how did that delusion relate to Lettie's new cognitive powers?

3 ~ The Cassette Recorder

The next morning, Kathy brought a cassette recorder with an attached microphone. The microphone could make it easier for Lettie to make herself heard and understood.

"Hello," said Kathy. "My name is Katharine Nashe. Call me Kathy."

She then held the microphone close to Lettie's mouth, smiled and nodded her head.

Lettie leaned forward until her lips touched the microphone and loudly said "Yes."

She pulled back in surprise at the volume. Then laughed, leaned forward again and counted to ten.

Then she took the recorder from Kathy and held it in one hand and the microphone in the other.

Kathy bent down and asked, "Who are you?"

"I am Kate. Kate Shakespeare."

"No," Kathy insisted. "Your name is Lettie McNamee, Mrs. McNamee. You're a Russian princess."

Lettie laughed. "You have imagination," she said. "You should be a writer."

"William Shakespeare died four hundred years ago. He died in the early sixteen hundreds. The year is now 1987. One thousand, nine hundred, eighty-seven."

Lettie laughed again. "Do you mean that I died? Heaven is much less interesting than I imagined."

"You didn't die. This isn't heaven."

"The Lord be praised," she laughed again.

"You are ninety-nine years old."

"No, young lady, you are wrong, very wrong. This body I am in may be that old. But this is not my body."

"Of course, it's your body," Kathy was trying to be patient. "Whose body do you think it is?"

"That name you said."

"Lettie?"

"Yes. That name."

"But that's you."

"No, that is Lettie. I am not Lettie. I am someone in Lettie's body."

"That's impossible."

"Yes. What is cannot be. Sounds like the plot of a play. Thank God I didn't wake up in the body of a donkey."

Kathy sat down on the edge of the bed. She was stumped.

Then Lettie started pushing the buttons on the cassette recorder, like she had pushed the buttons on the self-propelled wheelchair.

"My name is Kate," she said. "*That which we call a rose by any other name would smell as sweet.*"

And the machine said back to her, "*... by any other name would smell as sweet.*"

Lettie was delighted.

Kathy showed her which button was *play* and which *record* and which *rewind*. Lettie caught on quickly, and sang into the microphone:

"Under the greenwood tree
Who loves to lie with me
And turn his merry note
Unto the sweet bird's throat,
Come hither, come hither, come hither."

Then she rewound and played it.

Then Lettie put the microphone to Kathy's face and said, "Tell me about you, Katharine Nashe. Why are you here?"

Kathy played along. "It's my job," she explained, "my first job after college."

"College?"

"The University of Connecticut."

"Ah! You mean that in this place and time girls can go to school? They can learn to read and write without pretending to be boys? They can even go to university? What a brave new world. Would that I had a body like yours. Would that I was at the beginning of my life instead of the end. And what did you study there?"

"Psychology."

"What is that?"

"The study of the human mind."

"Ah, yes. Now I understand why you make friends with me, why you want to spend time with me. You think my mind is strange, and you want to study it. You will make copies of my words with this machine. You will write about me."

Kathy's primary reason for spending time with Lettie was the bond she felt with her. But challenged like this, she had to admit to herself that she had an ulterior motive as well. Lettie would make an interesting case study, might even become the basis for a dissertation.

Lettie continued with a smile, "Yes. You are embarrassed. You want to study me."

"Well, yes," Kathy half-admitted. "For your good, to understand what's wrong with you and figure out how to fix that."

"And for your own good, as well, I warrant. Not that I grudge you that, but I'd rather that you be honest with me. You want to study me. That's natural. I'm a mystery to solve."

Kathy was struck by how observant and perceptive Lettie was now. This was a rare opportunity. Here was a hundred-year-old woman with cognitive abilities that had suddenly improved, who had a bizarre delusion that she was dissociated from her body, that the body she was in was not her body, that she came from four hundred years in the past, and rather than imagining that she was the rebirth of some historical person, she believed that she was someone who never lived, who couldn't have. This was a fascinating, unprecedented case.

With a surge of relief and enthusiasm, Kathy leaned forward and gave Lettie a warm hug. This was the beginning of a great adventure and perhaps the start of a brilliant career.

That's when she noticed Miss Fowler, the administrative director, standing in the doorway. Miss Fowler, while adjusting the hair bun on the back of her head, glared at Kathy and told her, "I understand that you've been spending an inordinate amount of time with this resident, and neglecting your other duties. Do you have an explanation for your behavior?"

Kathy stood up abruptly and delivered an impromptu defense. "Mrs. McNamee is not an ordinary resident. She's a celebrity. In just a few months, as you know, we'll be celebrating her hundredth birthday. And, in the meantime, the *Transcript* is interested in publishing a story about her many talents and her long and interesting life. This could be valuable publicity for the Stratford. I was gathering information for the reporter, recording her memories. I suggested that the story be entitled *The Princess on Welfare.*"

"And when is this reporter supposed to come?"

"Soon. Very soon. I'll be calling today to schedule his visit."

4 ~ Enter Bill

The Stratford, thought Bill. How pretentious. And this assignment was just a publicity ploy. He was ashamed that he had to write such crap. Was this any better than grad school? He was always writing what someone else wanted him to write, and he never had time or energy to write the novels he sensed were in him. He felt his soul was being slowly and painfully squeezed out of him, like it was going through an old-fashioned clothes ringer.

The gate at the base of the hill was flanked by a life-size statue of Shakespeare waving greetings. The lobby had wallpaper that was a map of Elizabethan London repeated dozens of times, and large framed portraits of Queen Elizabeth, Christopher Marlowe, King James. He cringed at the sight of these decorations as he cringed at the sight of flamingos on lawns. Bill gritted his teeth and followed the directions the receptionist had given him to the office of the psychotherapist who had extended this invitation to the newspaper.

It so happened that his specialty was Elizabethan and Jacobean literature. That's what he would research, that's what he would write about, that's what he would teach for the rest of his days if he were to continue his graduate school career. He would stake out a territory and try to call it his own. He'd champion some little-known minor writer, deadly dull, deservedly little-known. What a fate. If he was lucky, given the fierce competition for very few jobs, he might end up teaching at a little college in the middle of nowhere and battle there for tenure. When would he ever find time to write his novels? How long before he would abandon that dream? What character could ever grow in that rocky barren field of his inexperience?

He had a steady girlfriend in college, Amy. She was why he had decided to try grad school rather than hitchhike across the US or Europe after graduation, to seek experience and soak up atmosphere, taking odd jobs when he ran out of money, then moving on. That had been his dream of a writer's life when he was in high school. But instead, he went to grad school to be near Amy, and it was hard to drop out with just an MA when she was going to diligently pursue her PhD. Leaving school had meant leaving her, and he still wasn't sure about that decision. He missed her.

He wondered if his current path was any better than grad school. Writing about PTA meetings and property tax hikes and fundraisers for the fire department and the library, and now this publicity story for an old folk's home. Who gives a damn about an old lady who once had the title of *princess*? What a waste of his talent, if he had talent. He wanted to get this damned assignment over with quickly so he could go home early and once again sit at his typewriter, trying to start his first novel.

It was easy to find the office. There was a Peanuts poster on the door. *Psychiatric Help 5 cents. The doctor is in/out.*

He smiled. A sanctuary of self-deprecating sanity in a world of pretense. He stood up straight, took a deep breath, and knocked.

The door swung open immediately. A tall thin figure appeared in the shadow of bright sunlight from the window behind. "Kathy?" he ventured. She backed away at the sight of him, as if she had been hit by a strong wind. He reached out to catch her before she fell.

He was a few minutes late. She must have been waiting for him. She couldn't be surprised by his arrival.

He held her and she held him a moment longer than necessary.

"Sorry. I must have tripped on the rug," she excused herself.

There was wall-to-wall carpeting, with no noticeable flaw.

Kathy was *lanky*. That was the first word that came to Bill's mind. She was tall and thin, with more angles than curves. She was as tall as he was, and he was five eleven. Her breasts were bite-sized, like Amy's. Her eyes were large, wide open, brown. They drew his gaze to them. Her smile was wide. She had a long face, high cheek bones. Her hair was red. Long legs. Athletic. Aside from her hair, she reminded him of Daryl Hannah in *Splash* and *Summer Lovers*.

She hesitated, as if she had forgotten why he was there, as if she'd like to put her arms around him again and have him put his around her. Then she stood tall, walked around her desk, and sat down. "Bill Greene, I presume."

He nodded with a smile, in no hurry to talk, still enjoying the sight of her. There was no ring on her ring finger. There was no photo of a significant other on her desk or on the bookshelves behind her.

"Kathy Nashe, I presume," he replied. "Any relation to Thomas?"

"Crosby, Stills, and Nash? That Nash is Graham. Who's Thomas?"

"Someone I studied. A contemporary of Shakespeare. *Pierce Penniless, The Unfortunate Traveler*. I could be writing a dissertation about him now, instead of pursuing the noble career of writing about princesses on welfare."

She stared at him and he at her, both with silly but flirtatious grins.

Then she, reluctantly, handed him a thick envelope. "It's all there. I've been taking notes. Here is everything I know about her, along with snapshots of her and her artwork, and copies of everything in her scrapbook. I'm sure you can write your article based on this. I could have and should have just sent it to you."

But Bill was in no hurry to leave, nor did she seem to want him to. Their eyes were carrying on a different conversation than their words.

"I heard that you requested me for this assignment."

"Yes. I read some bylined articles of yours in *The Transcript*. They were well written, and the editor who answered my call spoke highly of you."

Bill chuckled. "Yes, at the office, I'm known as *The Bard of PTA Meetings*. I'm tempted to write the next such report in blank verse, blankety-blank verse. And how did you end up making this request? I wouldn't expect that to be the purview of a psychotherapist."

"The Stratford is too small to have a PR person. I saw the opportunity and took the initiative. Lettie, Mrs. McNamee is a remarkable woman, and I'd like her to get the recognition she deserves. I'm new as a psychotherapist. I got my Master's in psychology last semester. I only wear this hat on Thursdays. Other days, I'm a member of the general staff."

"So, you're only mad when the wind is north-northwest."

"Is that a quote from Alfred Hitchcock?"

"Shakespeare. *Hamlet*, to be precise."

He paused. She paused. The silence was awkward. He didn't want to go before making a connection with her. And she didn't seem to want him to go.

Bill broke the silence with, "I'm sure you've done a marvelous job with your notes and such, but I really should meet the lady and ask some questions and take some photos of her."

"Unfortunately, that could be difficult."

"She's not sick, is she?"

"Not physically. But for the last week, she's been acting peculiar, and I doubt that you can get any useful information from her."

"In what sense *peculiar*."

"Well, you mentioned *Hamlet*. A few years ago, we had a resident who, influenced by the theme of this place, the Shakespeare decorations everywhere, suddenly decided that she was Ophelia."

"Mrs. McNamee thinks she's Ophelia?"

"No. She thinks she's Shakespeare."

"William Shakespeare?"

"No, Kate, his twin sister."

"But Will didn't have a twin sister."

"Exactly."

"Delightful! I must meet this woman."

5 ~ The Ballpoint Pen

The head of the bed was up, so Lettie could sit up, fully supported. The skin of her upper arms, her neck, and cheeks hung loose, as if there were no flesh underneath. Bill stopped in the doorway and stared. He had never seen anyone this old and decrepit.

The cassette recorder was resting on her chest, which once had been her bosom. A line from a sonnet ran through Bill's mind. *Bare ruined choirs where once the sweet birds sang.* She was speaking into the microphone, which she was holding close to her lips. He couldn't make out her words from that distance.

Then she noticed him and turned toward him. Her eyes made contact with his and sparkled, and for a moment he saw in her the young woman she once had been.

Finally, she spoke to him, loudly, with the help of the microphone, *Romeo, Romeo, wherefore art thou, Romeo.*

He replied automatically, *What light through yonder window breaks?*

She laughed and clapped her hands. "You know it! You've seen it. You've read it. Miracle of miracles. Kathy says four hundred years have passed. And people still know those words. Thank you for letting me know. That warms my heart."

As if mesmerized, he stepped forward, sat on the bed, took her hand, and kissed her on the cheek.

"What have you been recording?" he asked.

She pressed rewind, then play, proud that she knew which buttons to push.

The recorder played back; *They were waiting in the shadow of Notre Dame Cathedral when the sun rose. Mercutio arrived promptly, accompanied by a dozen other musketeers who came to watch him make short work of the rude Englishman. Each combatant held a sword in right hand and a dagger in left. They tapped swords and began.*

Bill looked puzzled. He took hold of the recorder, pressed rewind, then played that again.

Lettie beamed at him, delighted at his interest.

"What is this?" he asked.

"The story of my life. This is how I amuse myself. And perhaps my words will be saved and read, perhaps for another four hundred years." She laughed.

"But Mercutio in Paris? Why Paris, not Verona?"

"That's where we fought. The play came years later."

"An actual swordfight? Are you saying that Will Shakespeare fought a duel in Paris?"

"No. Not Will. I can't imagine Will doing such a thing. That was me."

"You?" Bill chuckled. "A woman fighting a duel? That's hilarious. You have such an imagination. Even Dumas couldn't come up with anything that wild."

"Dumas?"

"Alexandre Dumas. *The Three Musketeers*."

"Yes, musketeers. Mercutio was a captain of the King's Musketeers. But I never met or heard of Dumas."

"You've been recording stories like this?"

Kathy interrupted. "I have dozens of tapes she's recorded over the last week. She loves to record her words and play them back. But none of what she has said relates to her real life story, the subject of your article. It's all about her Shakespeare fantasy. She hasn't said a thing that could help me figure out what's wrong with her or how to cure her. What's more, she's lost her Russian accent and no longer understands her cousin and her friends when they speak Russian. And suddenly, her mind is fresh and sharp, I'd even say brilliant. It would make one hell of a dissertation topic, and Lettie has said she wouldn't mind, that she'd like to help me with the research. But if I'm ever to write about this, I'll need to come up with a logical explanation."

"Mrs. McNamee," asked Bill "would it be okay with you if I listen to your tapes?"

"Listen all you like, but my name is Kate. Please call me Kate."

He smiled indulgently. "Kate it is then."

"Would that I had quill and ink and paper. Then I could do a proper job of this. I am so itching to write. I am used to thinking with my hand, my right hand. Maybe I can think with this new hand if I practice. I want to write what I know, before I forget, and before I die, if I can die."

Kathy smiled. "I wouldn't worry about that. We're all mortal."

"Are we?" Kate asked seriously

"Kathy, can you get paper for her, please?" Bill requested. "And a ballpoint pen. And a hard surface that she can balance on her lap to write on."

It was difficult for Kate to hold the pen in her arthritic hands. She passed it from one hand to the other. She squeezed it. She kissed it. She licked it. She pressed the wrong end to the paper. Finally, Bill took hold of her hand and helped her grip it and brought the point into contact with the paper. She was delighted to see a mark on the paper, then waved her hand wildly, making marks with long broad strokes. Bill let go, and she swung back and forth over and over again. When the paper was full of marks, Bill replaced it with a new one. Gradually her movements became more controlled, but still they amounted to nothing—neither letters nor doodles.

Kathy was disappointed. "That was a good idea, Bill. I should have thought of that, instead of relying on the cassette recorder. Before the change, Lettie—"

"Kate! Kate! Kate!" the old woman insisted.

"Yes, Kate. Before the change, Kate had good control of her hands, despite her arthritis. She continued to paint watercolors of the Dalmatian coast. You see dozens of them on the walls here, and there are dozens more in the rooms of her friends. That's another symptom to add to my list, the loss of hand control."

"Wait a minute," said Bill. "Can you do that again?" he asked Kate.

She had made a broad loop. She made another and then another, each time smoother and smaller.

"Kate," Bill exclaimed.

"Yes, Kate it is," Kathy agreed once again, to indulge the old woman as Bill was.

"I mean she's forming letters, in the florid style of Elizabethan England, with broad loops over tiny letters. In grad school that was one of the most difficult tasks I faced, to learn to decipher the handwriting of that day, so different from our own, and with so much variation from person to person. She just wrote *Kate* three times in a row. And now she's writing *S-h-a-k-s-p-r*."

"So, she thinks that's her name and she doesn't even know how to spell it. I'll add that to the symptoms."

"Spelling was fluid in those days," Bill explained. "There are only half a dozen examples of William Shakespeare's signature, on legal documents. And every one of those has a different spelling."

"Next you'll tell me that that is William Shakespeare's handwriting."

Bill chuckled. "No. Of course not. This is Kate, not Will."

6 ~ Bodymates

Bill and Kathy spent three hours with Lettie in her room. Then they took her to the dining room for dinner, just the three of them at a table to themselves, far from Lettie's friends who Lettie didn't recognize now.

Bill brought the cassette recorder and Lettie regaled him with so-called memories of London long ago. She was amazingly creative and entertaining.

After dinner back at her room, Bill shut the door and talked softly with Lettie who was alert and tireless, on an adrenaline high. Mrs. Albrand was a sound sleeper. Kathy watched and listened, hoping for a clue that could help explain Lettie's condition. Bill stayed long after visiting hours.

Bill's persistence was impressive, thought Kathy. He was taking this matter more seriously than necessary for an article for *The Transcript*. Maybe the article had become an excuse. He was talking to Lettie, but his eyes repeatedly wandered to Kathy, to her long legs, to her breasts. There was a bulge in his trousers, and he knew that she knew. When he noticed her eyes aimed in that direction, he put her envelope of notes on his lap to cover it up. She smiled, almost laughed, and he blushed. How sweet. How patient and considerate he was with Lettie. But his staying so long was due to his interest in her, Kathy. He wanted to impress her and wanted a chance to be alone with her as much as she wanted to be with him. She felt a visceral attraction to this tall, fit, muscular man with penetrating blue eyes and jet back hair. In person he was striking. The little black and white photo in the newspaper didn't do him justice

Finally, at 2 a.m., Kathy insisted that they bring this session to an end. As she led Bill through the night-dimmed corridors, she hoped he would say something, do something, make a move, break the tension that both of them felt.

She was normally reserved, cautious, stand-offish. But not now. No way. The chemistry was undeniable, and she was sure that he felt the same.

As they approached her office, he finally took her hand. The touch was electric. Yes, she wasn't deluding herself. He wanted her as much as she wanted him.

She opened her office door, and no sooner did she shut it behind her than their lips and tongues met, and they were undressing one another. The only light was that of the full moon outside the office window.

They were all over one another, hands and mouths, devouring one another on her desk, on the floor. Kathy didn't recognize herself. She had just met this man. She had never acted like this, felt like this, with anyone, not even the college boyfriend she had once thought she was going to marry. But her emotional and physical needs were like a force of nature, like a cresting wave, unstoppable until it crashed on the shore. This was it. This was real. He was the one. She let go with full abandon. This was a moment to remember. This was the moment of her life. As she came, she almost blurted out, "I love you." Fortunately, she restrained herself. She hardly knew him and saying that too soon might sound insincere or might scare him away. Besides, what did it mean? She didn't believe in love at first sight. She didn't believe in soulmates.

But Bill was amazing. At the very least they were bodymates. And what more could anyone hope for?

They spent the rest of the night at his place. She had an apartment mate so it would have been awkward to go there. And there was no question that they needed to continue this in bed.

The next morning, Kathy wanted to call in sick so they could spend the day together. But Bill wanted to get back to Lettie and learn more from her about her supposed Elizabethan life.

7 ~ Reading Shakespeare

Bill brought with him the one-volume paperback *Complete Pelican Shakespeare.* He put it on Lettie's lap. It was too heavy for her to lift and hold. She opened it and turned the pages, carefully, slowly, with religious awe.

"This is a book?" she asked.

"Yes. Do you have reading glasses? Can I get them for you?"

"My eyes are not a problem. My eyes are just fine, thank you. It's the type. I've never seen anything like it. And the paper is so smooth, so thin, so uniform. How is that even possible? And joy of joys, here near the front, is what must be an engraving made from the portrait."

"Yes. That's Will. That's the only contemporary image of him that has survived."

"No, not Will," she chuckled. "That's me. Will didn't have time to sit for a portrait, what with every day performing one play and rehearsing for the next. So, I went instead. I got good use out of mustaches like that over the years, as did Will as well. By nature, he was beardless as a babe. And without a mustache no one would have taken him seriously. We both used the same mustaches, makeup, and clothes. If I had seen the two of us together, I wouldn't have been able to tell who was who. Read to me, please."

He picked up the book and sat down on the chair beside the bed. His intention had been to read to her with her looking at the pages. Now it occurred to him to test her. He'd read well-known passages and see if she knew the lines that followed. With all she seemed to know and claimed to know about Shakespeare, she may have read many of the plays years ago, may have acted in them in high school, in college, or even on the professional stage. Kathy would be delighted if the answer to the mystery were that logical, a delusion with a real-world explanation, that could be cured and described with psycho-babel in a dissertation.

For starters, he turned to *Romeo and Juliet*. She had quoted from that yesterday,

"*Two households, both alike in dignity. In fair Verona, where we lay our scene*"

And she replied, "*From ancient grudge break to new mutiny. Where civil blood makes civil hands unclean.*"

He read, "*Parting is such sweet sorrow.*"

And she replied, "*That I shall say goodnight till it be morrow.*"

He switched to *Hamlet* and quoted, "*I am but mad north-north-west.*"

And she said, "*When the wind is southerly, I know a hawk from a handsaw.*"

He threw out snippets from *Julius Caesar, Midsummer Night's Dream, Taming of the Shrew*. She knew all of them.

He thought he had her stumped with a line from *King Lear*. Then he realized there were two versions of that in the *Pelican*, a quarto and a folio. He had quoted the folio, and when he looked closely, he discovered that her reply was in the quarto. That was disconcerting.

Then he really stumped her with a line from *Troilus and Cressida*.

She apologized, "I don't remember much from that one. That was Will's baby. I didn't have much to do with it. Comedies, tragedies, and histories—those were for me. The ones that were neither fish nor fowl, those were Will's. But don't stop. Read me more. Read me anything and everything from that magic book. And give me that paper again and that quill without feathers, and that board thing to rest the paper on."

"What would you like me to read first?"

"One of the Harry plays, please. The Fifth if you have it. *Once more into the breach ...*"

He read Act I. Then he paused to ask. "What's that you're doing? Are you drawing? Kathy said that you painted these remarkable watercolors on the walls around us."

"Those aren't mine," she insisted, without taking her attention away from what she was working on. "The other lady who was in this body before me did those. Kathy says her name was Lettie."

"And what are you doing?"

"I'm writing."

"But how can you listen and talk and write at the same time?"

"Well, you can walk and talk at the same time, can't you? If I could only do one thing at a time, how would I ever get anything done?"

He read aloud all of *Henry V*, then *Richard II*, then *Richard III*.

"You say you wrote these plays?" asked Bill.

"Yes, Will and I together, mostly me, at least at first, when he had to spend all day rehearsing and acting other plays. It was far too much for one person to do, anyone, no matter how brilliant. I was amazed that people didn't realize he couldn't have done the writing, certainly not all of it. Gullible. No one suspected there were two of him, two of us."

They forgot lunch. Kathy appeared at suppertime and insisted that they all go to the dining room.

Bill was slipping into the habit of treating this woman as if she had actually lived in Elizabethan London and had known William Shakespeare and had helped him write his plays. Hearing him talk that way made her eyes sparkle and encouraged her to volunteer more intriguing details.

"Why did you want to write about history, English history?" he asked.

"I was a dreamer. Will thought it was dangerous doing English history, when these were the Queen's ancestors we were writing about. These flawed and all too human characters, with their lust and ambition, making war and murdering to seize the crown—they were the Queen's ancestors. And her claim to the throne was as precarious as theirs was. Will thought it wasn't worth the risk to write of such matters. But I thought it was far more important doing that than telling or retelling ordinary stories. I thought we could make a difference. I thought that this was a way we could make the world a better place than we had found it."

"You did, you know," said Bill. "Then again, maybe you don't know."

"What?"

"Royalty. Kings and queens. The people lost faith in them. No divine right. The ruler wasn't blessed and appointed by God, but rather was just a man or woman with the same faults as everyone else. Putting a crown on someone's head didn't put that person into contact with God, as God's appointed ruler. A few decades after your plays were performed, the people of England finally believed what you had shown so convincingly, that kings are ordinary humans. They rebelled and beheaded Charles I, the son of James, who ruled in your time."

Lettie or Kate or both Lettie and Kate, stood and hugged Bill, and kissed him on both cheeks. "Thank you. Oh, thank you for these thy gifts. There are no kings in England. Marvelous!"

"Not exactly," Bill tried to explain. "Kings came back later, but with less power. The myth of divine right was gone. And over time they became little more than title and tradition."

"But surely now, four hundred years later, there is no king of England."

"Not exactly. There is another Queen Elizbeth. The pomp and ceremonies of kings and queens continue, but the people rule."

"It is a *hollow crown*?"

"Yes, as you foresaw in *Richard II*."

Kate began, *For God's sake, let us sit upon the ground And tell sad stories of the death of kings;*

Bill said, *How some have been deposed; some slain in war, Some haunted by the ghosts they have deposed; Some poison'd by their wives: some sleeping kill'd;*

And Kate finished, *All murder'd: for within the hollow crown That rounds the mortal temples of a king Keeps Death his cour.t*

"As for America," Bill added.

"America?"

"Where we are now. The continent on the other side of the ocean, newly settled in your day. Here we never had kings, thanks, in part, I'd say, to your plays."

"Enough. I have no need of four hundred years of history."

***

That night, as Bill and Kathy cuddled in his bed, Kathy asked, "You're taking her seriously, aren't you?" She was beginning to wonder about the sanity of this man she was so strongly attracted to, who might become an important part of her life. "How can you take her seriously?"

"It's fun, isn't it? Who would ever have thought? A story like this just dropped into my hands, the story of a lifetime."

"But it makes no sense. How could she come up with such ideas? How could she write so well?"

"Are you kidding? She claims to be Shakespeare's twin sister. For all we know she may have written some or even all of Shakespeare's plays."

"Wake up, Bill. You know and I know, and everyone knows that Shakespeare didn't have a twin sister. And there's no sense in which that hundred-year-old Russian princess could be an Englishwoman who was alive four hundred years ago."

"Oh, you of little faith." He chuckled.

"Do you actually think that what she says is true?"

"Truth is overrated.

"But is there any truth in it?"

"Very little is known about Will Shakespeare."

Kathy repeated, "But could it, in fact, be true?"

"It's possible. Not probable, but possible.

"You mean in terms of history?"

"Yes, of course that's what I mean. You could sum up the facts of Shakespeare's life in a single paragraph. His wife Anne Hathaway was eight years older than he was. She was twenty-six and he eighteen when they married. She was three months pregnant at the time of their marriage. They had three children together. Susannah in 1583. Then twins in 1585. He left town soon after the birth of the twins. Then there were seven *lost years* before he became known in London. He only returned to Stratford and his wife in 1611, when he, at the age of forty-seven, retired as a writer. He died five years later.

"Kate has been mostly telling me about her childhood, and everything she has said has been plausible. It's amazing what she knows about that time. And she knows it, as if she lived there and then. Imagine it's possible for a soul to move from one body to another, regardless of space or time. That's what she claims."

"And you think that's plausible?"

"Try to look at it from her perspective. Imagine how you would feel if you woke up in the body of an arthritic old woman in a place and time that makes no sense to you. Isn't that what writing and reading fiction is all about—imagining yourself in someone else's skin, facing what they have to face? Suspend your disbelief. After all, the history works. And *There are more things in heaven and earth, Horatio ...*"

"*... than are dreamt of in your philosophy.*" Kathy finished the quote.

"This is a great story, a gift from the gods. It would make one hell of a novel. I hope I can do it justice."

"You want to write a novel about this?"

"Of course. With your help and her help."

"And I'm crazy enough about you to go along with that."

8 ~ Projection

Over the following weeks and months, Kathy felt like she was on a honeymoon. As for the dissertation, she was dropping that idea. Lettie's case made no sense to Kathy. She couldn't help Lettie much less write about her. But Lettie had led her to meet Bill, and meeting Bill was the best thing that had ever happened to her, and writing this novel was important to him.

Kathy told Miss Fowler, the administrative director, that the reporter found Lettie's story so interesting that he wanted to write a book about her, and hence he needed to do a lot more research. So, during the day, while Kathy went about her work, Bill was alone with Lettie, recording her words, deciphering her writing, editing and writing and transcribing on his IBM PC, which he brought from home and kept in her room, rather than lug the monitor, CPU box, keyboard, mouse, and wires back and forth.

Most nights, Kathy and Bill went to his place and enjoyed one another. But he often got up in the middle of the night to jot down new ideas.

Bill told his editor he needed more time to research this story. Then he called in sick. Then he didn't give a damn about his job. He had some money saved. He could go for a few months without income. He needed to write this book.

Kathy wanted to spend more time with Bill, at the very least to have a getaway three-day weekend with him. But he wanted to interview Lettie and work on the novel.

Cuddled, basking in the afterglow, Bill asked, "What attracts you to me?"

Kathy laughed, "Your body of course. Your magnificent body."

"Not my soul?"

Kathy laughed again.

"Seriously," he insisted.

"How can you be serious about that?" she replied. "The only people who talk about the soul in today's world do so as an excuse because they don't have the real goods, the thing itself. Love is body opening to body. It's the aim of evolution, the pleasure of being alive. Have you ever seen a soul? Have you ever made love to one? What nonsense. That's what comes of reading too many old novels. Love is a matter of touch and feel and taste. You taste very good, my love. All of you. My flesh wants your flesh, and yours wants mine. That's no mystery. Psychology 101. End of story."

"And you don't think we need to say *I love you* to one another?"

"Of course not. That's just words. You feel what I feel, the chemistry, the full body sensations and the surface touch. Love is orgasm, and we give that to one another in abundance." She kissed him, then cuddled closer. His only fault was that he was more interested in writing his novel than in being with her. But when they were together, they were perfect together. How could she begrudge him his passion for writing? If her only rival was a ninety-nine-year old, all was well.

Propped up in her bed, Lettie wrote all day while Bill asked her questions about her Elizabethan life and times. When she napped, and right after dinner when she went to sleep for the night, because of the frailness of her body, he entered on his computer what she had written in her archaic longhand, and he edited his notes of what she had told him.

She came to trust him and feel at home in this place, seeing analogs between it and the mansion where she said she had been raised. She described the long and winding corridors of the Arden mansion and said that she and her friend Molly would have loved to race around those corridors in power-driven wheelchairs.

"What is the last day and year you remember?" he asked her.

"My birthday— April 23 in 1616."

"The day William Shakespeare died."

"Will died?"

"Yes. Of course. Nearly four hundred years ago."

"He died on our birthday?"

"Yes, April 23."

"And where was he when he died?"

"In Stratford with his wife and children. Where were you that day?"

"I was on the dock waiting to sail to France. I felt a pull toward Will. I tried to project myself to him."

"You what?"

"It was like my father, my almost father, Sir James said about his bond with his falcons. When he launched a bird to the hunt, it was as if he saw the world through its eyes and felt the impact in his muscles and bones when falcon struck its prey. Will and I could do that with one another. I could get inside his mind and see through his eyes, and he could do that with me, regardless of how far apart we were. Will saved my life that way, from a great distance, when I fought my duel with Mercutio. I guessed we could do that because we were twins and because we were special. I guessed that no one aside from us could do it like we did. It was at the heart of our success as writers. Seeing the world through the eyes of others was our talent. We could take old stories that had been told many times and bring them to life for actor and audience. But that last time when I tried to project to Will, it didn't work.

"He had left London five years before. I had expected he would soon have enough of small-town Stratford and the wife he loathed, and he would return to me. But nothing, not a visit, not a letter, not even a projected brush of his soul. So, I tried one last time to project to him on our birthday, our fifty-second birthday, the day I was planning to sail to France, on what was to be a fresh start, a new life. But Will was dead, and I didn't know it. That's what was broken. That's what went wrong. I'm guessing that's how it happened. One moment I was standing on the dock with Molly and Hamlet, and the next I woke up here."

"Hamlet?"

"Hamlet, Hamnet, same name. My son. Our son. Named after the twin son Will had with his wife Anne, the son who died at the age of eleven. If Will hadn't had twins, we would never have learned that we were twins. But that's another story."

"The son of you and your brother?" Bill stared at her in disbelief.

"Yes, Hamlet was six when I last saw him. He was born in 1610, the year before Will left London and went back to Stratford for good. Will never saw him. I was forty-six when he was born. My monthly curse had ended. I was too old to have children. We restrained ourselves despite what we felt for one another as long as we thought that I could get pregnant. But nature played a trick on us."

"Was he ...?"

"Deformed? No. We were lucky. Hamlet is strong and healthy, with a brilliant future ahead of him. Molly will take good care of him. I'm sure she will."

In his mind's eye, Bill imagined this woman at half her current age, in the body of a fifty-year-old. She was brilliant, strong-willed, ready to start a new life, while her burnt-out twin was giving up and stumbling back to Stratford to die.

He imagined his Kathy, her young and lustful body, and with the spirt, the genius, and the willpower of Kate. For him, that would be the perfect woman—both a bodymate and a soulmate.

9 ~ The Stroke of Midnight

In the midst of a discussion about her duel in Paris and how Will saved her life, Kate sat up and stared at Bill. Panic filled her eyes.

"What's wrong?" he asked, standing and reaching for the emergency button on the table beside her bed. Was she having a stroke?

"Scared," she said hoarsely. "Scared of the dark."

"But it's morning, and the lights are on. Are you having trouble seeing?"

"Not that kind of dark. The real dark. The deep dark. The putting out of the light. The forever."

She was shaking. He leaned down and hugged her.

"That's why I took the risk."

"What risk?"

"I had no right to try it. It was a risk for you as well. I had no right to do it."

"Do what?"

"I wanted to know if I still could project. Bill, Will. I thought there might be some affinity between you and him. Maybe that was the reason I ended up here."

"You mean you tried to get into my mind?"

"Yes. To see through your eyes."

"I didn't feel anything. I didn't sense anything strange."

"That's because it didn't work," she said. "I don't have it anymore. It isn't in me. When I tried, I didn't see through your eyes, nor through my eyes, either. I saw the dark, the total dark. Black blacker than black. A tunnel without end. I saw through the eyes of death."

She shook again with her entire frail body.

He held her still tighter, and his arms got wet from the tears pouring down her face.

***

One night, as Bill and Kathy lay cuddled in the afterglow, Kathy said, "An angel just got her wings."

"What?" asked Bill.

"It's a line from the movie *It's a Wonderful Life*. At the end of the movie there's the line, *Every time a bell rings, an angel gets his wings*."

"But no bell rang."

"You didn't hear it. I don't know if I heard it, either. But I felt it. I felt something, only it wasn't his wings. It was hers, a woman's. Shit.! It's Lettie. Something has happened to Lettie. It's a premonition."

Kathy called The Stratford and insisted that a night nurse check on Lettie. Lettie was found on the floor of her room, non-responsive, but breathing

An ambulance took her to the hospital emergency room. Then she was moved to the ICU, then to a rehab facility. Kathy and Bill couldn't visit her because they weren't next of kin. It was a stroke. She had lost the use of her left arm.

Six weeks later, an ambulance brought her back to the Stratford. Although physically weak, mentally she seemed alert and feisty.

She told Bill that she thought she had brought the stroke on through her own foolishness. She had tried and failed to project to Kathy. That had probably triggered it.

While she was gone and they didn't know if she would survive, Bill had worked feverishly on a novel based on her story. He had finished it three days before she returned, and he was anxious to read it aloud to her.

PART TWO: Shakespeare's Twin Sister by Kate Shakespeare, as Told by Bill Greene

10 ~ Special Delivery

Stratford-on-Avon, April 23, 1564

A gentleman swung open the door to the inn and shouted, "A midwife! Is there a midwife to be had? Quickly. Run. Run and fetch us a midwife."

"Flo, sir. Flo Harrison," answered the hostess. "She be the midwife hereabouts."

"Fetch her now. My wife is in labor."

"She be at the Shakespeare house on Henley Street. Mary be birthing even now, so I hear. A long delivery—all day, and still not done."

"Shakespeare? Mary Shakespeare? She that was Mary Arden of the Ardens of Wilmcote? She's my second cousin. I've never met her, but family is family. Is her house far from here?"

"Not far at all. This be Stratford, sir. No place here be far from any other."

"Take us there quickly. Flo must do double duty today."

Sir James Arden was taking his wife to her mother's house for the birthing, which wasn't expected for another month or more. When the carriage was jolted by a rut, she fell to the floor. Her water broke. She went into labor.

The Shakespeare house was typical—with plaster filling the spaces between the crisscross oak timbers of the frame. The roof was of timber in contrast to the thatched rooves of the neighboring houses. The floor was broken limestone, covered with rushes.

When the Ardens arrived, Mary was in the marriage bed in the parlor, her screams coming at intervals of a couple minutes—the sound amplified by the wooden walls.

Her husband, John, fetched a bed from upstairs—a mattress of rush, stretched on cords across a wooden frame. He set it up in the main room, near the chimney. There was no way the lady in labor could negotiate the ladder to the bedroom up above.

Flo, the midwife, was a portly, no-nonsense take-charge mother of eight healthy children. Full-bosomed, with rosy cheeks and muscular arms, she was the image of well-fed health. She was a disciplinarian who handled her patients with the same authority and confidence as she did her children. In the birthing room, she had to be treated with respect, as the unquestioned boss; or she would simply leave. She didn't need the fee paid for her services. Her husband, the blacksmith, provided well. She did what she did out of a sense of duty, for the public good, because she and everyone else in Stratford knew that she understood the business of birthing better than anyone else for miles around. She took pride in her extraordinary skill, having ushered into life nearly everyone in Stratford under the age of twenty and that was half the town's 1900 residents.

It would be difficult dealing with two births at once, so the last thing she wanted was the *help* of expectant fathers. She exiled them to the other ground-floor room—the workshop for John's business as a glove maker. Then she dashed back and forth from one patient to the other.

No sooner did Mary give birth to a fine healthy boy, than the Arden lady screamed like she was dying. Flo tied off and cut the umbilical cord, put the boy down on blankets in a basket, and raced to the other room.

The Arden lady was pale and weary. She had lost a lot of blood. Flo spread the lady's legs wide, held her ankles, and urged her to push hard.

Out popped a tiny, fragile baby girl. Before its time. Not even five pounds, Flo would wager. A game fighter, crying feebly with all her strength, in what would likely be a brief life.

Flo washed blood off the baby, with warm water from a bowl, then swaddled her in a blanket and danced around the room, rocking her, trying to calm her.

"Flo, may we—" John shouted from the workshop.

"No! No! No! Let me do what I must do."

When the workshop door started to open despite her words, Flo gave it a whack with her hip, swinging so hard she lost her balance, barely righting herself, with a hand to the dining table, and avoiding falling with and on the baby.

"Stay out," Flo screamed.

Then, from the other room, Mary screamed even louder. Something was very wrong. Shocked, Flo lost her concentration. The baby slipped from her arms and fell head-first on the limestone floor. Blood gushed from its head. The baby was silent.

Frantic, confused, Flo left the baby—no doubt dead—on the floor, and raced to Mary, who continued to scream. She was crowning again—another head, another baby.

Going through the motions she had gone through hundreds of times before, trying not to think about the cracked-skull baby on the floor in the other room, Flo brought this unexpected new child into the world. A girl.

Mary was delirious. "What, Flo? What? What's happening to me?"

"It be the afterbirth," Flo improvised, without thinking. "Yes, the afterbirth was twisted and stuck. You'll be fine now."

She had to think fast. In this sound-box of a house, the fathers must have heard the cries of at least two babies. She had shouted, "a boy," for Mary's first and "a girl" for the Arden lady. She was silent about this one.

The Arden baby had come too early—a month or more before its time. Had she not dropped it, it would not have lived long. But this was no still birth, no natural death. A cracked skull doesn't come from birthing.

"I killed it with my negligence," Flo thought. "Man slaughter. Baby slaughter. Guilty as sin. But there be a baby too many here—more than expected, more than needed. And they be cousins, I hear. No one would be the wiser, not now and not when she grows up, so long as she favors the Arden looks. It be God's will. That's what it be—so perfect a fix, turning tragedy to joy."

She took the new baby girl to the other room, washed off the blood, swaddled her in a blanket, and put her in a basket near the Arden lady, who was barely conscious. Then she wrapped up the corpse and set it aside for disposal later and spilled on the floor bloody water from the bowl she had used for washing. Blood from birth looked like blood from death—it's all the same.

Next, she rushed back to Mary, who was screaming once again—this time from the real afterbirth; but who was confused enough to be convinced that she misremembered having delivered the afterbirth before. One pain was like another.

Only then did Flo let the fathers in—the one to meet his son and other to meet his daughter. And no one except Flo knew these were twins.

She took care of the finishing touches while the fathers danced about and showered affection on wives and babes. Men were so emotional.

The ritual of the complex details helped to calm her, to reestablish her self-confidence and to damp her feelings of guilt at the unfortunate death—anointing the babies with oil of acorns, then washing them with warm water, opening their nostrils, putting a little oil into the eyes, then re-swaddling them carefully so every part was in its due place and order, and all of this done tenderly and gently.

Then she gathered up the wet and bloody pieces of cloth which would need to be washed for use another day. She tied them in a bundle that included the wrapped-up remains of the baby that had died, and no one was the wiser.

The Arden lady died that night. That made Flo all the more certain that she had done right, that this was God's will. The baby that died from being dropped would have died soon anyway. It would have been too much for Sir James to lose both wife and child. And twins would have been hard for Mary to cope with.

Each infant had a half-moon birthmark near the base of its spine. But only Flo noticed that. And the two of them would never be seen together again.

11 ~ Behind the Arras

The Arden estate, Warwickshire, 1564 – 1574

Even before the death of his wife, Sir James had been reclusive. His mansion, three stories high, with six chimneys and a hundred-twenty glass windows, lay three miles south of Stratford, away from the road to London, surrounded by flower gardens, orchards, a hedge maze, and a deer park. It was a world apart.

One of his servants, Gertie, took charge of his infant daughter, Kate. Gertie had, in her wild youth, run off with a traveling troupe of players. Because of the ban on women appearing on the stage, rather than act, she had helped with makeup, costumes, and props. She loved the camaraderie, the vagabond life, and the sexual freedom as well, as she admitted when telling tales of that time. A few years after she ran away, she heard that her mother had died of the plague. In those days, the plague struck in the countryside as well as London; and it returned without warning, again and again. Those who were fortunate enough to survive the hazards of birth and childhood and contagions like the plague, often died in their forties, which was considered old age. Death was real and ever-present. Life was fragile and fleeting—a will o' the wisp, a fantasy, a dream.

Gertie's father needed help with her younger siblings, and she could have her mother's post in Sir James' household if she returned promptly. By then, she had had her fill of freedom. Besides, she was with child.

When she got home—buxom, full-figured, bright, and jolly—she was greeted without reservation by her old sweetheart, Jake, the cook. She moved in with him, had a miscarriage, then got pregnant again, this time with twins. One of them, the boy, died soon after birth. The girl she named *Molly*.

Gertie's breasts were overflowing with milk; and soon thereafter, Mistress Arden died in childbirth. So, it was natural for Gertie to nurse Kate as well as Molly, one to a breast.

There was an Arden resemblance to the families that had been in service to the Ardens for generations. Some would say that that was an effect of living together—like pet owners and their pets coming to resemble one another. Others might think that some of the lords of the land had dallied with the help and that, over the generations, Arden blood had mixed with the blood of the servants. In any case, Kate and Molly looked enough alike to be taken as sisters, both with black hair, blue eyes, long face, and light complexion. And Sir James, who never remarried and had no children but Kate, treated Molly like a second daughter.

Kate and Molly were inseparable—playing together and sleeping together in the same bed, often waking up in the morning in one another's arms, with legs entangled. Sir James read aloud to the two of them several hours a day, not just at bedtime. He varied his voice and made frequent eye contact with the two of them. He delighted in performing for them, making them smile and laugh, even when they were too young to understand English, much less the Latin, French, and Italian he often read to them. They enjoyed the attention and responded to his facial expressions, his gestures, and the tricks he played with his voice.

When they were old enough to follow stories, since there were no printed books intended for young children, he switched from reading to recounting, in his own words, tales from mythology and *The Bible*, and other tales that he made up. And when they asked to hear the same story again, he often came up with more episodes—the wilder and the more fantastical the better.

The house itself was in harmony with the temperament of Sir James and the girls. The chimney and stone superstructure of the banquet hall dated back to the thirteenth century, when a castle stood there. The rest of the mansion, built of timber and plaster, with wainscoting near the floor, had been tacked on later to meet practical needs, with little concern for the overall look of it. Winding corridors and secret passageways gave the house a fantastical air that the girls loved. It was the perfect setting for hide-and-seek and make-believe, with a dungeon-like cellar and towers and winding staircases, some of which led nowhere.

To the north lay the flower gardens. To the east lay orchards, including exotic trees imported by Sir James as a gift for his wife, planted a dozen years before, and now bearing fruit—plums, pears, walnuts. apricots, almonds, peaches, figs, oranges, lemons, and olives. To the west lay an extensive vegetable garden, tended by and for the benefit of the tenant farmers. To the south lay a vast hedge, eight feet high, trimmed in the shape of a maze. The girls mischievously placed scarecrow-like figures and booby traps in the maze, to the annoyance of the servants and to the delight of Sir James. "Livens the place up," he said. The girls made the grounds an amusement park before amusement parks were invented.

Surrounding all that was the deer park, and beyond the deer park were the tenant farms. Much of that land had been *enclosed*—serving as grazing ground for sheep, since wool was the most profitable farming product of that time. But there were also a dozen old-style farms, worked by tenants who paid rent and grew what they chose— mainly cattle, horses, goats, and wheat. They all shared in the produce of the vegetable garden and of the orchard, for their own consumption or for sale.

Frequently buried in his books, Sir James' one outdoor indulgence was falconry. He didn't hunt foxes with hounds or deer with bow and arrow. He hired a huntsman to harvest deer each fall so the population wouldn't get out of control, and he gave the venison to his tenant farmers. But he loved to hunt pheasant and duck with falcons.

He admitted that the sport was bloody and brutal, but he believed that it was magnificent, as well. He thought of the falcon as an extension of himself. He imagined that, briefly, his soul was in the body of his falcon, and he saw the world through his falcon's eyes. He was one with the bird and one with nature, and all of life and death made sense to him in an unthinking, instinctive way.

When released, the falcon would circle up above, *waiting off* for game to be flushed. Then, with a high-speed dive, it would catch and kill the quarry. Sir James described the experience, "When the strike comes, I feel the shock in my muscles and bones, and the dying prey quivering in my grasp. I feel so alive then, so part of the larger world, the ebb and flow of life through the ages."

Molly was squeamish. She was afraid of the falcons and found that way of killing disgusting and cruel. She thought it was far more natural to twist a chicken's head off, which probably hurt the chicken far less than getting ripped apart by a falcon.

But Kate delighted in the sport. Her father gave her a falcon of her own, who she named *Perry*—Perry the peregrine falcon. And he had a falconer's glove made for her by the finest glover in all of Warwickshire—John Shakespeare of Stratford.

She wasn't old enough yet to handle a falcon on her own. Perry would perch on her gloved hand, and her father would guide her motions as she launched him.

The most magnificent room of the mansion—the banquet hall— was where the girls preferred to play. The dining table could have fit all the Knights of the Roundtable, only it wasn't round, but rather rectangular, twenty-five feet long. A hundred years before, during the Wars of the Roses, it had often have been filled with relatives and neighbors either going to war or returning from it, either celebrating or grieving, probably including Richard Neville, the Earl of Warwick, known as the *Kingmaker*. The table was now an historical relic, well-dusted and polished, but never used. Sir James, Kate, Molly, and Mistress Jane the governess ate at a small table near the hearth. Sir James often coaxed Gertie to join them. She was reluctant, saying it wasn't fitting for the help to share bread with the master, though she often relented. The coaxing was a regular routine between them. He found her pride of caste and position amusing, since he had no such notions himself, and he enjoyed teasing her and making her laugh.

Large enough to be worthy of a royal palace, the banquet hall was made warm and memorable by tapestries that hung, ceiling to floor, on every wall. The girls felt they were in the presence of all of English history, and it was easy for them to imagine themselves as players in the events depicted.

The other public rooms of the house were adorned with painted cloths showing Bible scenes. But the tapestries in the banquet room depicted St. George and the Dragon; Robin Hood and his merry band kneeling to King Richard; King Arthur and his Knights on horseback before their battle with Mordred; Queen Eleanor of Aquitaine with her ladies-in-waiting on horseback and dressed as knights; King John signing the Magna Carta; Edward the Black Prince at the Battle of Crecy; Henry V at the Battle of Agincourt, a royal feast hosted by Henry VIII, and a fleet of war ships carrying William the Conqueror to England. The largest tapestry was an arras showing Queen Elizabeth sitting on her throne with a unicorn to her right and a lion to her left. This arras concealed an alcove as large as the room where Kate and Molly slept. That alcove was the girls' favorite place for staging make-believe games, with a rope and pulley to raise and lower the arras like the curtain in a theater.

While the other tapestries were family heirlooms, Sir James had commissioned the one of Queen Elizabeth as soon as he heard Queen Mary had died, and he promptly burned the one of Mary which had occupied the same space. It wasn't healthy to display anything that might imply nostalgia for the days of Mary and Catholicism. Everyone, even the lords of the land, were now expected to attend Protestant services every Sunday; and if they failed to do so, they were subject to fines and could come under suspicion of not being loyal to the crown.

The tapestries in the banquet hall were not just decoration. They, and especially the one of Elizabeth, were a political statement, a necessary expression of patriotism—for the queen was all-powerful and could, at any time, for any reason, confiscate this estate and have the owner and his family imprisoned or beheaded. Religion and politics were closely tied. When Henry VIII ruled, he broke with Rome and persecuted those who continued faithful to the Pope. Then his daughter Mary made the country Catholic again, burning Protestants at the stake. Now his other daughter Elizabeth had made the country Protestant again and considered Catholics as traitors. To survive, one needed to adapt quickly and convincingly.

With the ascent of Elizabeth, Sir James had disposed of all historical relics which might be construed as Catholic. And he hadn't simply put them into storage—which would have been dangerous. Rather, he had publicly destroyed them in a bonfire celebrating the Queen's coronation.

The feast of the bonfire on the occasion of the coronation and the feast he held six months later when he hung the arras of Elizabeth were the last times that Sir James entertained. On both occasions, his wore his right arm in a sling, as if broken, for fear that he might, from habit or thoughtlessness, make the sign of the cross and be denounced as a Catholic sympathizer. After that, he avoided all social contact, except the obligatory weekly church service, for fear of getting entangled in conversations that could be misinterpreted and prove dangerous.

"Good Queen Bess" was sometimes a benevolent despot, but she was always a despot. She was not only above the law; she was the law. If you crossed her or if she thought you crossed her, you were as good as dead, without trial or stated cause. And she had a habit of visiting mansions, with little or no warning. It was wise to stay prepared at all times.

That's why Sir James had culled from his library all books that had anything to do with religion, except, of course, *The Bible*. A large expensive Protestant *Bible* in English, open to the *Book of Psalms*, sat on a podium in the banquet hall, and was regularly dusted, but otherwise was never touched.

He felt safe and comfortable among the books that remained, contemplating the meaning of life, the fate of man, and the flow of history. He was nostalgic for the good old days that he had never experienced himself, when life was simple and wars were fought for power and conquest, before these frantic modern times when religious belief was a matter of life or death, and outward symbols of inner belief could prove fatal if and when the tide turned.

During the girls' early years, Gertie kept the girls in line and loosely managed their upbringing. Sir James taught them to read and was amazed at how quickly they caught on. But there was much they needed to learn that he and Gertie couldn't teach them—skills and tastes and manners appropriate to their station in life. And neither he nor Gertie was a disciplinarian. Both of them were too indulgent and loving for the girls' good. So when the girls turned seven, he hired a governess, Jane Wetherall, to guide their moral development and to teach the girls what all young ladies needed to know—manners, sewing, knitting, embroidery, painting, dancing, and musical instruments.

When he hired Mistress Jane, he made sure that she would provide no religious instruction. Ignorance and having no belief at all were the surest defenses against religious persecution from Protestants, Catholics, or from any of the angrily contending flavors of Protestantism. The girls should be taught to be polite and respectful in their demeanor, and silent, above all silent, about all matters of religion.

Jane, the widow of a clergyman, was respectable and accomplished, but inexperienced. She had no children of her own, no property of her own, and no relatives to turn to for support. No sooner had she buried her husband than she had to move out of the vicarage and find some means of supporting herself. She was intelligent and could read, which was unusual for a woman. She had been taught by her late husband. But since she was nearly forty and penniless, she was unmarriageable. As governess to Sir James' children, she got housing, food, and pay as well. This job was a godsend.

For the girls, having run free up to that point, the transition to structure was difficult. But eventually they worked out a compromise with Jane. They learned whatever there was to learn twice as fast as Jane would have expected; and as a reward, they had frequent long breaks during which they could amuse themselves however they pleased.

Kate and Molly would act out their favorite stories, dressing up in outfits that Gertie put together for them from old clothing in trunks in the attic. And since many of the characters they played were men, Gertie made them mustaches that extended sideways nearly to their ears and taught them how to stick them on firmly and how to remove them without pain and taught them tricks of makeup and costuming and wig making that she had learned in her days with the acting troupe.

In the banquet hall and its alcove or, when weather permitted, in the hedge maze, the orchards, and the gardens, the girls' role-play became elaborate, and carried over from one day to the next. Sir James taught them the rudiments of fencing; so sometimes, dressed as boys, they would wrestle and have sword fights with wooden swords he made for them, and with shields that were cushions with arm straps. Sometimes they'd be rivals and sometimes they would be lovers, the one having saved the other from villains or monsters. Often their play continued after supper, and in bed together at night.

They especially enjoyed stories of true love, soulmates, abduction, abandonment and exile. And then mistaken death, mistaken identity, shipwrecks, pirates, sudden changes of fortune, lost memory, birthmarks, love sickness, sword fights and destiny. Then there was wild coincidence, poisons, sleeping potions that produce the look of death without killing, live burial, changelings, and twins separated at birth.

***

On a typical day in this atypical mansion, two ten-year-old girls who were dressed as boys chased one another and wrestled and fought with wooden swords on either side of the arras. Their morning lessons were done and for an hour they were free to do what they liked and be who they liked in whatever fantasy they chose, so long as they didn't knock over the podium that held *The Bible* and didn't trip the servants going about their duties and didn't disturb Father in his study in the west wing.

The girls, playing pirates, raided the vegetable garden, as if it were a Spanish colony in the Caribbean. They took their ill-gotten goods to the family dining table by the fireplace in the banquet hall, but there they were spotted by Gertie.

"Vegetables? God's blood! Eating blooming vegetables?" she scolded them. "Over and over have I told you—vegetables be only fit for peasants, hogs, and wild beasts. Melons, cucumbers, radishes, carrots, cabbages—how can you stand to eat such garbage? Those of us that can, eat meat, lots of meat, only meat. We be lucky we be here and treated as we are. Sir James loves you like daughters. Molly's dad's the cook. You can have all the meat you want—beef, mutton, veal, lamb, kid, pork, rabbit, chicken, pig, venison, fish, wildfowl. Fresh meat or meat pies served on silver plates. And wine to wash it down. Never let me see you eating vegetables again, do you hear me? They're bad for your health."

The girls abandoned their plunder and retreated to the alcove.

"When I grow up, I want to be a pirate, a real pirate," said Kate. "Then I'll eat all the vegetables I want, whenever I want."

"And I want to be a princess," answered Molly.

"But you can't be a princess," Kate objected. "Not unless your father's a king. And your father's a cook."

"That's what you think. That's what everybody thinks. But I'm special. A wicked witch stole me when I was a baby, but some day my true identity will be revealed."

"And how, may I ask, will it be revealed?"

"By a birthmark."

"But you don't have a birthmark," laughed Kate. "I'm the one with the birthmark, and I'm already the daughter of a lord, so I don't need to be anyone other than who I am."

"Well, I'm special," Molly insisted. "I know I am. I feel it in my bones."

"Let me feel those bones." Kate tickled her belly.

Molly squirmed away. "Enough. Enough. Well, if I can't be a princess in the real world, if I have to be the daughter of servants, then let me have my choice of who I'll be in our play."

"And who would you be today, milady?"

"I want to be Henry the Fifth at the Battle of Agincourt, and you can be my French princess, my Kate."

"I'll be no silly princess. I'm the Duke of York."

"But the Duke of York dies."

"To hell with death Once more into the breach."

"For St. George and England," shouted Molly.

"For Harry," answered Kate.

Back-to-back, fighting invisible enemies with their wooden swords, they edged out of the alcove and to the main door. Then they sprinted to the hedge maze to do battle with one scarecrow French knight after another.

When the battle was done and won, the girls became rabbits and crawled carefully, so as not to be seen by an imaginary Farmer Brown, and raided the garden once more, this time for a melon that they cracked open on a rock and feasted on, sitting on the ground near the cabbages.

Then, Molly leading the way, they raced back to the banquet hall where Molly hid behind the arras and called, "Help! Help! Sir Knight. A witch has imprisoned me here and an invisible dragon is about to eat me."

"Fear not, fair lady," replied Kate, slipping into the alcove with her. In good fencing form, with a call of *en garde*, she fought the invisible dragon to the death.

"My hero," exclaimed Molly, batting her eyelashes, letting down her hair, and looking very lady-like and helpless.

Kate tossed aside her trusty sword and shield and rushed to embrace the fair lady. They kissed and hugged and hugged some more—a welcome relief after a hard day of make-believe battles. It felt good to hug and to be hugged by someone you cared for. No wonder knights went to such trouble to rescue damsels in distress. And no wonder damsels went to such lengths to get into trouble so they could be rescued.

***

Walking through the banquet hall, Mistress Jane was shocked by the silence. She was coming to reprimand the girls for being so loud, but now she didn't hear them at all, and couldn't see them, neither inside nor out. That was most peculiar. They were only silent when they were up to something they knew they shouldn't. Not that anything they did was ever truly bad, but they might accidentally hurt themselves or one another. She needed to keep an eye on them. It was her duty to protect them.

She pulled on the rope to raise the arras, and there they were, wrestling.

No, they were hugging and kissing. And that didn't look like make-believe.

Shocked, Jane let go of the rope, and the arras fell. Then she pulled again and tied the rope in place. They were still hugging and kissing. They hadn't even noticed her.

"Break it up," yelled Jane.

"This is our game," Kate objected. "It's a play we're acting out."

"Nonsense," Jane insisted. "It's unnatural for young ladies to get physical with one another."

"You mean we should recruit servant boys to play those roles?"

"No. That would be even worse. Young ladies shouldn't do plays at all. I should have insisted on that long ago."

"But it's make-believe. And father tells us stories like this all the time."

"That was fine when you were little girls. But now you're ten years old, on the brink of becoming women. Not too long from now, you'll be old enough to have children of your own. It's time to put an end to this childish foolishness and prepare for life in the real world."

Jane grabbed hold of them, dragged them out of the alcove, pulled them apart, and glared down at them in disbelief and anger. She needed to find words that could drive these girls to shame and contrition, to make them beg for forgiveness and promise reform.

Then a wave of fear swept over her. If she reported this sinful, unnatural behavior to Sir James, and demanded that the girls be separated—Molly cast away and Kate subject to close scrutiny and discipline—he might side with the girls, and dismiss her, the governess. He might pay her a month's wages, maybe two, but he would send her out into the world where she had no one to turn to, where it would be impossible to find another post like this. She would be reduced to the life of a drudge, at best, washing other people's laundry or sewing all day and into the night by candle light, or doing chores for the family of a blacksmith, for a pittance, barely enough to stay alive, a miserable life that likely would end soon, in exhaustion, hunger, and illness.

Meanwhile, Molly was weeping loudly and trying to free her wrist from Jane's grip. She was in anguish, imagining the consequences for herself—her exile, the loss of her dear and only companion, the wreckage of what should have been a wonderful life. Molly's reaction made sense, but Kate's did not.

Kate was calm. Kate looked up at Jane with sympathy, tenderness and good will. This little girl seemed more concerned about what was likely to happen to her governess than to herself. How could a ten-year-old know so much? How could she project herself into her teacher's skin?

Rather than pull away, Kate reached up, standing on her tiptoes and gently stroked Jane's cheek.

Jane started to lose her balance; and Kate, with all the strength in her body, helped Jane recover and stand straight; then led her by the hand to a nearby ottoman, with Molly trailing behind, still held firmly by Jane's other hand.

When Jane sat, Kate sat on her lap, and hugged her, and cuddled close.

"Don't fret," Kate told Jane. "This can turn out right, better than right. I'm here for you, and you for me and Molly. I know what you face. It's not easy being a woman in a man's world. We need to stick together."

12 ~ Projection

That night Kate had a dream that she remembered vividly for the rest of her life.

The dream started with Perry, her falcon. She was the falcon. She saw through the falcon's eyes.

Then she was in the banquet hall with Molly and Mistress Jane, and she saw the shock, anger, and fear on Jane's face.

Then she was looking at herself, not Jane. She was seeing herself through Jane's eyes.

It had always bothered Kate that if she held an open book to a mirror, she saw everything backwards, reversed. That meant that when she looked at herself in a mirror, she saw the opposite of what others saw when looking at her. She didn't really know what she looked like. She had never truly seen herself. But now, in her dream, she did, for the first time.

She was wearing a brass medallion that was a prop for her make-believe games. It had REX engraved on it in large letters. Looking at herself through Jane's eyes the letters on that medallion appeared not backwards, not reversed, but rather as they would appear when seen directly.

One moment Kate was a little girl looking up at her tall, thin, aging, angry governess—a shadow blocking a beam of light through the window behind her. The next moment, she saw herself through Jane's eyes—saw herself as small and helpless, but unafraid.

Remembering that dream years later, Kate wasn't sure that it was a dream. How could she imagine herself not mirror-reversed, but seen directly—the way others saw her, the way she had never seen herself before? And why had Mistress Jane changed so abruptly, from scolding her to hugging her and reassuring her. When she saw herself through Jane's eyes, she had felt a bond with Jane like she had never felt before with anyone—she became Jane. Then snap, she was back in her own head again.

Molly wanted to believe that she was a princess. Kate wanted to believe that she had a special power that she was born with, that she was a wizard who could project herself, who could throw her soul into another person or another creature. She wanted to be able to control this power, to do it at will. But this first time it happened without her consciously doing anything to make it happen; and it may not have happened at all—it may have been a dream. In any case, she wanted to include that power in her make-believe with Molly, and to do so plausibly, without stretching the imaginative limits of their fantasy, she needed to know more. Surely, someone must have written about such a power.

Kate sought out her father in his study. She had faith that he knew everything there was to know about myths and folklore.

His study was on the second floor of the west wing, with books not only on shelves, but also stacked on the floor, in patterns that only Sir James understood, and that the servants didn't dare disturb. The windows looked out on the maze hedge.

He turned his chair to face her, pulled her close, and touched his nose to her nose, smiling broadly. "You mean the notion that someone's soul can move at will from body to body? Soul transfer? That's a fascinating idea, Kate. Quite clever, my dear. I've imagined something like that as a metaphor for the union I feel with a falcon when I launch it. But from metaphor to reality is a long leap."

He stood and paced back and forth in his study, among his shelves and stacks of books, scanning his memory for something similar. "Some religions believe that when you die, your soul goes into the body of a newborn baby and you live again," he continued. "The ancient Greeks believed that when you fall asleep your soul leaves your body, and when you wake, it returns. And Christians—all flavors of them, even me—believe that each of us has a soul which is separate from the body, which leaves the body when the body dies, and which lives forever. But the idea that a soul could leave a living body and enter the body of another living person and see through that person's eyes, maybe even think that other person's thoughts and then return— that I've never heard of, never read of. But I could think of that as a metaphor for what happens when a great author creates an unforgettable character, empathizing with someone different from himself to such an extent that it's as if he had lived in that man's skin and experienced life as he did. Most interesting, my Kate, most interesting. Perhaps you have in you what it takes to be a great writer."

"Honestly, father," she replied, "I'd much rather be a great wizard."

13 ~ Brave New World

1574

Kate and her father were interrupted by a knock on the door to the study. Mistress Jane requested, "Sir, may we walk together in the garden? I need to discuss an important matter with you about the girls. And it will be easier for me to talk—I'll feel less self-conscious—if we walk together."

Kate cringed. Seeing her reaction, Sir James asked Jane, "Have they misbehaved? Are they not working hard enough on their lessons?"

"Nothing of the sort, Sir James. Kate, in particular, has extraordinary intelligence, and not just intelligence of the mind."

"Then there should be no reason not to include her in the conversation. I'm sure she'd like to hear good things about herself." He smiled.

"I had hoped to talk to you first and then to her. Not that there is any reason to keep this from her. Just that I wanted to be sure that you're in agreement before I raised her hopes and expectations."

"Fine. Fine," Sir James agreed. "Run along now, Kate. We'll get back to you soon, I'm sure."

Once Kate had left, Jane continued, "Kate has emotional intelligence as well as the rational kind of intelligence that we strengthen through schooling. She has remarkable insight into what others are thinking and feeling, how others experience the world."

"Indeed," Sir James agreed. "She was just talking to me about such matters. And what do you conclude from that, Mistress Jane? Do we have a budding wizard on our hands? Should we look for some way to give her an education in magic?" He chuckled.

"Seriously, sir. I was thinking that we should strive to prepare her for a different kind of life than what young ladies are normally limited to. I believe that she can and should be enabled to live an independent life, if she should so wish."

"Independent? You mean financially independent? Without a father or a husband to guide and protect her?"

"Think of her as a boy, sir. If she were your son rather than your daughter, what would you do for him now to prepare him for the life ahead of him? That should be easy for you to imagine given how often in their play Kate and Molly dress and act like boys."

"Play is play, and life is life."

"But perhaps all of life is a play."

He chuckled. "You're playing with words, my dear."

"Well, I'm proposing that you and I play with life, for her sake. Rather than thinking in terms of what is done, of what is always done and is considered acceptable, let's think of what could be, what should be. If there were no constraints imposed on us by society, imagine how you would raise Kate, and Molly, too, because they are inseparable. Imagine them as boys. Imagine what would be possible for them if the world thought they were boys."

"You mean send them to school?"

"At the very least. School could be the starting point."

"But you and I have already taught them much."

"Enough to make them accomplished young ladies, but not enough for them to get on in the world of men. Latin for instance."

"I've given them the rudiments of Latin. They know their conjugations and declensions."

"But they aren't fluent in Latin, and knowledge of Latin is a matter of social status and is important in foreign trade and law and government. They would need to be able to speak it, to write it, to think in it, if they were to be treated as equals to men in the world of men."

"They could only arrive at that level of facility if they were totally immersed in the language."

"Indeed, as they do at the King's New School in Stratford."

"But they only accept boys at that school."

"Indeed, Sir James. That's why you must think of them as boys, and they must act in such a way that others, too, think of them as boys.

"But that's impossible."

"If we were talking about anyone other than Kate and Molly, I would agree, sir."

"What you are proposing is extraordinary."

"Indeed, sir."

"A challenge like no other. An amazing adventure."

"Indeed, sir."

"And you believe they're up to it?"

"I do, sir. And I believe they will take on this challenge with gusto."

He laughed at the thought, then took hold of Mistress Jane and kissed her on one cheek and then on the other and hugged her tight.

14 ~ Sex Change

Sir James sent Jane to fetch Kate, Molly, and Gertie.

Kate had wrapped a sheet around herself as a cape and was running with arms spread like a bird flying. "I'm a falcon," she shouted at Molly, who ducked under the banquet table to evade her clutches. "I'm going to grab you and rip you to pieces," Kate threatened.

"Well, I'll stop you with the *Spell of Avalon*," Molly countered.

"There is no *Spell of Avalon*," said Kate.

"Yes, there is, if I say there is."

"Then I'm an elephant," countered Kate, abandoning the sheet and getting down on all fours.

"You can't just change from one creature to another. That isn't fair."

"Then I didn't become an elephant," said Kate. "Instead, my spirit moved to an elephant's body. My spirit moves from one creature to another. I'm the same, but I see through the eyes of a falcon, or the eyes of an elephant, even through your eyes. That's my superpower—to see through the eyes of others."

Jane smiled seeing the girls at play, as if this were a day like any other day, as if yesterday had never happened. "That's enough battles for now, girls. Saving the world will have to wait until afternoon. Sir James wants to see both of you in his study. Right now."

When they opened the door to the study, they saw Gertie was there as well as Sir James. That was out of the ordinary. This was a serious matter.

Molly whispered to Kate, "What's happening? I thought you said we'd be all right, that Mistress Jane wouldn't tell on us."

Sir James snuck up behind Molly, leaned down, and whispered, "Have no fear. No one snitched on you. Whatever you did is still a deep dark secret. And even if it weren't, certainly it would be forgotten and forgiven." Then he stood tall, turned Molly around, and explained to both her and Kate, "You're here because it's high time we talked about your future. Mistress Jane has reminded me of how brilliant you both are and that soon you'll be young ladies. And I'd like to do what I can to enable you to make the most of your brilliance in our benighted times. But this needs to be about you, not me. I don't want to try to fulfill dreams of my own through you, as proxies for me."

"Proxies, sir?" asked Kate.

"Sometimes grownups push their children to do things that they wished they had done themselves. They don't do that on purpose, but rather because it's human nature to act as if life were a relay race, and you want to pass the baton to the next generation, for the child to finish what the parent began or what the parent was never up to doing. That's all too tempting. So, before I propose to you what Mistress Jane and I have been talking about, I want to find out what the two of you want for yourselves."

"Do you mean wealthy husbands, healthy children, and the like?" asked Molly.

"No. I'm not about to marry you off. Not at your age." He chuckled. "And I'm thinking bigger and broader than that. I'm wondering if the two of you might want lives that are very different from the ordinary."

"In what sense, father?" asked Kate.

"Well, not to put ideas in your heads, please tell me—if you could be anyone who has ever lived, who would you choose to be?"

Molly answered, "That's easy, sir. I'd be Helen of Troy."

"The face that launched a thousand ships," Kate mocked her.

"What?" asked Molly.

"That's what I think when I think of Helen—a face without a brain. You could do far better than that."

"And you, Kate, who would you be?" asked Sir James.

"Are there limits, father? Does it have to be somebody real?"

"No limits at all. It could be someone from myth or story, as well as history."

"Then Tiresias. I would like to be Tiresias," Kate declared.

"The man the gods changed to a woman and then changed back to a man again?"

"That's the one," Kate confirmed.

"But why him, or should I say *her*?"

"To look at life from both sides."

"And you'd rather be Tiresias than Helen of Troy?" her father insisted.

"Of course. I'm not into princesses, like Molly is."

"I can understand your wanting to be a boy. But why would you want to be a woman, too, with all of woman's weaknesses both physically and before the law?"

"To feel what it's like. Why live just one life if you could live two or even more?"

"Honestly?" Jane interrupted.

"What, Mistress Jane?" asked Kate.

"I remember when we went over the story of Tiresias. There was something else that interested you, wasn't there, Kate?"

"You mean the wager between Zeus and Hera?"

"Indeed, my dear. And what was that wager?"

"They wanted to know whether men or women get more pleasure from sex. But what is sex, Mistress Jane? You never answered that question."

"In due time my dear. But, honestly, Kate, is that why you'd want to be Tiresias?"

"Because of his answer?"

"Yes, my dear. And what was that answer?" asked Jane.

"That the pleasure for the woman is ten times as great as the pleasure for a man."

"And so, you're curious?"

"Yes, Mistress Jane. Of course, Mistress Jane," affirmed Kate. "What's the pleasure of sex? Is it better than the taste of cherries? Better than King Arthur stories? Better than launching a falcon on a bright summer day?"

"Enough, Kate," Jane put an end to that line of questioning. "As I said before, when you're older you'll know. At your age, you simply wouldn't understand. You're a clever little minx, I warrant. You only said *Tiresias* in hopes of getting answers to your questions about sex."

Kate smiled innocently and nodded.

"Most interesting," noted Sir James. "Kate, so much goes on in that head of yours that I would never imagine. But I liked what you said about wanting to live more than one life. It's delightful, simply delightful that you would think of that. Mistress Jane and I were just talking about helping you to do something very much like that—to enable you to live as boys and get a boys' education."

"And Molly, too, father?" she asked.

"Molly, too, of course."

"But, sir," objected Gertie, "what be this you be saying? Magic? Alchemy? There ain't no natural way of turning girls to boys. And I don't want my Molly mixed up in black arts."

"No magic needed, Gertie. I'll dress them as boys and send them to school as boys—to the free grammar school in Stratford, the King's New School, where they'll be so drilled in Latin that they'll be as good at it as any gentleman in England."

"They be bright, sir. I grant you that," said Gertie. "My Molly as well as your Kate. And they have the gift of acting. I be seeing that every day, the way they lie their way out of every trouble, and they be into trouble all the time." She chuckled. "But if you be so lucky as to fool the world that they be boys and get them into that fancy school, what do you expect them to be learning in just a year or two?"

"What do you mean a year or two?" asked Sir James. "They're only ten. And most boys continue until they're fourteen or fifteen."

"Ten, yes, sir. And going on eleven. My very point, indeed," said Gertie.

"Of course, the boys in that school started at six or seven. But I'll wager my Kate and Molly can catch up because of the firm foundation I've given them and their will to learn."

"But, sir, those be boys, and these be girls, no matter how you dress them, no matter how they act."

"Why, Gertie, I'm surprised at you. You've seen them at their play, as I have."

"Now, yes, of course, sir. They be ragamuffins, and more like boys than girls. But in a year or two the change will be coming. They'll sprout up in no time at all."

"As will the boys their age. They'll fit right in."

"And the boys' voices will crack and change."

"So Kate and Molly can fake their voices when the time comes," suggested Sir James. "It's difficult for a man to fake the high voice of a girl. But a girl can make her voice sound deep. They can do it. They're born actors."

Gertie laughed. "I can hear it now, sir. But how will the girls fake it when they be getting the curse?"

"The curse?" asked Kate. "What curse?"

"The woman's curse," answered Gertie. "The monthly curse. There will be no faking out of that when it comes. The very smell will mark them," she laughed again. "I can see it now—the very dogs be swarming to them and sniffing them, and the boys their schoolmates be staring."

"Yes. You're right to point that out, Gertie. Their public schooling will have to end when that begins. So, we are talking about maybe two instead of four years. But I want them to have their chance however long or short that might prove."

"But that first time, when the curse comes, and none can tell the coming of that. If that be at school? God! That be a mess of explaining to do."

"It won't be a surprise to Kate and Molly. They'll know what to expect. You and Jane can see to that."

"And how could they hide it, sir? Blood's blood, no matter how lordly it be. It makes one hell of a mess, and stink, too, sir."

"There must be a way. They're clever, devilishly clever. Tiresias ..." He laughed. "Given the challenge, I'm sure they'll come up with a way deal with it; and they'll rehearse their roles and play their parts to perfection."

"As if they be actors on a stage?"

"Yes, indeed, Gertie. They'll be acting every day for a year, two years, maybe even more. And the day when the curse comes for one of them if it's at school that'll be the climax of their play. For them, every day will be a play and all the world will be their stage."

"Be careful what you ask for, girls," Jane interrupted, "because once you enter that school, there will be no turning back. Sir James, we need to make sure that they know what they're agreeing to. This isn't a game that will be over in an hour. It'll be hard work, morning to night, day after day."

"Indeed, Mistress Jane. But if I know my girls, once they set their minds on something, there's no stopping them. Stubborn beyond belief. So, give it to them. Lay out all they'll be up against and see if you can talk them out of it."

Jane turned the girls around to face her, then glared at them as she continued, "That school does Latin, Latin, Latin. They drill you. They drown you. They force you to memorize and compose, to learn page after page of nonsense. You go from six to eleven in the morning and then from one to six in the afternoon. That's ten hours a day, every day but Sunday, every month of the year. Is that what you want, young ladies?"

"Latin is the language of gentleman and the language of gentlemen's business," answered Kate. "Everything that matters is in Latin. I want to matter. If others can learn it, I can learn it. I can do anything."

"And you, Molly?"

"Whatever Kate can do, I can do better."

"Not better," insisted Kate.

"Yes, better," Molly countered.

Jane laughed. "I'm glad you have such gumption and self-confidence. And your competition with one another could help keep you on course. But academics will be the least of your problems. You need to act like boys."

"That's easy," insisted Kate. "Molly and I do it all the time. You've seen us at play. Gertie can help us with the clothes and the makeup, like she always does."

"This won't be a matter of just dressing like boys and play-acting. You'll need to have the gestures and mannerisms, the temperament of boys. You'll need to be recognized as boys not just by the schoolmaster, but also by the boys in the school. You've led sheltered lives. You've never spent time with boys your own age. And you would need to fool dozens of them, ten hours a day, six days a week."

"You'll teach us," said Kate, with confidence.

"Much as I wish I could teach you; I must admit I know nothing about boys from age ten to age fifteen."

"Then we'll have to find a tutor for them," Sir James suggested, with confidence.

"A tutor for how to be a boy?" asked Jane. "I'd really like for this to happen, Sir James. But the more I think about it, the more problems I foresee."

"Lew," said Gertie.

"Lew?" asked Sir Janes.

"The stable boy. He be fifteen. He be knowing what it be like to be a boy. Let him teach them how to walk, how to sit, how to stand, what to do with their eyes and their hands."

Jane was skeptical. "Even if this boy, Lew, were a brilliant teacher, which I doubt given his role as a helper in the stable, I cannot imagine how ten-year-old girls, even absolutely amazing ten-year-old girls, could possibly learn what needs to be learned. I'm sorry, Sir James, for having suggested this. I should have thought it out more carefully. I should have known better."

"Father, don't listen to her," Kate insisted. "We can do it. Molly and I can do it. And it could be great fun, I imagine. It would be far better that than doing things with cloth and needles and learning manners and dance and playing music. Bring on the Latin. We want to learn, to really learn. We're as good as any boy, right Molly?"

"Better," answered Molly.

"Those are my girls." Sir James chuckled. "My feisty ten-year-old girls—ready to take on the world. More power to you, I say."

"Then we can do it?" asked Kate.

"If you and Molly can prove to me that you're up to it, I'll back you two hundred percent."

"And how can we prove it to you?"

"Mistress Jane will be your coach. Don't take her for granted. She's not only well-read, she has instinct and insight you can benefit from. She'll drill you in the basics and enlist the help of Lew for the fine points of boy behavior. Gertie will put together costumes for you; not just what's good enough for your make-believe. She'll make you realistic everyday boy clothes. When we agree that you might be ready, I'll take the two of you to the school myself to meet with the master, Simon Hunt, on a regular school day. We'll see how the boys react to you, whether you seem out of place or if they might accept you as one of them."

"Sir James," added Jane, "remember your position and the position of your girls. There will be no need to fraternize. Kate and Molly—"

"Kit and Matt," he corrected her.

"Yes, sir, we need to practice calling them by boys' names. Kit and Matt can be standoffish at school. They needn't sit near the other boys, who aren't their social equals. They won't need to talk with the boys or interact with them at all except in the context of the lessons and the school routine. That will make this extraordinary adventure more doable. Lew can accompany them, as their servant and guard. And with an appropriate payment to the schoolmaster, you can assure that they get special treatment, with no flogging."

"Yes, indeed, no flogging," Sir James agreed.

"Flogging?" asked Kate.

"A pedagogical method much in favor in our benighted times, but not appropriate for the likes of you, most certainly not."

"Flogging?" she asked again, in disbelief.

Sir James laughed. "That's the least of our worries. Now, let's celebrate our decision. Boys," he addressed them with a smile, "fetch your swords. Mistress Jane get your lute. Gertie, bring Jake from the kitchen."

When they had all assembled in the study once again, with background music provided by Jane, the girls knelt solemnly before Sir James, and he tapped both shoulders of each girl with the wooden swords; and, as if he were knighting them, he dubbed them Matt and Kit. Then they rose with big grins, proud that now they were boys.

15 ~ How to be a Boy

As for the physical difference between boys and girls, Kate and Molly knew the rudiments from having seen, held, and changed the babies of the servants in the house. Yes, boy babies had a tiny limp appendage that piss went through. It seemed bizarre that God had given them such a silly and useless piece of flesh. The ten-year-old girls had no idea that it was connected with true love and the making of babies. As far as they were concerned, boys were defective girls. They had lost interest in the difference between boys and girls years before. Magic, spells, dragons and sword fighting were far more intriguing and fun.

Now on the brink of masquerading as boys so they could go to school, Kate expected to focus on Father's lessons on Latin and memorization, and Lew's lessons on how to act like boys. But her curiosity in anatomy was aroused.

"What's a boy?" Kate asked Jane, as they walked downstairs from her father's study.

"Don't be silly," Jane put her off, incredulous at her naivete.

"I'm not being silly," Kate insisted. "Aside from dressing differently and acting differently, what's a boy? And what does marrying a man have to do with having babies?"

"You actually don't know, do you?"

"Of course, I don't know. I don't have a brother. And there are no boys here to tell me or show me. I feel like you and father and Gertie are all talking in code. What's the change that will be coming to Molly and me? And what's the curse? What's the difference between boys and girls, the real difference?"

Overhearing this exchange, Gertie caught up with the others, "Have you paid no heed to the babies in the house, those of the servants? Have you never been holding them and rocking them in your arms?"

"Of course, Molly and I did, years ago, when we were little girls, and liked to play with babies. But now we have better things to do—battles to fight, worlds to save."

"Be coming with me now," Gertie ordered.

Kate and Molly followed her to the kitchen where a scullery maid was nursing her infant boy.

"Watch," ordered Gertie.

"Yes. Milk comes from breasts, I know that much," said Kate.

"Well watch now as she be changing his wrappings. Look close now. You be seeing that little thing between his legs? That be where the piss comes out of a boy."

"Yes. We've seen that before. But what's the point of it?"

"That thing be called a cock, and out of it comes the baby juice that goes in a woman to make her with child."

"Piss and baby juice come from the same limp little thing?" asked Molly.

"Not always so little and not always so limp."

"So that's the deep dark secret nobody wants to talk about?" asked Kate. "Enough of that. We don't need to know how boys piss for us to act like boys. Let's see Lew and get on with our lessons."

Lew was tall, gangly, thin, and muscular, with a long neck and a prominent Adam's apple. He looked older than fifteen, except for his pimples. The girls had never had occasion to talk to him before, but they had seen him around and knew him as *Pimple Boy*. He wore a black felt cap, which had belonged to his father before him. It was his prize possession.

Jane and the newly minted boys met him in the stable, where he was brushing Sir James' favorite riding horse, a gray mare.

Jane explained to him, "Kate and Molly here need to look and act like boys so they can go to school. We'd like you to teach them how to be boys."

He laughed. "No offense, ma'am. But I ain't about to teach nobody nothing. I can't even read, much less teach."

"Would you like to learn to read?" asked Jane.

"Yes, ma'am. Indeed, I would, ma'am."

Jane replied, "We could help you with that. But first, you have to get out of the habit of calling these young gentlemen *ma'am*. Their new names are *Matt* and *Kit*."

"This be a joke, right? But why be you coming to the stable to make jokes with me who you never talked to before?"

"This is no joke," insisted Jane. "By order of Sir James, you will help instruct Matt and Kit on acting like boys. And then you will escort them to school each day, and sit through the lessons with them, as their servant and guard."

"But I be a stable boy. I be learning to be a groom. That be my life, ma'am. I be apprenticed to Sir James' groom."

"Not any longer. Now your full attention will be required for instructing Matt and Kit."

"Begging your pardon, ma'am. But my job is horses—has been these last two years, and always will be."

"Not anymore. Have no fear—you'll be paid for this. And we'll give you reading lessons. Then in a couple years, when this project is done, I warrant that Sir James will pay to apprentice you for whatever trade you wish."

"You mean I can become a blacksmith?"

"If that is what you want—yes."

"And I can learn to read?"

"Yes, we can help you with that."

"But for that I need to teach these girls how to be boys? So, all I want can be mine if I be doing what can't be done. A fine bargain you make, ma'am."

"You only need to teach them what you know already—from being a boy yourself. Just explain and show what boys do and how they do it."

"But I never be thinking about what it be to be a boy. I be knowing nothing about it. I just be doing what be natural to me. How can I teach what I do not know?"

"You're a boy of an age like the ones who will be their schoolmates. Tell these girls—now boys—what you think and feel and how you act. They've grown up sheltered here. They've had their reading and their fantasies, but they know no more about boys their own age than they do about elephants or giraffes."

"I be not their age ma'am. I be fifteen and they be what? Maybe ten?"

"Yes, ten. But that's a minor detail."

"I beg to differ, ma'am. They be two different beasts—a boy of ten and a boy of fifteen."

"And what do you mean by that?"

"A boy of ten be sticking with boys, doing boy things with other boys. He be caring about hisself and his pals—being stronger than them, being better than them at this and that, but being one with them. They stick up for one another, get into trouble together for the heck of it. They run in tribes—us and them. They be who they join with and who they be against. And above all, they be against girls—leastwise girls who act like girls and stick together and show no interest in boys and boy things. The worst insult to a boy of ten be to call him a girl."

"Heavens," exclaimed Jane. "And what about boys of fifteen?"

"We be thinking of girls."

"And what do you think of them?"

"Most times there be nothing else in me head but them. Not little girls. Womanly girls that been through the change, that been sprouted up and with grown woman parts and shapes. The legs, the bosoms, the buttocks—whatever we can see of them, and whatever we can imagine under their clothes."

"Excellent," Jane replied. "You see, Lew, you do know. You can help. You have helped us already. We needn't worry about the older boys guessing that Matt and Kit are really Molly and Kate, at least not until Molly and Kate go through the change and become interesting to them. The older boys will be too wrapped up in themselves and thinking about womanly girls to pay attention to a couple of newcomers—little boys.

"And the boys who are ten years old are tribal, you say. So, we'll make them think of Matt and Kit as outsiders, from a different tribe—wealthy and privileged. The pair of them will be outcasts as far as the ten-year-old town boys are concerned, not to be mixed with.

"But tell me, Lew," she continued, "do you really think of womanly girls and womanly parts all the time?"

"Begging your pardon, ma'am. I can't help it. My mind's not mine to order about. I be like a mare in heat—not that strong, but like that, and not just for a week each month—all the time."

"What's heat?" asked Kate.

"Never mind," Jane put her off.

"And what's the change?" Kate persisted.

Jane explained, "When you're a little older, you'll grow tall quickly and start growing womanly parts."

"By womanly parts do you mean breasts?" asked Molly.

"Not just breasts," Jane explained. "You can think of it as your body changing. Or you can think of your soul moving from one body to another and you having to learn how that new body works and how it feels and how it thinks."

"Is that the only time in life that something like that happens?" asked Kate.

"No. It will happen again. When you go beyond your child-bearing years and then in old age, if you're lucky enough to live that long. You'll find yourself in different bodies, and you'll have to adapt to those new bodies and how they move and feel and think. Life is a series of changes. Over the years, you'll move from one body to another and another. But you'll always be you. That's the great adventure of life—one challenge after another."

Over the following month, Lew spent ten hours a day with Kate and Molly and Jane. Jane had him walk and sit and gesture with his hands when he talked. And she had the girls mimic his actions over and over again. She also had the girls practice focusing their full attention on the schoolmaster, as if the boys in the room didn't exist— how to look superior and detached, with no interest in the peasants around them; and how to look bored like everyone else, while paying close attention to the lessons.

Jane also had the task of spreading the word in the neighborhood that the Arden girls were now staying with cousins, and that, in return, Sir James was hosting two boy cousins, so they could attend the excellent King's New School at the Guildhall in Stratford.

Sir James' servants were liberally paid for their silence and took pride in being privy to the secret of the house—Sir James' experiment at turning girls to boys.

The girls enjoyed Lew's mode of speech and the word play it inspired. They talked of *the mare of London* and the Queen minding her *bessy-ness*. They promised to work *arder and arder with ardor for the Ardens*. They talked of *cat licks* preaching *sir mans on son day and daughter day*. They talked of *skipping to the Lew, lewsing on Lewsday*, and going *lew-ny*. They talked of *girly girls with curly curls* and *boiling boys bitching boisterously*.

They had two wooden swords made for Lew so he could hold one in each hand and the girls could both fight him at the same time. He became their giant, their ogre, their sword-wielding dragon, and Molly and Kate teamed up to disarm him, to tie him up, and to tickle torture him. Soon it was hard for them to imagine their make-believe without him as resident villain and victim.

One day Molly asked him, "That lump on your neck, what's that?"

"That be me Adam's apple. That be a man thing. It be a way to tell a man from a boy and a woman from a man. He that be having one of those be a man for sure. But not all men be having them, not sticking out so, like me. No need you be having one to be thought a boy. But I be proud of my Adam's apple."

Being six inches shorter than Lew, that's the first thing Molly saw when she looked up at him. She reached out and touched it, caressed it. Then every day after that, when she saw Lew, she would touch his Adam's apple for good luck, a personal superstition.

In their lessons with Lew, they mocked him by exaggerating the mannerisms and gestures he demonstrated—walking and sitting and standing up like proper boys, marching with high-legged goose steps, running in place and getting nowhere.

Jane tried to keep the girls focused and serious, but she couldn't help but laugh at their antics and mimicry, while being amazed at how quickly they learned, despite their shenanigans, which in honor of the stable boy they called *horseplay*.

16 ~ Admissions Test

To Kate and Molly, Stratford was a major metropolis—six streets with nearly 220 houses and 1900 residents. It was far larger than the dozen-house village on the estate. The Guildhall, the largest building in Stratford, was smaller than the Arden mansion; but it wasn't divided into rooms. The downstairs, where meetings were held and plays performed, seemed enormous, and the loft above was also huge. A corner of the loft served as home for the grammar school, while the rest of the space was rented to the town's merchants for storage.

Sir James and the girls arrived promptly at eleven in the morning, when the students had just been dismissed for lunch break. The Earl of Oxford's Men, from London, were noisily rehearsing a play in the hall below, so Magister Simon Hunt led them across the street to talk. There they ordered lunch—lamb and ale, Sir James' treat.

"So, these are your wards—the young gentlemen you wish to enroll in my school?"

"Indeed, Magister Hunt. These are my cousins—Matthew and Christopher, Matt and Kit we call them. Where their parents live, there is no school comparable to yours. They are staying with me to have the opportunity to study with you, and my daughters, who, of course, cannot be admitted here, are taking the boys' place at their parents' home."

"You say they have a firm foundation in Latin?"

"They have completed William Lilly's *Short Introduction of Grammar,* and they know Caesar well."

Simon Hunt stared Kate in the eye and ordered, "Recite for me the first paragraph of the second book of *De Bello Gallico.*"

She did, without hesitation.

He turned to Molly, "And you now—the first paragraph of the third book."

She, too, did as ordered.

"Excellent. Many prospective students come prepared with the beginning of Book One. But ask them for Two or Three, and they stammer or clam up. Well done.

"Sir James," the schoolmaster continued, "I can see that these are fine lads. They only speak when spoken to. They know how to stand straight and sit still and look attentively. They project obedience. Do you deem that they are ready for Cicero?"

"Indeed, Magister Hunt."

"That is an appropriate level for their age. I understand that they are ten?"

"Yes. Eleven in six months."

"A solid Latin background is important. I have forty—now forty-two—students. They range in age from seven to fifteen, with a wide range of ignorance and ability. It's a challenging task to bring them all along, with just myself teaching. I cannot afford to devote significant time to any individual. They memorize their individual lessons. They recite. They translate. Latin and only Latin is spoken in the school room. If your boys do not have a firm foundation, they will flounder and, of course, they will be subject to frequent floggings."

Sir James objected, "I must insist that you forgo the flogging, even if they should occasionally deserve it."

"No flogging, sir?"

"I am willing to pay handsomely that an exception be made in their case."

"But flogging is the very cornerstone of modern pedagogical theory and practice. How do you expect boys to learn without flogging?"

"They learned well at home under my guidance. But I have taken them as far as I can with my limited knowledge and my lack of experience in teaching."

"Limited experience, indeed. I'm amazed to hear that you got them through Caesar without flogging. That's unheard of. Spare the rod and spoil the child. When you get whipped for an error, you remember, and you never make that mistake again. You are doing a boy a gross disservice not to flog him. That's my main function as a teacher. Many is the night I go home with an arm sore from administering floggings."

"I must insist," said Sir James, putting five gold sovereigns on the table.

"If you insist," Simon Hunt agreed, quickly pocketing the coins. "But you must realize that not only will they not learn as well, but also, they will be ostracized by the other boys, who get flogged as much and as often as my arm can stand it. My boys take great pride in how well they take their beatings, without crying, without so much as flinching—brave little lads that they are. Sparing your boys from my flogging will open them to bullying from the other boys. And in the end, Matt and Kit may well get far more and far worse beatings from the other boys than they ever would from me."

"I do not expect Matt and Kit to fraternize with the other boys, given the difference in their social positions. I bring them here because of your remarkable reputation, Magister Hunt. I understand that you are able to offer free education to all, due to the largess of your patron. But I prefer that my boys keep to themselves. They will be accompanied by a servant to help them maintain their distance and ensure their safety."

"As you wish, sir, much as I disagree with your approach. In any case, I invite you and your boys to join us today, as spectators, when my scholars return from their lunch break. They will be performing _The Menaechmi_ by Plautus, in Latin, of course. Drama is an important part of our program, requiring memorization, which is at the heart of all learning. Flogging is the first pedagogical principle, and memorization is the second. What matters isn't the material remembered, but rather the mental exercise involved. They must build their memory muscles.

"As for this play, it is Plautus' best. I'm sure you'll enjoy it. It's a story of mistaken identity, with twins separated at birth. It's believed that originally the dialogue was sung rather than spoken. Unfortunately, the music has been lost."

"But, Magister," Sir James apologized, "I'm afraid that I and my boys would be lost. The Latin we know is written Latin. We would be lost listening to a Latin work performed. That's why we are here—for you, with your immersion technique, to enable them to write in Latin as well as read it, and to speak Latin and to understand spoken Latin."

Magister Hunt laughed. "Plautus knew how to write a rollicking good play. You won't need to know a word of Latin to enjoy it. At any theatrical performance, many in the audience can't hear or understand all that's said, depending on where they sit or stand. And many might not be educated enough or bright enough to get the verbal jokes. So, the story must be carried by the action which you see, like watching mime; and the humor must be conveyed not just by words but by the gestures, the expressions, and the movement—physical comedy; slapstick some call it."

17 ~ Will Shakespeare

1574-1575

The school was in session all year round, six days week. There was no beginning nor end. So, Kate and Molly began the very next day. Lew carried their supplies: candles, books, writing materials, a writing book, a glass for ink, an ink horn, half a quire of paper—12 sheets. The three of them sat together on chairs to the right of the teacher, near a window, so they would only need candles on foggy days. The rest of the boys sat on benches, facing the teacher.

Everyone ate a breakfast of bread and ale. Then Simon Hunt began the day with roll call—each boy answering his name with *adsum*.

Each student recited a passage that had been assigned to him the night before. Then the teacher said *Bene. Traduce,* and the boy translated. If he made a significant mistake, his name was added to the flogging list—the beatings to be administered at the end of the day.

Once Molly made the mistake of asking a question in English. Magister Hunt glared at her, and the class broke out in laughter. She never made that mistake again.

Over the course of the day—out of the corners of their eyes, never looking directly, never staring—Kate and Molly studied the boys' mannerisms, as they had been asked to do by Mistress Jane. They had never before seen boys their own age in their native habitat, in groups, interacting with one another—poking and pushing and tripping one another; laughing with and at one another; challenging one another, threatening one another, then acting like it was all meant in good fun; slapping one another on the back, then acting like that was a gesture of friendship. This was like observing a strange new species in its natural habitat. They wondered if this was the way low-class boys behaved or if all boys were like this.

From time to time, Kate's eyes wandered to one particular boy, on the third bench back, who she saw in profile. Something about him was eerily familiar. She tried not to stare at him, not wanting to draw attention to herself. He looked a lot like Molly, and Molly looked a lot like her. And none of the other boys looked anything like them.

Near the end of the day, Kate sensed the presence of someone else beside her—no, inside her. Someone was in her head. That couldn't be. Someone else had her power and was using it on her? And why her? Did someone suspect her? Had she blundered? Was she crossing her legs wrong? Were her legs too tight together so she'd squeeze her balls if she had balls? Was she holding her quill too high up, too daintily? Not gripping it near the tip and pressing forcefully, with authority, as a boy would? Was there something else about her looks or her manner that gave away the fact that she wasn't a boy? Would he out her? She grasped the sides of the seat of her chair and squeezed, trying to force this thought out of her head, trying to calm herself, trying to shut the door to her mind that someone had opened. Who? A boy on the third bench back was staring at her out of the corner of his eyes. *Will* was the name he answered to. *Will Shakespeare.* John Shakespeare was the glover who made her falconer's glove. That was the son of the glover. She forced herself not to stare back. Glover. Her glove. Perry. Flying high, looking down at the hedge maze at home.

"Christopher," the schoolmaster spoke loudly at her, with the tone of a reprimand. She woke to the here and now and focused on the passage from Cicero that she must translate, aloud. The foreign presence was no longer in her head.

When her father asked what was most memorable about the first day, Kate said nothing about that eerie experience, but rather replied, "The boys' bare bottoms—when their breeches and hose were pulled down for the flogging. I was amazed there was no crying, though there was plenty of bleeding and bruising. They didn't try to avoid it. Rather, they acted like taking their beatings calmly, without complaint, was a sign of their manhood or boyhood. And all of them have lots of scars on their little butts. Thank God you paid our way out of that— the humiliation, the pain."

Sir James laughed. "We couldn't exactly pretend you were boys if your breeches and hose were pulled down, now could we?"

"And, father, one of the boys in the school looks a lot like me, even more like me than Molly does."

"Do you know his name?"

"He answered to the name of *Will*. And I think his last name is *Shakespeare*. I suspect he might be the son of the glover."

"Yes, indeed, John Shakespeare made your falconer's glove. He's a fine craftsman in leather goods of all kinds. In recent days, he has been alderman and high bailiff. He's an important man in Stratford. And Will is a cousin of yours through his mother, who is an Arden. No doubt that's where the resemblance comes from."

The sight of Will was distracting to Kate, and she couldn't understand why, except that looking at him was like looking in a mirror—the same black hair, blue eyes, long face, and light complexion. She was used to Molly's resemblance to her. But for a boy to look like her was annoying, as if he were guilty of deliberately cheapening her identity by duplicating it.

She tried so hard not to think about him that her very effort reminded her of him. At roll call, she was alert not just to Magister Hunt intoning his name, but also to Will's voice—the high-pitched and girl-like voice of a ten-year-old boy, but with a tone and rhythm that resonated in her ears, too familiar to her to be the voice of a random stranger.

At break time and at lunch, before everyone dashed off to home to eat, half a dozen of Will's friends gathered around him and laughed at his punning jokes and expected him to express what they all were thinking and fearing and hoping. Clearly, he had a way with words, though Kate couldn't catch much of it due to the general cacophony and the distance that she, Molly, and Lew kept from the others. She wanted to get closer and listen in. She wondered what it was about him that drew others to him. But her fear of discovery was greater than her curiosity, at least for now.

The first time she saw Will flogged, he was on the other side of the room. She could see his face, but not his bare bottom. She turned her head away, not wanting to watch. But despite herself, her eyes stayed fixed on his face. He cringed with each stroke. He bit down on the wooden handle of his penknife so as not to cry out in pain.

Kate grabbed Molly's hand and squeezed, then let go and pushed her away. Boys didn't hold hands. Lew had drilled them over and over on that. Did Will notice? Their eyes met. He was staring straight at her, with a puzzled look. Despite herself, she smiled back at him, and he quickly looked away, as the beating continued.

Why did he look away? What was he thinking? That she was a boy who liked boys instead of girls? That by smiling she was flirting at him in a boy-boy way? Lew had said such things were possible, but he hadn't talked about it. Much wasn't talked about. Too much. And if Will thought that of her, of her as Kit, what could she ever do to undo that? Did that mean they could never be friends—plain old boy-boy friends, buddies like he was with the half dozen boys who clustered around him whenever they had the chance?

It was by chance that they first spoke to one another, soon after she turned eleven. As usual, at the end of the day, when the boys all rushed to get to the door first and squeezed past one another to get out the door to freedom, Lew, wearing his black felt cap, and towering above most of the boys, led the way for Kate and Molly, pushing everyone out of the way. By accident, he pushed Will so hard and at such an angle that Will collided with Kate, and they fell over. Helping each other up, before Lew realized that anything was amiss, Kate and Will were pressed up against one another by the tangle of boys around them.

For a moment, they were face to face, staring at one another, their noses nearly touching.

She hesitated. There was something strange about his eyes. Then she realized that it was her own eyes she was looking at. She was seeing herself through his eyes.

Suddenly, he shook her, and she was back in her own head, and he whispered at her, angry, but not wanting others to hear. "How did you do that?"

"Do what?"

"The eye thing. I saw myself through your eyes. That makes no sense. How did you make that happen? Are you a crazy-eyed witch?"

Lew reached back, grabbed hold Kate by her shoulder, and glared at her urgently. She was breaking the rules they had agreed to. She was interacting with a boy from the school. Their ruse could be uncovered.

But Kate had learned that a boy of eleven would never back down to a challenge. He would fight back, matching insult with insult. She had been drilled so well in that that she shook free of Lew's grip and responded to Will by reflex. "Crazy? You talk about crazy? You're the glover's son, aren't you?"

"Yes."

"And you help you father in his glove work?"

"Of course. So what?"

"Well you know what happens to hatters?"

"Hatters go crazy. But what does that have to do with glovers?"

"The chemicals that hatters use make them go crazy. Everybody knows that. That's why we say *mad as a hatter*."

"What's your point?"

"Hatters make felt hats, and glovers make felt gloves. Same materials. Same chemicals. It will drive you mad."

He slapped her hard on the cheek, and said, "So tell me how that felt."

"You son of a bitch," she shouted back, and kicked him in the balls.

Lew forcefully pulled Kate away, and they ran for it, before Will could recover and retaliate. Kate and Molly rode, and Lew ran along side, guiding their horse.

The next day Will asked the teacher's permission to sit, permanently, at the far end of the back bench, as far away as possible from Kate. He asked in perfect Latin, having composed and memorized his speech the night before. Magister Hunt smiled and granted his wish.

Sequestered as she was, with Molly and Lew, on chairs off to the side of the school room, chances were that she and Will wouldn't encounter one another again. That was good. Something about him made her feel uncomfortable, insecure. That brief moment of projection into his head had been unsettling. And the crazy look in his eyes. And his quick temper. She never wanted to see him again.

18 ~ Dear Glover Boy

1575-1576

A year after Kate and Molly started at school, the teacher, Simon Hunt, moved on and was replaced by Thomas Jenkins, who had studied at St. John's College at Oxford. His rules were more lenient than Simon Hunt's. He allowed whispering so long as it wasn't loud enough to disrupt the lesson. And he did less flogging, using it not as an instrument of education, but rather to enforce discipline. Misbehavior and disobedience, rather than mistakes in lessons, triggered beatings. But those beatings were longer and harder. He sought to break the will of his victims, not letting them take pride in the *manliness* with which they took the strokes. Rather he beat them until they begged him to stop.

The most memorable of Magister Jenkins' beatings occurred a year later. Kate and Molly were both five foot eight now—very tall for the age of twelve, average for full-grown men, and four inches taller than the average adult woman. Their exceptional height helped their disguise.

Will, too, had sprouted. He was just as tall as the girls, and taller than all his friends. He was now pimply and awkward. He had not yet learned how to deal with this new body he found himself in, and his voice often cracked, comically, when he recited his lessons.

Half a dozen of the older boys, old enough to be apprenticed, were caught passing notes to one another—notes from or intended for delivery to girls who were their sisters or neighbors. Magister Jenkins was furious, determined to make an example of them. To humiliate them, he read the messages out loud for all to hear. Then he had them line up, with their hands on the bench at the front of the room, their breeches and hose down, and their bare bottoms in the air, for a double dose of flogging. Will was at the end near where Kate, Molly, and Lew were sitting. That meant that Kate got a good look at Will before his turn for flogging came, and she noticed a black spot near the base of his spine. She whispered to Lew to walk around, as if he were bored, and sneak a better look. She wanted to know if the spot was filth, or if that was the color of his skin.

Lew whispered back. "To me that be looking like a birthmark."

"And what's it's shape?

"Half moon, maybe."

"That sounds like yours, Kate," whispered Molly. "What are the odds?"

Kate gulped. Her eyes opened wide. Will looked in her direction. Their eyes locked for an instant. He seemed to look right through her. She shut her eyes tight and turned away. She didn't want him in her head, and she didn't want to be in his head. Something about him aggravated her. She didn't want to think about him.

Molly mused, "Maybe lots of people have half-moon birthmarks on their buttocks. Maybe we haven't seen enough bare bottoms to know."

Kate was outraged, as if it were an insult to her that this peasant, this ordinary run-of-the-mill boy should have her mark, as if he had gotten that mark on purpose to annoy her. She knew very well that this made no logical sense. But she was in no mood for logic. The boy aggravated her, whether he intended to or not. And she would get back at him.

When it came time to leave, while Magister Jenkins was busy elsewhere, and no one seemed to be watching, Kate scooped up the scraps of paper with the notes from the podium and stuffed them in her pocket.

After she got home, she shared the notes with Molly, and they read them out loud to one another, in mocking voices. Most were written by boys. A few, from girls, were recognizable from the handwriting and the style—primitive and unschooled. One of them began, "Dear Glover Boy" and was signed "Bridget." Kate copied that one over and over until she could credibly mimic the handwriting. Then she composed her own message:

Dear Glover Boy,
Do what you will with me.
Bridget

The next morning, Kate dropped that note on the floor near the podium, where Jenkins would be sure to find it. He read it out loud,

88

then immediately beat Will, furious that so soon after the last beating, he had committed the same offense.

Kate was delighted. And she was even more delighted when he came to school the next day with a black eye, most likely inflicted by Bridget. She couldn't help but chuckle. Will heard her and looked, then glared at her. She looked away, but she was pleased with herself, and pleased that he knew.

The next day, at school, Kate found tacks on the seat of her chair. And while they were at lunch at the tavern across the street, someone untied their horse and chased him away. It took Lew hours to find the horse and bring him back. Kate had no doubt that this was Will's doing. After that, during the two-hour lunch break each day, she had Lew follow Will and keep an eye on him.

19 ~ Sex Education

1577

At the age of twelve, nearly thirteen, Molly's breasts started growing noticeably. Each morning, Gertie wrapped cloth tightly around her chest, to contain them and press them flat. And expectations rose that Molly would soon have her first period.

Sir James wanted to end the experiment then and there. But Gertie and Jane pointed out that it might be months or even a year before the first period came. And the girls wanted to continue their schooling for as long as possible. Sir James relented, and Gertie and Jane advised the girls on what they could and should do if the bleeding should start at school.

Jane agreed that the schooling must end as soon as one of them had her first period. But she didn't think they'd need to take extraordinary measures in anticipation of that event. She said, "For most people, the first period is light—just some spotting."

"Most people, you be saying. Likely, you be saying. This be my daughter you be talking about," Gertie objected. "I had a gusher, and early, too. And I wager she shall, too."

"We need to plan for the worst case," Sir James decided.

So, every school day, Molly carried under her doublet a sheepskin container intended for water, only it was filled with chicken blood. Both Kate and Molly carried penknives, used to sharpen the tips of quills for use as pens. Boys also used such knives to play mumblety-peg. When Molly started to bleed, Kate was supposed to use her knife to puncture the sheep skin—lightly, only letting out enough chicken blood to mask the blood from menstruation. They probably wouldn't need to spill quarts of blood, but they could if necessary. In any case, they'd claim that Kit had been playing with her penknife and had accidentally stabbed Matt in the belly. Lew would pick her up, throw her over his shoulder and run, with Kate at his side, to get their horse and head back to the estate, leaving teacher and students stunned and confused.

In rehearsals, Gertie demonstrated how carnival magicians tricked their audiences to look somewhere else while they did what they had to do. Lew would carry dozens of pebbles in his pocket and toss a handful toward the back of the room to shift their attention before Kate made the stroke with her knife.

With maturation came increasing curiosity about sex. Now they didn't look away when the boys had their breeches and hose pulled down for flogging, and their bare bottoms and their penises, as well, were on display.

Kate and Molly asked Sir James how babies were made. He was embarrassed and talked about birds and bees and cattle and horses. "They all have offspring," he said. "Men stand to pee. And their piss goes through the same tube as the baby juice and cleans out the passage, removing the dried residue."

"But how does the baby juice get into a woman?" Kate insisted. "And do women have any choice about whether to have babies or not?"

"You'll learn these things when you're married. Your husband will tell you and show you."

"And if we don't marry?"

"Why then, I suppose, you'll never know, except by hearsay; for there are no books about it. The censors would never permit the printing of books about such matters."

Kate and Molly confronted Lew in the stable.

"Okay," Kate asked. "Boys have cocks, and baby juice goes through them. But how does a man put his limp little cock into a woman? Do you know? Have you ever done it?"

"No. Not me. Not yet, ma'am" Lew looked away in embarrassment.

"But you've seen it done, haven't you?"

"Seen people fucking? Are you mad?"

"But have you seen beasts fucking? Beasts that have cocks? Horses?"

"Horses, yes. ma'am. A stallion with a mare in heat."

"And when does a mare go into heat?"

"From spring to fall, a mare be in heat every three weeks. Six days on, then fifteen days off. If'n the seed takes, she be carrying the foal eleven months. And she can bear a foal each and every year."

"So, heat is like a period," Kate guessed. "When a woman gets her period is that when she goes into heat?"

"Period? What be your meaning, ma'am?"

"The monthly bleeding, the curse. Does a woman bleed because she's in heat? Is that when she can breed?"

"No, ma'am. People not be getting into heat. They be mating any time."

"And how do you know a mare is in heat?"

"That be easy ma'am. They be raising the tail and pissing and squatting and acting all hyped up when a stallion be coming near. And above all there be the winking."

"Winking?"

"The lady hole, down between the hind legs, it be winking—open and shut, over and over, she so itching to have it filled."

"Are any of our mares in heat now?"

"There be one what is."

"Well, bring a stallion to her so we can see what happens."

"Sir James will not be wanting that. That mare be his favorite. If she be pregnant, she not be good for riding. He be planning which mare to put to stud and when, and which mare to match with which stallion."

Kate chuckled, "And the day will come when he'll want to find husbands for the two of us, so we can breed. How civilized. Well, Molly and I want to know what's in store for us."

She handed Lew a gold sovereign. He grinned and led the way to the stallion at the other end of the stable. Kate and Molly took a good look at it, especially the penis.

Kate said, "That thing is limp. How could that get into a mare?"

But as Lew led the stallion to the mare's stall, the stallion started to sniff and pulled to move faster, and the penis got longer and harder. By the time they arrived, it looked too big and hard to fit in the mare.

After they had witnessed the mounting, and the stallion was back in his own stall, Kate noted, "It's hard to imagine how doing that could give pleasure to the mare. She looked like she was in pain, serious pain. If people breed like that, I don't understand why anyone would want to do it, how the human race keeps going. And Tiresias must have been dead wrong."

"Tiresias?" asked Lew.

"An old story the point of which was that in sex the woman gets far more pleasure than the man. I don't believe that now. Everything grownups say about sex—and they say damned little—makes no sense. Why do grownups lie about this to their children? Or do they only lie to their daughters—so we'll consent to marry and have this done to us? I won't put up with this forced ignorance. I have to know more."

"Things be as they be."

"Not if I have anything to say about it."

Molly asked, "Does it hurt for the man as well as the woman?"

"It be great pleasure for the man, or so I be hearing."

"And if it's such a great pleasure, why haven't you done it?" Molly pursued.

"I still be young."

"But not too young for that," Kate insisted. "Your voice has changed. You have the voice of a man, and you must have the bodily parts to match."

Molly added, "The stallion's member got long and hard. What about yours? Does your man part get big and hard?"

"What?"

"Take down your breeches and show us your man parts," Kate ordered.

He stared in disbelief, that little girls should say such things, should think such things, should want to look at his private parts.

Molly stepped forward, took hold of his breeches, unbuttoned them, and pulled them down.

He didn't try to stop her. He shut his eyes and tried to convince himself that this wasn't happening, that it couldn't happen. Never before had he been as frightened as he was right then, nor had he ever been this sexually excited.

Kate and Molly backed off and watched, surprised at their own audacity and yet very curious about what they saw, for, as they watched, his member swelled and rose, on its own, with no other stimulus than the knowledge that they were watching. Then liquid came from it, and more slowly than it had risen, it lowered and shrunk.

Kate broke the awkward silence to ask, "Is that the sperm—the baby juice?"

"The spunk, it be called," he answered as he quickly and awkwardly bent down and pulled up his breeches.

"And that's the thing that goes inside a woman?" asked Molly.

"Yes, that be my cock."

"And does putting it in hurt the woman?" asked Molly.

"The first time, I be thinking. So it be said."

"And after that it gives a woman pleasure?" asked Molly.

"I cannot be knowing that, not being a woman," said Lew.

"Does it hurt when your cock gets hard like that?" she asked.

Lew stood stock still, leaning back against a support post. "No, ma'am. But when that be happening, I be itching to put it to action."

He was unsure of himself. He would never have talked about such matters to the young ladies of the house, much less expose himself to them. But they were in control. He was their servant. And they certainly wouldn't tell anyone about this, any more than he would.

Kate, still brimming with curiosity, asked, "And does that happen when you're alone, when you're in bed at night?"

"If I be touching it meself and thinking like I be with a woman."

"Fantasy, you mean? Just thinking things, make-believe, imagining can give boys the pleasure of sex? They don't need a woman for it? The idea is enough? How romantic. Boys are weird. Life is weird."

20 ~ Birthday Present

There had been so many floggings since Kate and Molly started school that they had stopped paying attention to them. One boy's bare bottom was like another. The Glover Boy was the exception. When he got flogged, Kate couldn't keep her eyes off him. And he had become Magister Jenkins' favorite victim. His voice still cracked sometimes, and when he responded to questions shrilly and loudly, Jenkins believed he was doing so deliberately, as an insult, requiring discipline.

Meanwhile, at Kate's prompting, Lew went out of his way to get to know Will's friends and then Will himself. Lew told him he was the servant, not the friend, of Kit and Matt. He talked them down as snobs and sissies. He mimicked how they walked and how they talked. He made fun of the very gestures and mannerisms he had taught them— which, indeed, were boy-like, but not his style. He said he preferred the company of Will and his friends. To them, Lew was someone older, stronger, and more worldly-wise. They were unused to someone his age treating them as equals. The other seventeen-year-olds in town considered themselves full-grown men. They worked all day and paid no attention to school children. Gradually, Will and his friends came to accept Lew's companionship, and to joke and roughhouse with him at lunch breaks.

Will lived just four hundred yards from the Guildhall, and his best friend, George, lived three houses away. George had a sister named Bridget, and Will spent more time with her than with George. Lew reported their doings to Kate, who wanted to hear about Bridget, though the main purpose of Lew's surveillance was presumably to protect Kate and Molly from further pranks by Will.

Will was the third of eight children, six of whom survived childhood. In 1577, Gilbert, eleven, was going to the same school as Will—the only school in town. Joan was eight, Anne six, and Richard three. The youngest, Edmund, would be born three years later.

Will's father, John, had been one of the most important men in town, serving as alderman and even as bailiff, which was the equivalent of mayor, in addition to running his glove-making and leather goods business. He was wealthy enough to buy the houses on either side of his house and connect them all to make a single house big enough to accommodate his expanding family and expanding business. But he was beginning to act strangely, not showing up for alderman meetings and neglecting his business. Will noticed a tremor in his father's hands after a long day's work, a general weariness, and an inclination to go to bed early, rather than joining friends at the tavern down the street, which had long been his habit. Seeing these signs of decline, Will wondered if Kit might have been right—that his father might be suffering from long-term effects of the chemicals used in glove making. When Will brought up that question, his father got angry.

"Glove-making's me trade, me only trade," John insisted. "That be who I be. People been making gloves that way for generations, and so will they be hundreds of years from now. If you don't want to lend a hand to your father, Will, if you don't want to apprentice with me as a glover after you be finished with school, then fine. So be it. I have more than one son. Gil will welcome the training, and the business too, when time comes. And Dick, too, will want it someday. My ungrateful disrespectful oldest son can do what he damned well pleases, for all I care. Think on it, lad. Not many have a chance like this. Don't throw it away. It be two more years before you be fifteen and have all the schooling you be needing. Tell me then what you be wanting."

For now, Will was far more interested in girls and one girl, in particular, than in his future livelihood. Physically, Will was a tall, gangly, pimply boy, and Bridget was an *older woman*, nearly two years older—fourteen, going on fifteen, with womanly breasts. He daydreamed about those breasts, which he had not yet seen, but which he had felt through her clothes. He doodled those imagined breasts absent-mindedly at school, and several times got caught and flogged for it. He proudly reported those incidents to Bridget and showed her his drawings in hopes that she would let him see the real thing. She laughed him off, pleased rather than insulted by his fascination with her womanly parts, but limiting him to handholding, hugs, and kisses. She was far more impressed with his way with words than his drawing, though she knew very well that he would never make a living from either talent. She didn't know how to read, having never been allowed to go to school, and having parents too poor to hire tutors for her. But she appreciated a clever turn of phrase and was flattered that he wrote lines of poetry for her.

After he had gobbled his lunch at home, he'd stop by at her house before returning for the afternoon session at school. She'd play the mandolin, and he would read her his snippets of poetry. And for his thirteenth birthday, she promised, for the first time, to grant him the freedom of her breasts.

Normally, his birthday, April 23, was St. George's Day, a national holiday, when there would be no school. But this year, because of the proximity of Easter, the holiday would be celebrated not on Saturday the 23rd, but rather on the following Monday. Bridget suggested that they go to the woods on Monday when they could spend the whole day together.

But Will didn't want to wait. If she was going to do something that special for him, the sooner the better. "Let's do it tonight, the eve of my birthday eve," he suggested. "Then we can be together those other times as well."

She smiled at his ardent appeal, gave him a kiss, and agreed. Tonight, her breasts would be his, to enjoy as he pleased.

That night, when their respective families, as usual, had gone to sleep early, they slipped out and met in a nearby woods, part of the Forest of Arden, named for Will's mother's family, who had been local gentry even before the Norman Conquest.

Will had prepared the way, leaving a trail of papers with lines of poetry on them, to guide her down a path to a cluster of trees on which he had carved her name.

She brought her mandolin and a basket with bread and ale.

He read aloud to her from the papers she had retrieved along the way:

Love alters not with his brief hours and weeks.

My mistress' eyes are nothing like the sun.
Parting is such sweet sorrow.
We are such stuff as dreams are made of.
Shall I compare thee to a summer's day?
If music be the food of love, play on.
Under the greenwood tree, who loves to lie with me?

She gave him a kiss—a tongue kiss—for each line he read to her. At that point, she was ready for the dramatic unveiling.

But Will, with what he thought was romantic flare, insisted that first they sit close and stare into one another's eyes. He believed he loved her. And he wanted to project that emotion through his eyes to hers and for her to do the same. He had imagined what that might be like after the annoying incident with that rich boy Kit at school. If it was possible to feel like you were inside the head of someone you hardly knew and didn't like, and who was a boy, then surely it must be possible to do it with the girl of your dreams, your destined soulmate.

She would rather kiss and hug and get on with the unveiling. She was curious what that might be like, never having shown her breasts to a boy before, much less let him touch and kiss them. She kept turning her head, breaking the stare. He held her head tightly, with their noses touching. But she kept breaking the spell by talking and blinking, and she got irritable when he tried to discipline her.

"I don't want to do this," she insisted. "Whatever you imagined would happen, isn't happening. So, let's get on with your present."

She opened her bodice, put his hands where they belonged, and smiled invitingly.

He went through the motions he had been daydreaming about for months. But he was in a foul mood. He is disillusioned. He had wanted more than friction. He had hoped for a magical experience. Despite his adolescent physical need and curiosity, this was a letdown. But he played his part like a talented actor, and Bridget was pleased and thought he was pleased.

When they were done, Bridget left behind the papers with his poetry. She considered them a sweet gesture. She thanked him for them enthusiastically, but she couldn't read them, so why should she keep them?

What he had meant as a grand romantic gesture hadn't amounted to much. But paper was costly. He gathered up the papers and took them home. He could write more in the blank space and on the backs.

21 ~ Twins?

The next day, Lew reported to Kate, "If Will be smiling today, Bridget's the why of it."

"And what did the sweet little slut do for him?" asked Kate

"Word has it she be giving him her breasts."

"And what was the occasion?

"His birthday."

"And what do you mean by that?" asked Kate.

"Tomorrow be Will's birthday."

"But tomorrow is April 23."

"Indeed, ma'am. He be thirteen years old tomorrow. And last night, Bridget be giving him his present."

"April 23?" Kate repeated, incredulous.

"Yes, that be Will's birthday."

"But that's my birthday. Tomorrow is my birthday," she protested.

"Don't be thinking you own that day, ma'am. More than one body can be born the same day."

Kate was puzzled. Will looked very much like her. Her father had explained that they were cousins, on Will's mother's side. But born on the same day in the same year? And both with the same birthmark? That was too much coincidence to take without question.

Hearing about the birthday, Molly jumped to the conclusion, "Twins. You must be twins. Separated at birth."

"You've read too many stories."

"Well, ask your father. He would have heard if a cousin of yours was born in Stratford on the very day that you were born there."

After dinner, Kate approached her father when he was alone in his study. "Will Shakespeare, the son of the glover, who is at school with me, looks like me—same height, black hair, blue eyes, long face, and light skin."

"Yes, my Kate, you told me that, and I told you that he's our cousin, through his mother who is an Arden."

"And do you know that his birthday is today, like mine? He and I were born on the very same day—April 23, 1564."

"Yes. And you were born in the same house as well."

"What? Why didn't you tell me that before? And how could that have happened?"

"I didn't think it was important." He chuckled. "It was a coincidence. Your mother and I were passing through town, and our coach hit a hole in the road, and she fell out of her seat, and the impact triggered labor. The midwife was at the Shakespeare house, delivering Will. That's where we rushed, and she delivered you there as well."

Kate almost mentioned the birthmark but stopped herself. She suspected her father wasn't telling her the whole truth. This was the first time she had ever doubted her father, who she had worshipped as wise and honest and caring—the best of all possible fathers. It bothered her that she doubted him now. She felt guilty. Whenever they had differed in the past, she had been wrong and he right. That was normal. That was as it should be. And she didn't want to challenge him now—she didn't want to prove to him that he was lying to her. She wanted to believe that she was wrong, and that everything could go on as it had before.

Talking that night in bed, Molly found it hard to believe that Kate hadn't mentioned the birthmarks to her father.

Kate defended her decision, "Birthmarks don't mean anything. That's just a random physical defect. We aren't exactly the same. We aren't even the same sex. We could be twins and not have the same birthmark. And we could have the same birthmark and not be twins. A birthmark doesn't mean anything one way or the other."

"Kate, you sound like a lawyer," Molly countered. "But this is common sense—born the same day in the same house and you look so much alike. The birthmark is the clincher. Tell Sir James about that. Then he'll have to fess up. There's no other explanation than that you're twins, and it must be his doing that the two of you were separated."

"Nonsense. I don't want to force the issue. I don't want to think about this. I don't want to know as much as I know already."

Molly teased her, "Admit it—you like Will. That's why you're acting this way. You have a thing for him—more than a thing. A budding romance. And you haven't said anything to me about it. You're blushing. I've never seen you blush before. And now you won't look me in the eye. You don't want to admit that he's your twin brother because then the two of you could never marry, could never have children. It's against the church, against the law, against nature."

"Nonsense," she answered too loudly. Then she said again, more softly, more normally. "I don't think of him that way."

"If that's so, then fine. No problem," Molly snickered to express her disbelief. "But if this were a story you were acting out and not real life, you would tell him you are a girl, but you wouldn't tell him that you're his sister, and you'd hope by some miracle it turns out that you really aren't brother and sister."

"That would be duplicitous."

"That's a lovely Latinate way of saying it would be lying. But it would only be white-lying—a sin of omission, not commission. What he doesn't know—and what you didn't know until today—won't hurt him."

"No, I can't do that. I can't lie to him by omission. I couldn't live with myself if I did. If I tell him anything, I have to tell him everything. It's my duty to him as his sister."

"And what about your duty to him as a possible lover? He could be your soulmate, your one and only," Molly carried on, caught up in the plot of a make-believe romantic story. "Do you want to throw away that chance?"

Kate remembered the moment when she had—she believed—seen through Will's eyes, and he through hers. She blushed again.

Molly advised, with all the certainty of a thirteen-year-old, "Be discreet. Be selective in your truth telling."

"Molly, you sound like the voice of the devil. This isn't a fairy-tale romance where it's finally revealed that the lovers aren't really brother and sister, and so they can marry and live happily ever after. No. This time—in the real world—the revelation is the reverse. We are, indisputably, twins, and we can't magically change that."

"You say that with such passion. You the truth-teller," Molly mocked her. "You who for two years have pretended that you're a boy. I think that this obstacle to you two getting together as lovers makes you want him all the more."

"Nonsense. I don't want him. I don't love him—not as a lover. But I should love him as a sister, and I feel I have to be honest with him."

"And what is honesty here? Sharing a few facts, or getting to the heart of the matter? If you are twins, and I certainly believe you are, that means that one or the other of you was raised by the wrong parents."

Kate replied, "Well, there's no way a glover's family would take and raise as their own the only son and heir of a wealthy lord. Will isn't the son of Sir James Arden. He's a Shakespeare. I have no doubt of that. That means that I'm the glover's daughter. I'm a Shakespeare. We know that Lady Arden—the woman I was told was my mother—died in childbirth. I have no reason to doubt that. But if I'm Will's twin that means I'm not the child that Lady Arden died giving birth to. There must have been another baby who died, and I was the replacement. The switch was probably made right there and then."

"I wonder how much Sir James paid for you," Molly added. "What were you worth to him? How much was enough for your true parents to give you up?"

"Enough," Kate objected. "I don't want to go down that path. I don't want to believe that my father—the man I always thought was my father—could have taken me away from my real parents. And I don't want to believe that my real blood parents could have been so crass and money-grubbing as to sell me."

Molly urged her, "Go to Sir James. Tell him about the birthmark. Tell him what you know and what you've guessed from that. Maybe there's another explanation."

"I don't want to know any more about this. I wish I didn't know as much as I do. I don't want to be Will Shakespeare's sister."

"Then leave well enough alone," Molly suggested. "To all the world, you're the child of a rich lord. That's what Sir James wants the world to believe, and that's what you should want to believe. So it has been, and so it shall be."

Kate replied, "I don't know how I'll feel in the morning. This is too much to swallow in one gulp. But you're right. Will's parents must have sold me to Sir James. They must have split us up for money. They abandoned me. And they've never seen me, and I've never seen them since the day I was born. Will needs to know what kind of parents he has, what kind of parents both of us have. This is a matter of Will's identity as well as mine. Will and I could and should be close to one another, as close as brother and sister can be, from this time forward.

"I feel no bond to the parents who sold me or to the man who bought me. The only bond I feel now is to Will, my brother. And I won't betray him by not telling him the truth now that I know it. We have a natural, an almost supernatural bond. We should never have been separated. We should never have been lied to.

"I can no longer trust the man I thought was my father, and Will should no longer trust his parents, who are my parents as well. Now that I know this, I can't keep it from him. I have to tell him, even if doing so will mean letting him know that I'm a girl, not a boy, and that I have no business attending school.

"And how will Sir James react to my knowing this and telling Will about it? Sir James is not my father. He has no blood bond with me. He could disown me. And even if he doesn't disown me, if word gets out, everyone will look at me differently. I'm not the daughter of a lord, but rather the daughter of a tradesman, a glover. And I was abandoned by my real parents. I was sold, like slaves are sold.

"I've lost my identity, and all I have to latch onto is this brother, this twin brother, this boy who I hated before I found out he's my brother. He's my flesh and blood, and he's been lied to as much as I have. He's my natural ally. I have to reach out to him."

Then and there, she wrote a letter to Will:

Dear Glover Boy,

You know me as Kit, but I'm Kate.

You know me as your cousin and the daughter of Sir James Arden. But I am really the daughter of John and Mary Shakespeare, your parents.

You and I are twins.

We were born in the same house on the same day and have the same birthmark—a half-moon at the base of the spine.

Your parents sold me to Sir James when his baby daughter and wife died in childbirth.

I just learned the truth and feel compelled to tell you.

I don't know what will happen to me or to you because of this knowledge.

But whatever we feel about one another, however much we've aggravated one another in the past, we're connected by blood, as closely as any two people can be connected.

Let's talk, after school today or at a time and place of your choosing.

Your twin sister,

Katharine Shakespeare

22 ~ Curses

1577

Every day for months, they had gone through the ritual of dressing Molly with her sheepskin full of chicken blood. Her first period, which they had thought was imminent, now seemed remote. They took for granted that this routine would continue day after day.

Molly complained to her mother, "Do I really have to do this? Mistress Jane thinks it won't amount to much when it finally happens. Why don't I just wrap a cloth around my nethers? That should take care of spotting or a few drops of blood."

"Take care, Molly. Don't be dropping your guard. Like Sir James be saying, be ready for the worst, then all be right no matter what."

The morning of Kate's birthday, Kate took the message for Will with her to school. She had folded it in half three times, so it fit in the palm of her sweaty hand. She wasn't sure if she would deliver it, or if she would shred it, discard it, forget the whole idea of twins, focus again on her studies, and get on with her life as the only child of a wealthy lord.

As usual, boys straggled in one by one, then arrived in a bunch right before Magister Jenkins rang his bell and did roll call. Then there was a pause as everyone had their bread-and-ale breakfast. The boys could mill around and talk together, softly. As usual, Will's friends gathered around him, in front of the benches. The rising sun shone through the east-facing windows.

Kate stood. Molly took her hand to squeeze it, as a sign of support, knowing that she intended to give a note to Will and that that could change everything for her as well as for Kate. There was no telling what Sir James might do if he had an angry split up with his supposed daughter. Molly was only treated as a daughter because she was so close to Kate.

The hand Molly squeezed happened to be the one in which Kate was holding the note. The note fell. Kate bent down and quickly picked it up, frowning at Molly. She didn't need distractions. She needed to concentrate. She needed to keep to her plan, to put one foot in front of the other, and soon it would be over. Regardless of the consequences, the agony of decision-making would be over.

Kate started again.

"Kit!" Lew called. He had no idea what she was up to. He knew nothing about the twin business. He was still operating under the old plan—no fraternizing with the boys, keeping to their seats away from everyone else, avoiding direct eye contact with any of the boys. Unless Magister Jenkins called on them, they were to remain still, quiet, and attentive. For now, Kate should eat her bread and drink her ale like everyone else. But instead, she was walking, alone, toward at a cluster of boys.

"Kit!" Lew called again. She turned quickly to signal him to be silent, to let her do what she must do. But in so doing, the note once again slipped out of her hand. And when she turned back, before she could bend down to pick it up, her eyes met Will's eyes, and she froze.

It might have been a few seconds, but it felt like hours, before she could force herself to look away, then to look down, where the note must be. That was when she saw red spots—blood—on the floor by her feet; and she felt a trickle of liquid rolling down her thighs. She looked up, the realization dawning on her that her first period had started. Maybe she had started bleeding as she sat in her chair, maybe even as she and Molly rode the horse from the estate, but only now did she see it and know it. She was embarrassed, as if she had peed while standing in a crowded room. She was scared and confused. In their rehearsals they had presumed that Molly would be the first. But no. It was Kate.

Will was staring at her. What would he think? What would any of these boys think if they saw blood at her feet? She shut her eyes tight, to break their contact with Will, then turned and looked at Molly, in dismay.

Molly—practical, reliable, common sense Molly—immediately guessed what was happening. She kicked Lew in the shins and whispered to him, "Now. It's starting now. Throw the pebbles."

He threw them to the back of the room.

Everyone turned toward the noise, wondering what was happening.

Kate ran to Molly. With one hand, Molly reached around Kate and hugged her close; and with her other hand, with her penknife, she slit open the sheep skin full of chicken blood.

Blood poured onto both of them.

Magister Jenkins shrieked at the sight, took two steps forward, then three steps back, frightened by the sight of so much blood, and undecided what to do. "Help! Do something. Everyone, do something! What will people think? Accidents happen, but they never happen on my watch. Whatever this is, it's not my fault. Remember that, boys. I was nowhere near when that happened. I was preparing my lessons. I had no idea what they were up to. Calm. Calm. We must have order. We must restore order."

Lew threw Molly over his shoulder and took Kate by the hand. As they walked toward the door, Kate looked back, remembering the note on the floor.

No. It wasn't on the floor anymore. Will had it.

Mission accomplished, in spite of everything.

But no—he didn't open it, he didn't read it, and he didn't put it in his pocket.

Rather he tore it, then tore those pieces, then tore those pieces. And he put the pieces in his mouth one at a time and chewed and swallowed.

He believed that Kate was trying to set him up for another beating.

He smiled and stared at her as she went out the door; and swallowed, as if gloating that he had put an end to her treachery.

23 ~ Change of Plans

After Kate and Molly were cleaned up and dressed as young ladies, the family conspirators convened in the banquet hall, at the huge, little-used table, to emphasize the importance of the decisions they now must make.

Half a dozen banners of the St. George Cross—a white background, with two red lines crossing perpendicularly in the middle—hung lengthwise from the rafters. Monday would be the national holiday, and each year Sir James took this precaution in case an unexpected guest representing Good Queen Bess might appear checking for symbols of national loyalty.

Under Elizabeth, St. George was the primary patron saint of England. The banners of all the other saints had been abolished in 1552 because they were tainted with memories of Catholicism. This was before the Union Jack, which, under James I, joined the diagonal crossing lines of Scotland's St. Andrews Cross, with the horizontal and vertical lines of England's St. George.

By legend, St. George had appeared on the battlefield and helped the Crusaders under Richard I and he was invoked by Henry V before the Battle of Agincourt in the Hundred Years' War. Kate was proud to have been born on St. George's Day, and Sir James was pleased that when he made a fuss about her birthday that could be interpreted as an act of patriotism.

Now, Kate, Molly, and Lew were subdued and anxious. Molly had ripped the lambskin open completely and all of the blood had poured out. Their exit from the school had been hurried and messy, without a word of explanation.

Rumors, likely to grow to the size of legends, were spreading even now. In any case, their public education was over. Kate presumed that that was the reason for the meeting. Her speculation about Will being her twin was no longer paramount. What direction would her life and Molly's life take now? The girls had known that sooner or later the curse would come, and their education experiment would end. But they hadn't given much thought to what would come after that.

Sir James, Jane, Gertie, Lew, Kate, and Molly were gathered at the table, all looking somber and serious. Waiting for Sir James to speak, the silence weighed so heavily on Kate that she blurted out, "What will you tell them, father? What will you tell Magister Jenkins and the townspeople? There was blood everywhere. People must think that Molly or I or both of us are dead from losing so much blood."

To her surprise, Sir James laughed. "I've sent word already that both of you are fine. I said it was a superficial wound. No organs damaged. Jenkins is not to be blamed. Boys playing with their penknives. No fault of Jenkins. That's all he'll care about. I'm sure that as far as he's concerned, the less said about this the better. Maybe he'll ban penknives from the school, have the boys sharpen their quills at home. But Matt and Kit need to be disciplined for making such a scene, and for having been so careless. This accident could have proven fatal from loss of blood. So, the boys will return to their parents. And Kate and her friend Molly will return home."

"And that's it, father?" asked Kate, shocked that it could be so easy. "We magically turn back into girls, to be raised as prim and proper young ladies?"

"That's the easy part," confirmed Sir James. "We're gathered here to deal with the hard part—what can we and what will we do?"

"Will?" Molly sighed, not meaning to say it out loud. She had been obsessing over the twin question and the consequences for her if all were revealed. Her fate was tied to Kate's.

"Yes," Sir James affirmed, misunderstanding her and cutting her off before she could say more. "What *will* we do, together as a family, to ward off the danger that's upon us?"

"Danger?" asked Mistress Jane. "I can't imagine that the scandal of this incident will lead to danger. Even if word should get out that Matt and Kit are girls, that wouldn't be a crime, would it? Not a serious crime? Little more than a prank, I'd call it. At worst, a minor fraud that you could make go away and be forgotten, with the right payment to the right people."

"That's not my concern at this point," Sir James corrected her. "Kate and Molly, do you remember Simon Hunt, Magister Hunt, your first schoolmaster?"

"Of course, father," Kate and Molly responded in unison.

"He left a year ago, and he's been quite busy since that time."

"Doing what, Sir James?" asked Jane.

"Treason, it could be called."

"Treason?" Gertie exclaimed, throwing her apron up to cover her face, as she started trembling with fear.

Sir James patted her on the shoulder, then gave her a hug to comfort her. "There's no need to panic, Gertie. But this is serious. We need to be cautious. The Arden family is large. It has many branches. And some of our cousins have been careless in matters of religion. They're sincere in their religious beliefs, at a time when sincerity is dangerous. And they've been indiscreet. While I've gone out of my way to publicly demonstrate my support for the Protestant Church and for Queen Elizabeth herself, they have not. If the next ruler of England happens to be Catholic, I'll quickly and publicly switch my banners, my beliefs, and my allegiance accordingly. That's how to survive in times like this. I'm hyper-sensitive about such matters because the actions and beliefs of our Arden cousins reflect on us and put us under suspicion."

"By cousins do you mean the Shakespeares of Stratford?" asked Kate, alarmed at the direction of the conversation.

"No," Sir James reassured her. "To the best of my knowledge, Stratford is not a hotbed of traitors. John Shakespeare is an upstanding citizen, and your cousin Will is just a mischief-prone ragamuffin like the rest of your schoolmates. But prominent individuals in another, wealthier branch of the family have been careless and have drawn suspicion to themselves as supporting the Pope, who has excommunicated our Queen and called for her violent overthrow. Such opinions are dangerous. Saying the wrong words in the wrong company could cost you your head, literally. And that could bring ruin on relatives both near and far. We need to work hard to keep up appearances and distance ourselves from anyone under such suspicion."

"But you do that, father. You're very good at doing that. What's changed?" asked Kate, still puzzled.

"After he left Stratford, Simon Hunt went to France, to the University of Douai, where he studied to become a Jesuit priest. As far as the Queen's government is concerned, Douay is a training academy for Catholic spies and revolutionaries, and Simon Hunt is one of them. Any Jesuit found in England will be burnt at the stake—beheading would be too good for them. I just got word that Simon Hunt, your Magister Hunt, intends to return to England and wants to meet with me. We mustn't be here when he arrives. If I could, I'd like to erase any memory that we knew him, that children under my care were schooled by him, and that we might be considered friends of his."

"What do you propose we do, Sir James?" asked Jane.

"We need to leave the country as soon as possible."

"Do you mean me, as well, Sir James?" asked Jane.

"Yes. Of course. Kate and Molly will need your continued guidance and instruction. And Lew, to provide them with protection if and when they should venture forth on their own, disguised or undisguised, as I have no doubt they will want to do. They are too much in the habit of independence to change that now. And, Gertie, I'd like you to come as well, if Jake can spare you, for Molly's sake, and mine as well."

"You be ever so kind to me and my Molly."

"And you make my life a joy," he replied, then quickly corrected himself, realizing that that sounded too affectionate and might be misinterpreted. "The two of you, I mean. The both of you. With you, we will have the core of our household, and much can continue as is our wont, regardless of where we may roam."

"Rome?" Molly, asked wide-eyed. "Are we going to Rome?"

Sir James laughed. "Of all the places in the world, that's the last place we should go, given the political climate. The farther we stay from the Pope and papists, the better. We're not abandoning our home. We'll return here when I deem it's safe to do so."

"When?" asked Kate, wondering if she and Will would ever cross paths again.

"In a few years. Maybe a little longer. I'll manage business matters from a distance for a while. We just need to get out of the public eye until these religious and political issues cool down."

"Sixteen? Eighteen?" Kate thought out loud, calculating how old she might be if they returned in three or five years.

"Yes. You and Molly will be young ladies by the time we return. While we're gone, we'll see to raising you and educating you as gentlewomen of distinction, so you'll make a grand entrance when you return."

Kate pursued, "You mean you're going to train us as obedient, submissive women, like other women, so you can marry us off and we can have children and live quiet, forgettable, respectable lives. That's the very fate I thought you were saving us from."

Molly took hold of her hand and nodded in agreement.

Sir James laughed again. "I don't think anything could make the pair of you conventional, submissive women. But I'd like you to have a choice. I'd like you to be able to shine in society if you should so wish. And I'd also like the two of you to be as well educated as any women have ever been. That's all part of the plan. What you do with your intelligence, your education, and your wealth will be up to you. Mistress Jane will find tutors for you—French and Italian, first. Then as your tastes dictate—history, philosophy, literature."

"Art?" asked Molly.

"Art, too, if you like."

"And fencing?" asked Kate.

"Yes, fencing, too. Whoever heard of education without fencing?" he smiled.

"But where will we go?" asked Jane.

"We'll sail to the Dutch Republic, to Amsterdam. Staunch Protestants. It will be good to make it known that that is our destination. From there we could go to Bruges, to Brussels. And when the two of you are ready to take your studies to the next level, and if relations between England and France improve, I'd like to take you to Paris, where, if you like, you can do your boy-girl thing again."

"And go to the Sorbonne?" asked Kate, with enthusiasm.

"Well, the Sorbonne is the Faculty of Theology. I doubt that you would want that; and politically that would most certainly be impossible. But that's just one part of the University of Paris. And I'm sure with your brilliance and your skill at disguise, you will be able to attend lectures there in whatever subjects you choose. You could never do that at Oxford or Cambridge, where students room together in groups of three or four and with a fellow who guides their studies. You could never pass as men in an environment like that. But in Paris, students live separately in rented rooms scattered around the neighborhood. And the only education is provided in lectures. Yes, with your facility in Latin and what you could learn from tutors over the next couple years, the University of Paris should be well within your abilities."

Kate was beaming. A life she had never before dreamed of was opening to her. This man, who called himself her father, was a god-like genius. He was offering Molly and her an education and a life the likes of which no woman had ever had before. How could she have doubted his good intent, his natural nobility, his fatherly love. Blood mattered not at all. He was far kinder and more generous than any real father could ever be. She was blessed, and she rejoiced.

24 ~ Dear Will

Kate tossed and turned for hours that night. She knew her father wasn't her father, but he didn't know that she knew. And now she would never tell him.

She had a twin brother, but he didn't know they were twins. He didn't even know that she was a girl. From the look in his eyes as he swallowed, unread, the pieces of her note, he hated her.

She had tried to tell him the truth, but that hadn't worked. Now since she wouldn't be going to school in Stratford and she would be leaving the country, she would probably never see Will again. And now Sir James was offering them the unheard-of opportunity of taking their independence to the next level, leading to university in Paris.

She got up from bed, lay on her belly in front of the fireplace and wrote a letter to Will:

I am about to leave the country for a few years, perhaps forever. I am writing to you now to clear the record. I feel I owe you that much.

Although we only spoke to one another once, and that was brief and angry, I felt a bond between us when our eyes met. You must have been confused by my interest in you. Boys don't look at boys that way, or so I'm told.

I would need to be told because I'm not a boy. I'm a girl who wanted an education and could only get it by posing as a boy. Lew can confirm that. He helped coach my best friend Molly and me, on instructions from my father, Sir James Arden, who came up with this clever ploy. You knew Molly as Matt. My real name is Kate.

The incident with the blood at school was a charade. Neither Molly nor I was hurt. We staged that incident—which need not have involved so much chicken blood—to mask the fact that one of us had the woman's curse for the first time. We've reached the level of maturity when it would be impossible to continue to pretend that we're boys. Even if we weren't leaving the country, we would have had to stop going to school, so as not to be found out.

Please don't tell anyone about this. I don't want to unleash a scandal that might hurt my father, who was willing to go to such great lengths for Molly and me.

You have a very expressive face. You could become an actor. And in your face, I saw an interest in me perhaps equal to my interest in you. I'm guessing that it was confusing to you to have such an inclination toward me, when you thought that I was a boy. I want to assure you that your instincts knew better than your reason. This was not a matter of unnatural feelings, as Lew would put it. It was a natural urge of your new manhood, which, I'm guessing, is similar to what I feel toward you.

If I weren't leaving, I don't know how much longer I could have kept up this charade without opening up to you. But I am leaving. In all likelihood, we'll never see one another again. Or if I do return to Stratford, by then you'll have a wife and children, and will have forgotten me.

I hope you have a long and fulfilling life.

All I ask of you is your silence about this matter. I sense that I can trust you.

Never yours (such is the way of the world)
Katharine Arden

She was relieved at how easy it was to write to a boy she'd never see again. She could say anything. She could declare undying love or bitter hate if she liked, and she would face no consequences. She could unburden her conscience about the gender-swap and the confusion that might have caused, without having to say anything about their being twins. Yes, she was still certain that they were twins, but she no longer felt she needed to tell Will. As long as she said nothing, only Sir James and Molly and she would know. She could act the part she had been trained to act as the only daughter and heir of Sir James Arden, and she would be the grateful recipient of a future such as no woman had ever had before.

In the morning, she gave that letter to Lew for delivery to Will.

***

Lew and Will were friends now, so it was no surprise when Lew showed up at Will's house on Sunday after church services. But the letter was a surprise.

Will had wondered what was in the message he had torn up and swallowed and what the bloody scene was about. He wondered if anyone was badly hurt. Reading the letter, he realized why Kit's—Kate's—eyes looked spooky. A girl. That was a girl! For two years a girl had been making eyes at him, and he never knew it. He wondered what she would look like dressed as a girl, or, better still, undressed. And all those times she had seen him with his pants down for flogging. No other girl had ever seen him with his pants down. Humiliating. Titillating, too, that she wanted to watch.

And she must be some genius as an actor—both she and her friend—that they could pull that off for nearly two years, and he never suspected.

So, maybe as she said, he was attracted to her, but had fought that inclination, thinking she was a boy, and a weird boy at that. And all the while he was sensing but not consciously realizing that she was a girl. That's why she aggravated him so much.

But she was going away now for years and maybe for good. He couldn't see her before she went, and he would never see her as a girl or talk to her like talking to a girl.

"It ain't none of her choice, Will," Lew explained. "She be doing what her father says. That be the way it be. We leave in the morning. I be going with them."

"But can I write to her? Will she write back?"

"And what be the point of that, Will? She likely never be coming back."

On impulse, Will gave Lew the pages with lines of poetry that he had written for Bridget. "Here. Give her these to remember me by. And tell her to have a good life."

With that Will ran down the street to George and Bridget's house. He needed to see; no, he needed to feel Bridget again, and forget this mind-spinning nonsense about the boy who was really a girl, who admitted that she had feelings for him, but who he would never see again. He needed to get that out of his head. Bridget was uncomplicated and available. Kate was fantasy. Bridget was reality. Kate had feelings for him. But Bridget he could feel, here and now.

***

Kate knew very well that Will hadn't written these lines of poetry for her, and she doubted that they were his creation. He probably copied them from a book. But still she was pleased that he had sent them to her as a parting gift.

She wondered what it would be like to be his friend, to be his more than friend, to be his Bridget. He was the first boy she had thought of in a girl-boy romantic way. And the lines of poetry were good. He had taste, even if he had no talent. There was more to this country bumpkin than met the eye. Maybe someday he would make something of himself. Afterall, the same blood was in his veins as in hers, and she knew that she was exceptional. She wished him well.

Kate showed Molly the lines of poetry. She didn't consider them personal or private; but even if she had, she would've shared them with Molly. She shared everything with Molly. The poetry was like a trophy. She felt proud that the first boy she had ever paid attention to had made this gesture to her.

She gave the pages to Molly to do with as she pleased. There was no one else she wanted to show them to. And there was no reason to cart them around the continent.

***

Molly was obsessed with thoughts of their upcoming trip and the life that lay ahead for them. But after Kate's talk about she and Will being twins, and now having read Will's poetry, Molly started thinking about Will. She wondered what he might look like in three to five years, after the pimples were gone and the gangly body had filled out with muscle; and if, he might acquire some manners and couth. What a fine gentleman he might be when he grew up. And would he still write poetry? And might that poetry be moving and memorable? And might he write poetry for her?

Regardless of how much time Molly spent with Kate and Kate's father, and no matter how well Sir James treated her, Molly was and always would be the daughter of a cook and a house servant. She knew her place in life, and she'd never forget it. Gertie had instilled that wisdom in her.

In teaching Molly that, Gertie was passing on what her mother had taught her. But while Gertie had paid no heed to her mother's words and had run off with a troupe of players and sowed her wild oats, Molly took Gertie's words to heart.

She was submissive, accepting her lot in life and enjoying her present good fortune without expecting it would last. Molly would ride high as long as she could and enjoy the ride. But she knew very well that Sir James treated her like his daughter only because she was close friends with Kate. Sooner or later Kate would go off on her own, to have her own glorious life, and Molly would return to her natural state, with no breeding, no fortune, and no suitors of substance.

In her daydreams, Molly imagined hiding at the place in the woods where Will and Bridget met for his birthday present and watching them. She couldn't understand why boys were so interested in breasts. Hers were fine. Probably as well developed as Bridget's. And her mother, whose lead she was likely to follow, had the fulsome breasts of a midwife. Would that suit Will's fancy?

Molly didn't consider Kate as competition for Will's attentions. She was confident that when Kate blossomed into a fine lady, she'd forget the country bumpkin from Stratford. Besides, the blood tie ruled out the possibility of romantic entanglement between Kate and Will.

But there were no barriers to Molly and Will pairing, should they meet again. She wasn't his twin, and she wasn't his social superior.

She admitted her interest in Will to Kate. They laughed about it. They make-believed about it, with improvised skits of flirting, wooing, and happily-ever-afters. And Molly packed the poetry pages with her books in her trunk.

25 ~ Amsterdam

Amsterdam, Dutch Republic, 1577, age 13

Once they settled in a rented house in Amsterdam, Sir James let their tastes dictate the girls' studies. Kate and Molly had tutors in French, Italian, and dance. Kate did fencing as well, much to the surprise of the fencing instructor who had never taught a woman of any age, much less a thirteen-year-old.

One day Molly suggested to Kate, "Write to Will."

"Why should I? I hardly know him."

"We have no one else our age to share our adventures with."

"What adventures? Studying morning to night?"

"The adventures that we could have, the things we don't do, though we're tempted to do them. Making things up would be fun, and Will would believe anything you tell him."

"You write to him."

"But it's you, not me, he's interested in."

"He has no interest in me."

"The poetry."

"He wrote or copied those snippets for Bridget."

"He knows you. The two of you have a connection."

"And he has no idea what that connection is."

"No matter, Kate. Write to him. when Sir James sends dispatches home, include your letters and pay the courier to deliver them to Will and to bring back replies. Imagine his surprise getting a letter from Amsterdam, getting a letter at all. He's probably never received a letter in his life."

"Nor have you or I."

"All the more reason to write to him, so he'll write back."

Kate's first letter was brief, using Lew's delivery of the poetry pages as the excuse for writing, as well as the subject matter:

Dear Glover Boy,

What's this you send me by way of Lew? Lines, unconnected lines. Not a single poem, just the beginnings or endings of poems. And not written to me or for me. When you wrote these, —if you actually did write them, and not copy them from a book— you didn't even know that I was a girl. So how could you pretend that you were passionate about me? You wrote them for someone else—Bridget no doubt, she of the fulsome breasts. I'm not so built. You should know that. If it's breasts you want—and I can't imagine what the attraction of breasts is—you should look somewhere else.

Say hi to Bridget for me. And have a good life.

The line about breasts was Molly's idea. She was proud of her own burgeoning womanliness.

It took a month for their letter to be delivered and another month for them to get a reply. Kate paid the courier for his silence as well as for delivery. She didn't want Sir James to know. Not that he'd object, but rather because secrecy gave the correspondence an aura of the forbidden.

His reply was brief:

Dear Kit-Kate,

Don't be calling me "Glover Boy." I won't be apprenticing as a glover, no matter what my Dad might say.

Bridget sends her love.

England had close commercial ties with the Dutch Republic, and the two nations were almost co-religionists—the Dutch flavor of Protestantism being moderate like that which currently prevailed in England, as opposed to the more severe Calvinist or Puritan flavor. The house they rented was in a district where English merchants outnumbered natives. There was no need to concern themselves with the local language since they would only stay here for a few months while Sir James kept an eye on the political climate to gauge when they could move to Flanders, also known as the Spanish Netherlands, and eventually to France.

Sir James hired as a language tutor, a French refugee, Lucien, formerly a Protestant lawyer in Nimes. He also hired a French gentlelady, Simone, to serve as a personal maid to the girls and to perform some of the menial tasks that Gertie had always done before. He was now treating Gertie more as a close friend than a servant.

Simone was the widow of a Huguenot merchant from Lille. He had been killed in the St. Bartholomew's Day Massacre, when over 30,000 Protestants across France were slaughtered on orders of King Charles IX and his infamous mother Catherine de' Medici. His property had then been confiscated by the state, leaving Simone destitute.

Lew was often recruited as a dance partner for both the girls and as a sparring partner for Kate's fencing lessons. He also became an enthusiastic student of French, finding that French phrases impressed the servant girls in their neighborhood.

Some dances required more than two dancers, involving intricate patterns of movement, leading to kaleidoscopic changes in the pairings. Sometimes the language tutor Lucien as well as Lew, Jane, Molly, and Sir James himself all joined in for dance practice, with the dance instructor playing the harpsichord.

Sir James spent far more time with Gertie than before, and they were more openly friendly, exchanging looks and touches and smiles. Finally, Kate and Molly woke up to what was going on. Kate concluded, "They've been sleeping together for months, maybe years. I don't understand why they didn't tell us before."

"They were keeping it secret from my dad," Molly guessed.

"Maybe this is the reason why we're on this trip, not religion and politics. It's so they can be together, without Jake around. But they should have told us. We're old enough to understand."

"And she's old enough to know better. It's hard to imagine that my mother, at her advanced age, would do such things."

"And how advanced is that age? Do the math, Molly. Just because she's your mother doesn't mean that Gertie's an old lady. You're thirteen, so Gertie's been with Jake maybe fourteen years. She was eighteen when you were born. That means she's thirty-one now—a woman in her prime."

"God," exclaimed Molly. "How long do you think they've been doing it?"

"You mean how long has she been two-timing Jake?"

"I mean how long have she and Sir James been making the beast with two backs? You realize what this might mean, don't you?"

"Of course. You might be his daughter—not just treated that way, but his blood daughter."

"Which could mean we really are sisters," Molly concluded.

"You forget so quickly. I'm not his daughter. I'm a Shakespeare. That means you're his one and only child, his heir."

The next morning, the girls waited outside Sir James' door and waylaid Gertie as she left his room. Gertie blurted out the whole story, presuming that they had figured it out already. She seemed relieved, rather than upset. She didn't like lying—not among friends and family. She had been at a loss how to bring this subject up. Now that they had guessed, she could simply tell the truth and get it all out in the open.

They crowded into the girls' room, sat on the bed, and Gertie explained. When Molly was born, Gertie had no doubt that she was Jake's daughter. She made love with Jake nearly every night, and she had only done so twice with Sir James to comfort and help him. Lady Arden had had three miscarriages and no live births. Both Lady Arden and Sir James wanted a child badly, but he was so concerned about her health that he couldn't do his business with her. The look of her, much less the touch of her in bed at night made him shrivel, so there was no way he could sire a child.

What Gertie did was therapy. When he was depressed and drinking heavily, Gertie climbed into bed with him and pleasured him. He rose to the occasion and entered her. All was well again. He was a complete and functioning man.

A couple of weeks later, when Lady Arden wanted to try again, Sir James, on Gertie's advice, shut his eyes and imagined Gertie and instructed his wife to do things that Gertie had done for him. Lady Arden was glad to do anything and everything, delighted that he was once again able to do what they must do for her to conceive. That's how the pregnancy began that ended on April 23, 1564, the day that Kate was born. Two weeks before that, Gertie had given birth to Molly.

Gertie was eighteen when Molly was born. At that tender age that was her second pregnancy. Her first was when she was a runaway and ended with a miscarriage. Gertie was a healthy happy young woman with a virile husband who serviced her nearly every night. She had every expectation that, like other women, she would have a pregnancy nearly every year and more than half of her babies would live, leading to a large and happy family. But despite literally thousands of attempts with Jake, Gertie never got pregnant again.

As Molly got older and looked like an Arden, Gertie began to suspect and then to believe that Sir James, not Jake, was Molly's father. Sir James and Jake, too, came to that same conclusion.

Gertie and Sir James should have gotten together long ago. But first Sir James was grieving for his wife. Then he was reluctant to steal another man's wife.

Then, a few months ago, they started up again, and didn't want to stop, they simply couldn't stop. Jake wasn't surprised when she told him. They had drifted apart long before and their union had never been blessed by church or state, so their breakup required no official sanction. With an enthusiastic recommendation, Jake would soon find new work. And with a generous settlement, he would land a new woman to share his bed. No harm done. Jake and she remained good friends.

And, yes, this trip was an extended honeymoon for Gertie and Sir James, the start of a new life for the two of them. She was glad the girls now knew, and she and Sir James could be open about their love for one another.

"You be sisters now, blood sisters," Gertie concluded. "All the more reason for you to be loving one another and for me to be loving you both."

Once Sir James knew that the girls knew, he began to treat Gertie openly, around the house, as if they were man and wife.

It soon became evident that Gertie was pregnant.

26 ~ Brussels

In late fall, while the weather was still warm enough for the waterways to be free of ice, they set out for Flanders by barge. They maneuvered through the maze of streams and canals, their barge pulled by a donkey led by a farmer and walking on the path beside the waterway. The bargeman steered them away from snags, nudging now and again with a long pole.

Stopping when the mood struck them, as tourists in no hurry enjoying their travel, they went by way of Antwerp and Ghent. By the time they got to Bruges, the canals started to freeze. So, they went by coach to Namur, then to Brussels.

***

Dear Will,

After a dawn-to-dark fifty-mile, bumpy ride by coach, on a frozen dirt road from Namur, in a snowstorm, in the dark we saw a brightly lit tower in the distance. As we got closer, more buildings glowed—the light reflecting off the falling snow—and we heard a rumble, which became music, which became the voices of thousands of singers. It was Christmas Eve, and it seemed like the entire city had assembled in the Grand Place and all were singing Christmas songs, led by a vast choir. The tower was part of the town hall, which looked more like a Gothic cathedral. The buildings around it were illuminated by candles held by every singer. In the center was a creche, with a tableau of actors portraying Mary, Joseph, baby Jesus, the shepherds, and the Wise Men.

Before we arrived here, I would have described Bruges as magical. It's a walled medieval city, very much as I imagined King Arthur's Camelot. But the Grand Place of Brussels at night, with candlelight reflecting off falling snow and thousands of voices singing in unison, was beyond belief.

"Perfect," said father. "What a perfect place for a child to be born."

This is where we'll stay, probably for a year or more, until Gertie's child is born and has safely survived its early months.

Then on to Paris.

Father says that relations between France and England are improving. Protestants, at least English Protestants, are no longer subject to arbitrary searches and harassment and are no longer targets for random mob violence. He says that the king's brother, the Duke of Alençon, joined the army of Protestants—known here as Huguenots—and to avoid further war, a treaty was agreed on giving the Protestants basic rights. Rumor has it that the king wants that brother of his to marry our Queen Bess, to establish peace between our countries. Can you imagine? The Duke is 22 and Bess is 44. He's the heir apparent to the French throne, but I hear he has a pitted face and a deformed spine. His nickname is "The Frog." Maybe if she kisses him, he'll become a prince in looks as well as title. And maybe that same kiss will take twenty years off her age. It's going to take serious magic on both sides to make that work. It will take even more magic for Bess to get pregnant at her advanced age and bear an heir, which, I think, would be the whole point of such a match.

Father thinks Bess is just toying with the Duke, not intending to marry at all, but stringing him along to keep peace between the countries. I hope she keeps that going long enough for me get an education at the University of Paris.

Maybe Bess actually could still bear a child. Mistress Jane is pregnant, and she must be forty. And the proud father, Lucien, the French tutor we've brought along with us from Amsterdam, is as young as the Duke. So, first Gertie and now Jane. And for a few days Molly thought that she was pregnant was well. It was like pregnancy was contagious.

As it turned out, Molly had had dreams of making love with Lew, who you knew at school. He used to be our stable boy and now he's our bodyguard and dresses smartly and can speak French, brokenly, but with enthusiasm. Between her dreams and all the talk of pregnancy, she convinced herself that the dreams were real and that she was pregnant, too. Gertie calmed her down and assured her that dreams, even realistic ones, can't get you pregnant. You need physical contact. Gertie also explained that stress can mess up the schedule of your monthly curse. So, we only have two pregnancies here, which is plenty enough.

At first Lew was puzzled when he heard that Molly thought he might be the father of a child of hers. Then he seemed proud to learn that he was the subject of Molly's dreams, and he whispered to me that he wished it were I who was having such dreams. How silly. I have no idea what Molly sees in him.

By the way, I've been dressing as a girl for a year and a half now, since we left Stratford. That's starting to feel natural, which is a bad sign. I value my independence, and I'll have to be a man again when we're in Paris, so I can go to the University. I want Father to get two sets of travel documents for me, one as Christopher and the other as Katharine. I want choice.

For now, in addition to French, Italian, and dance, I continue to take lessons in fencing. For that I can dress and feel like a man, with a man's height, strength, and agility. Lew takes those lessons with me. If he's to be a bodyguard for Molly and me, he has to be able to fight at least as well as I do.

Molly, meanwhile, delights in wearing finery, goes shopping with her mother, and dreams lewd dreams about Lew. What became of my dragon-slaying companion-in-arms? Where is my friend of yesteryear?

Christopher Arden

***

Dear Kit or Kate, whoever you are today,

University? I wish I was in your shoes. Best of luck to you.

My Dad's on hard times now. A few years ago, when he was riding high, he might have set his sights on sending me to Oxford or Cambridge, not so much for my good as for the status that would be for him to send me there. But he isn't himself these days. Sometimes he acts like he's sleepwalking, in a haze. Other times he lashes out at me and Mom for no reason at all. Long-time customers and old friends shy away from him. He's no fun to be with. His work is shoddy so he can't get top price for it. The worse the money situation, the grouchier he gets; and the grouchier he gets, the fewer people bring their business to him. I think you were right about the chemicals affecting his mind.

I'm nearly fourteen now, nearly a full-grown man. It's time for me to make life plans, and I can't count on any help from my dad. I'll be leaving school within the year, and I certainly won't apprentice with him. There's no way I'll have anything to do with the glove business. And working for dad would be total hell.

I've been running errands for a solicitor, cleaning up his office, shoveling snow when there's snow to shovel, doing whatever I can for him after school to make some money and in hopes of working for him as a clerk after I leave school. There's not much legal business in Stratford, aside from wills and real estate. But that would be better than breathing the fumes of glove-making and being berated all day by my irascible father. And maybe I'll find a way to make a few pennies writing on the side.

By the way, Bridget is history. She'll be seventeen soon. For nearly a year now she has only been interested in older men, who have already established themselves in some business. George says that their father wants to marry her to a baker, and she's already helping out with the baking and learning the business.

Good luck in Paris.
Your envious friend,
Will Shakespeare

***

"A *baker*?" Kate exclaimed to Molly after reading that letter out loud. "The famous Bridget, she of the fulsome breasts, is marrying a baker? The true love of the great would-be writer, the poet-laureate-to-be of Stratford has cast him aside for a *baker*. And why does he tell us that? He's available is what he's saying. He wants us to know that he's an eligible bachelor, with no complicating attachments and a great future ahead of him as a clerk in a law office. Are you interested, Molly? He's yours for the taking. Or do you still have your sights on the stable boy?"

27 ~ Letter from Paris

Paris, February 1579, age 14, nearly 15

Dear Will,

Are you still there? What a silly question. Of course, you're still in Stratford. You'll be there for the rest of your life. Isn't that an exciting prospect?

It was a year ago that you last heard from us. Then we were in Brussels. Now we're in Paris. Glamorous Paris. It's not that much different from Stratford, except it's a lot bigger and there's a wall around it. But that's not a picturesque medieval wall with a moat, like Bruges. No. It's low and rambling, crumbling in places. It would be no use at all in war. It's just an obstacle to people going where they want to go as quickly as they'd like to go, limiting comings and goings to the gates. And inside isn't much different from outside—single houses with vegetable gardens and farm animals both inside the houses and out. Many of the men leave the city proper every day to work in the fields outside the city walls. It's much more rural and Stratford-like than I would have imagined, except for the filth. The streets—all of them as far as I can tell—are open sewers, with garbage and waste, both animal and human so mixed with the mud that you don't know what you're stepping in, and you can't even tell by the smell because the whole city stinks. Only the main roads are paved at all, with cobblestones. There the filth accumulates on the sides, flowing in gutter streams when there's rain or piling up during dry spells. It's especially bad in the heat of August. Everyone who can afford to leaves the city then. We went to the coast in Normandy. It was good to breath clean air for a few weeks.

Of course, there are grand buildings, palaces like the Tuileries and the Louvre, the Cathedral of Notre Dame, and the lecture halls of the University of Paris. Those who can afford it get carried by litter or ride by carriage from building to building and so they never set foot in the street. In terms of sanitation, Stratford is Heaven compared to Paris.

By now you've recognized that the handwriting in this letter is different. This is Molly, formerly Matt, not Kate who is now back to being Kit. She gave up on writing to you. That's why you haven't gotten a letter for over a year.

She told me, "Will's a country bumpkin, yesterday's news. I don't want to waste my time on him. If you want to write to him, go ahead. He's all yours if you want him."

In any case, I'm in the mood to confide in someone today. So why not you?

My mom, Gertie, had her baby last spring. A boy, to Sir James' unabashed delight. They named him James, little Jimmy. She insisted on breast-feeding him herself.

Mistress Jane and Lucien, the French tutor, also had a son. Jane takes care of both the babies, except the breast-feeding. Gertie handles that for both of them, as she did for me and Kate. It feels natural to her to have one for each tit.

In case you are wondering—your imagination having been prompted by Kate's last letter—no, I myself am not with child, and I'm not likely to be with child soon. As of now, there are no eligible suitors for this fifteen-year-old beauty—yes, beauty, I'll have you understand. It will be another year before they put Kate and me on the market. I look forward to flirting with handsome and witty men and having them scramble to outdo one another to impress me and win my hand.

"What a noble ambition," Kate remarked. Mating and breeding are beneath her. Not that she knows what she wants to do with her life. Just that she knows she doesn't want that.

Honestly, I find this whole husband-hunting business absurd. It makes no logical sense. But still, I'm looking forward to it. It will be an adventure to learn how to make myself attractive, like learning how to fish with myself as bait. And then to learn what to do with men once I've caught their attention and learn how to go far enough to keep them hooked, but not too far, until I'm ready to pick one and haul him in; how to toy with them for fun, without committing myself, or sullying my reputation.

As for Lew, who was the man of my dreams, he doesn't love me and never will. He looks at Kate the way I would want a man to look at me. But she doesn't think of him that way. What nonsense—me chasing after him and he chasing after Kate and Kate too in love with herself to chase after anybody. That sounds like the plot of a bad play.

Not yours, not anyone's yet,

Molly

28 ~ Royal Invitation

The house Sir James rented in the Latin Quarter was seven stories high but only wide enough for one room per floor. Kate insisted on having the top-most room with a view of the Seine and the Notre Dame Cathedral from her garret window.

For the first time, she and Molly didn't sleep together. Molly's room was on the third floor, with far fewer stairs to climb. Her interests and Kate's had diverged. Molly, dressing as a girl, continued dance, music, and art lessons and looked forward to being a young gentlewoman pursued by suitors.

Kate dressed as a boy in anticipation of attending the University and also because she felt comfortable and could be independent that way. At sixteen, Kate was taller than the average man and muscular. Because she was flat-chested, it was far easier for her to pose as a man now than it would be for buxom Molly.

Sir James and Gertie shared the second floor. Jane and Lucien shared the fourth floor. Simone had the fifth, and Lew the sixth.

The cook, the housemaid, and the coachman shared the basement. They kept chickens in the yard, along with a pair of goats, who were often in the kitchen begging for scraps.

The first floor served as both kitchen and dining room.

Kate was impressed by the looks of the Kings Musketeers, parading in their blue cloaks with a gold cross, their red breeches and high boots, a jaunty hat with a plume on top, musket at the shoulder and sword at the side. Whenever she had a chance, she watched the public exhibitions of their skills.

Despite the fact that it was impossible for her to become a musketeer, Kate took her fencing lessons seriously. On the lawless streets of Paris, ability with a sword could be a matter of life or death. In her exercises, she imagined herself as a public-spirited citizen who intervened in street fights and combatted crime—an urban hero. Lew continued to join her for lessons and practice.

Kate could have started attending lectures at the University, but she was enjoying her freedom in the big city—able to go where she pleased when she pleased, so long as she dressed as man and was accompanied by Lew, and they both carried swords, and they stayed away from the worst districts.

She hadn't read a book since they arrived in Paris, though she continued her lessons in French and Italian with Lucien.

She had a carriage and driver at her disposal. But when the weather was clear and warm, she preferred to walk along the Seine and browse the bookstalls, rarely buying and never reading what she did buy, but enjoying looking and considering the possibilities. On the best summer days, she and Lew would ride horseback outside the city walls into the countryside.

Kate was drifting. She wanted to know everything, but she didn't need to know anything because she wasn't preparing for anything in particular. Thanks to Sir James, she had no need to earn money, and never would. And the professions were all closed to women. She couldn't become a soldier or a clergyman or a lawyer or a physician or a scholar. She couldn't apprentice for any skilled trade. As a gentlewoman, she'd be expected to be idle, aside from sewing in its myriad forms and reading. Thanks to Sir James, she had the luxury of learning anything and everything that could be learned. But because of her birth gender, she couldn't do anything with that learning. That undermined her motivation and left her drifting. Rather than mull over this dilemma and be depressed, she chose to enjoy the moment and live the life of a student without the work of actually studying. During the day, after French, Italian, and fencing, Kate and Lew would explore the city or its surroundings. Then in the evening, they'd settle at a tavern frequented by students and drink wine or ale and sing drinking songs and share stories. Kate quickly learned the names and eccentricities of the professors from the tales the others told and made up stories of her own that were plausible enough to be accepted without challenge. She enjoyed the camaraderie and soon found it hard to imagine how she had gotten along all those years with just Molly as a friend.

When the talk turned to women, she listened and laughed when the others laughed, and added nothing. When women joined them at the tables to drink and flirt and be fondled in warmups for more strenuous exercise later in their rooms, Kate kept her distance, as did Lew, following her lead. The students seemed pleased with her non-competitive restraint, because many of the young women flirted with Kate/Kit, and trouble could have broken out if she/he had flirted back and stolen one of those lasses.

Sometimes a few members of the King's Musketeers stopped by. They stayed together and wouldn't fraternize with lowly students. But Kate couldn't help but stare at them in admiration. Inspired by them and with the help of Gertie, she *grew* a mustache and goatee, musketeer style. Gertie made the fake facial hair get longer gradually, so the *growth* seemed natural until the mustache extended from ear to ear.

Many of the regulars at the tavern were foreigners—Italian, German, Swiss, Spanish. Kit and Lew were the only English. The students all knew enough French for practical purposes, but Latin was the only language that everyone except Lew was familiar with. Lew smiled and gestured and pretended he understood. The others knew him as Kit's friend and fellow student, not as his/her servant and bodyguard.

The Latin of students in taverns was a bastardized slang, dealing loosely with cases and tenses. Kate caught on quickly to that dialect.

When it was time to head home, Kate and Lew would sprint, racing one another. Although Lew with his longer legs was faster, he always let Kate win, without letting her know he wasn't trying his best.

These were the best of days for Lew. He adored Kate, but even when drunk he would never overstep the boundaries of his role as her servant. He never expected reciprocity. But he could enjoy her company and her friendship all day and every day.

When going to the tavern, just a few blocks from their house, Kate and Lew didn't take their swords, since students went armed only with daggers. So, that was the riskiest part of the day, returning from the tavern, inebriated and swordless, in the dark and stinking streets.

Kate's drifting ended with the announcement that the entire Arden family was invited to a royal ball. Sir James explained, "As you well know, our glorious queen isn't married and doesn't seem inclined to marry. That means it's an open question who her successor will be, and what will then be the religion of the land. The Duke of Alençon, brother of the King of France and heir to the throne, wants to marry her, despite the fact that he's nearly twenty years younger than her. He's taken up residence in England and courts Queen Bess with diligence and enthusiasm. That's his only occupation, and he's the only suitor attending her in person. To show support for his suit, Catherine de Medici, mother of both the King and the Duke, is throwing a royal ball on mid-summer's day, and inviting all the English gentry who are in temporary residence in Paris. Our family can have as many invitations to the ball as we like."

"Count me out," Kate shouted.

"No, my dear. You are most definitely in."

"But, father, Catherine de Medici? The Jezebel herself? We are to honor her?"

"No. She's honoring us. And Jezebel is far too tame a word for her. She was the architect of the Saint Bartholomew's Day Massacre. She's arguably the greatest bigot and the most heinous murderer in this age of religious war and religious massacre. But we have been invited, and we shall all go to her ball. That includes Gertie, Mistress Jane, Lucien, Simone, and Lew as well. For this occasion, Gertie will be my cousin Gertrude, Countess of Arden. Mistress Jane will be a cousin from York, and her spouse will be Lucien de Montaigne from Montpelier. Simone will be a cousin from Lille. And Lew, yes, Lew we'll introduce as Louis d'Artagnan, a renowned swordsman from Navarre. We'll have suitable clothes made for all of you. Think of this as a coming out party for you Kate and for Molly as well. This will be your first chance to socialize with gentlemen your own age. If you wish to forego this opportunity to be seen and scrutinized as a young lady of station and fashion, you may go as a man, but go you will. In that case, please make an effort to learn to dance as a man dances and do us proud as a man."

29 ~ Duel Identity

Paris, June 1580, age 16

The ball was held on mid-summer night, June 22, 1580, at the newly built Tuileries Palace, the king's residence. On the night of the ball, the glitter and the glory of the palace was in sharp contrast to the filth in the streets outside. Long winding staircases converged in a vast marble hall. For this occasion, mirrors and gold-leaf reflected the light of thousands of candles.

For some of the young ladies, like Molly, new to the marriage market, this was the first time they had appeared in public and also the first time they had to wear the full regalia of their opulence for an extended time. It wasn't easy for them to maintain their balance while decked out in a farthingale—a contraption of hoops, stuffed with cotton and rags, intended to hold the skirt out in a wide circumference. It made walking an acrobatic feat. In addition, the weight of half a dozen petticoats and other paraphernalia made it difficult to move gracefully in time to the music through the complex patterns of multi-partner dances. Ruffs, too, were obligatory—disks of stiff starched cloth around the neck that forced the upright posture that was a symbol of social status.

The complex kaleidoscopic patterns of the most popular dances shuffled and reshuffled dance partners, so if the music played long enough, everyone danced with everyone else. Kate, dressed as a man, did not participate, didn't even watch, standing stock-still by a window and looking out into the darkness, ignoring the grandeur around her.

***

During breaks, one young lady was drawn to a handsome and enigmatic young man with mustache and goatee. He had a world-weary look of indifference. For the other men his age, this ball was a unique experience. They were wide-eyed with excitement at the lavish displays of wealth not just in the furnishings and decorations of the palace, but on the ladies as well, who were decked out in all the glory that money could buy in colorful silks and jewels. But this one handsome man had a look of extreme boredom. Obviously, he was here under protest. He wanted to be somewhere else, anywhere else. All this extravagance and luxury was beneath him.

This young lady boldly addressed him, without having previously been introduced. He didn't acknowledge her presence, persisting in looking out the window, where nothing could be seen. Then she grabbed his hand and catching him by surprise, pulled him into the disciplined complexity of a dance, and, breaking the rules, she maneuvered back into his arms, again and again, to the shock and annoyance of the other dancers. This young lady unabashedly demonstrated her interest in this one young man, oblivious of what others might think.

He danced well, and until the music stopped, he did what he was supposed to do, and improvised around the antics of this strange woman who had singled him out. Then, before she could catch hold of him again, he walked away, maneuvering through the crowd to a small room beyond the converging staircases. He shut the door, sat on an ottoman, and chuckled, thinking of the spectacle that strange young lady had made of herself.

Moments later that same lady joined him there in that room, shutting the door behind her. He stood and walked away, puzzled at her shameless behavior and her persistence. What did he have to do to make it clear to her that he had no interest in her?

She raced after him, caught up with him before he could leave the room, grabbed him by the shoulders, turned him around so they were facing one another. Then she took hold of his head with both her hands and kissed him on the mouth.

He tried to push her away, but she held tight, pressed her lips even tighter to his, and even tried to insert her tongue in his mouth. At that, he used his full force in self-defense, pushing so hard that her body went in one direction while her heavy clothing swung in another. She started to lose her balance, and in wrenching herself forcefully to bring under control the wild mass of the farthingale with its padding and hoops and the layers of petticoats, the strap on her left shoulder broke, then the strap on her right, and the entire assemblage of clothes fell to the floor, leaving her standing in her undergarments, with bare breasts.

She was too shocked to scream.

He burst out in laughter and made no move to help her.

She scrambled to pull up her clothes and hold them up, covering her breasts. Then she left the room through a back door, quickly and quietly, hoping that no one but this heartless but handsome snob had witnessed her humiliation.

He went back to the ottoman, lay down, shut his eyes, and smiled, rehearsing in his mind the crazy lady's unheard-of behavior.

A few minutes later, the front door to the room swung open with a bang and in walked an officer of the King's Musketeers, with the crazy lady following him. The straps of her dress had been tied back together.

"That's the man," she shouted, pointing at him.

***

Kate was tempted to correct the lady's mistake, but that could lead to even worse consequences. So, she waited to see how this would play out. It was hard not to laugh again, but she knew that would aggravate the already infuriated lady.

The lady continued, "I hear that he's an Englishman, but I don't know his name. Without so much as saying a word to me, he pulled me into this room and groped me and kissed me as he would handle a whore in a tavern. He grabbed me so forcefully that the straps of my gown broke, and my naked breasts were exposed to his eyes and hands. Maybe he's used to treating women with such barbarism in England, but here he needs a lesson in French manners and the consequences of treating a French lady with disrespect."

The musketeer directed her back through the door. "Enough, Juliet. Go back and wait for me near the musicians. I'll make short work of this." Then he turned toward Kate. "I recognize you. You're a student, a scum. I've seen you getting drunk with other such scum at a tavern in the Latin Quarter. What are you doing here? And dressed like a gentleman, with a sword at your side? Be careful you don't cut yourself with that, boy. You have no business here. And you have no business molesting my sister."

He took off his glove, strode toward Kate, and slapped her with it.

Kate snatched the glove from his hand, examined it, and threw it back in his face. "No thank you, sir. You can have your glove back. Very poor workmanship. I have no use for such a glove. We make them far better in Stratford."

"And where the hell is Stratford?"

"A long way from this hellhole you call *Paris*."

"Enough insolence." He turned and looked back toward the door where another musketeer was now standing. "Tybalt," he called. "This English scum has a death wish. This mere student, who dares go to a royal ball, dares to insult my sister. And now he dares to insult me to my face. Tomorrow will be the last day of his life. Set the time and place and the weapons. If he has a second, deal with his second. Otherwise, simply dictate terms. I'm leaving now with Juliet."

Kate bowed, tipped her hat, and said, "Parting is such sweet sorrow."

"Even more insolence. I must away or in my rage I'll kill him here and now without the niceties of a duel."

As soon as that musketeer left, Kate asked his second, "Aren't duels illegal in France?"

"Of course. But honor is honor, so duels go on. Thousands take place in Paris every year. And as you prepare yourself for this one, you should keep in mind that half the time both the duelists die from their wounds, slowly and painfully. But you needn't worry. Mercutio is one of the finest swordsmen in France, a captain in the King's Musketeers. He'll finish you off quickly and nearly painlessly—an honorable death for a lowly student, far better than one of your rank could hope for."

"Ah, Mercutio. Thank you. It's good to know a man's name before you kill him," she said with bravado, as if she were in a play, for this incident didn't feel real to her. Her life didn't feel real to her, having been one make-believe or charade after another. But the games she had played up until now had never been played for keeps.

"Do you have a second?"

"I have an hour, if you like," she replied with a smile.

"Do you have a second?" Tybalt repeated loudly.

"Yes, of course, my dear sir. He's here. I'll get him now. His name is Lew."

"Lew? Lew is a name?"

"The renowned swordsman Louis d'Artagnan. From Navarre."

30 ~ In the Shadow of Notre Dame

Paris, June 1580, age 16

Kate and Lew told no one about the impending duel. They left their house late at night, a few hours after they got home from the ball. When the sun rose, they were waiting at the designated spot, in the shadow of Notre Dame Cathedral. Mercutio and Tybalt arrived promptly, accompanied by a dozen other musketeers who came to watch Mercutio make short work of the rude Englishman.

As seconds, Lew and Tybalt had set the rules. Each combatant held a sword in right hand and a dagger in left. They tapped swords, said *en garde*, and began.

Mercutio was three inches taller than Kate, and his arms were longer than hers. Kate tried for a quick lunge, only to see her initial strike parried casually. Overextended and wide open, she barely managed to block his counterattack—a slash toward her neck. Her own sword came dangerously close to her own flesh as the blades clashed. Without realizing it, she soon fell into a pattern with him in complete control—strike, strike, strike, block, block. Every stab, every slash she tried was only what he allowed, his sword moving to intercept almost before she thrust and always angled just right a second before her slash had any momentum. And when he took his turn, every attack seemed to come at the pace of some tune in his head, his footwork was dance-like and graceful. She couldn't get near him, and she couldn't make him retreat a single step. At most, he would sidestep as he avoided a blow, without bothering to block, and he would force her to quickly get her sword between his and her body. Those dodging strikes were much more difficult for her to deal with than his return thrusts. And he kept her at sword's-length distance, never allowing a close-quarters clench, within reach of a dagger stroke.

Kate realized that he was toying with her, and that he knew that she knew. He was mocking her. She didn't know what she could do to turn that around, but she had to come up with something soon. Her breathing was becoming ragged, while his was as steady as if he were sitting on a bench and reading a book. Undoubtedly, he knew that she was tiring, that she didn't have the stamina of a full-grown man, that soon her sword would feel heavy, and her responses would slow down. Mercutio was in no hurry. He would finish this fool off at his leisure.

Suddenly, images flashed through Kate's head—boys at school in Stratford, playing with their penknives before school resumed after lunch, throwing at a target nailed to a tree behind the Guildhall. She was seeing through the eyes of one of the boys. He threw and hit the bull's eye repeatedly, cheered on by his fellows, who called him *Will*. She was seeing through Will's eyes a scene that Will remembered.

Distracted by that vision, she blundered a parry, and Mercutio's sword cut her left cheek, just below the eye. She jumped aside, scared now as she had never been before. Blood was pouring from the wound.

With that blow to the cheek, her mustache fell to the ground. From the expression on his face, she knew that he now knew that the mustache was false. Mustached, she looked like a man in his mid-twenties. Without it, she looked like a mere boy, no more than sixteen.

Mercutio laughed and struck at her clothing with teasing strokes. He slashed her right sleeve, then her left sleeve, deliberately and masterfully, cutting only cloth, not flesh, not skin.

His face showed that this match was too easy for him to take seriously. It was an insult to his skill to face a mere boy, a rank amateur.

Then suddenly, without thinking about it, without deciding to do it, without even imagining that such a move was possible, she threw both sword and dagger in the air, like a juggler, and caught the sword with her left hand and the dagger with her right.

***

The thought passed through Mercutio's mind that this boy may have been toying with him. Maybe he was left-handed and would now show his true skill. He had heard of such a ploy but had never encountered it in combat. It was disconcerting to face a left-handed swordsman, without warning. If he had expected it, he would have prepared for it, both mentally and physically.

He hesitated. He thought, and he thought about the fact that he was thinking. He never thought in sword fights. He depended on his training and his instincts. Thinking made him slow and vulnerable. He needed to be above thought, in the zone where he became pure action. He longed for the high he usually felt when his sword moved as if on its own, with speed and strength, and he was like a spectator of his own fight.

He was thinking, staring at the sword in the Englishman's left hand, when suddenly a dagger was flying at his head.

Shocked, he watched it come at him in slow motion. Unreal. His senses were heightened to the point that a second felt like an hour. And while he could have ducked, a thought ran through his head, *Who is stupid enough to throw at the head—a small target, always on the move, and easy to move. You should throw a knife at the body, the biggest target and the slowest to move.*

He felt pain in his left eye.

That thought continued after his heart had stopped. His mind had not yet gotten the message that he was dead.

***

Silence. No one moved. Kate didn't know how she had done what she had done. The entire situation felt unreal to her—fighting a duel with a musketeer, and killing her opponent with a knife, although she had never thrown a knife before. What the hell just happened?

The other musketeers stared, stupefied. The Englishman, without his false mustache, was little more than a child. And yet he had held his own against one of the finest swordsmen in France. Held his own? He had killed a captain of the King's Musketeers, in a fair fight, and with a move that none of them had ever seen before—juggling sword and dagger as a distraction and then throwing the dagger with pinpoint accuracy. The boy had guts. The boy had talent. With training he could become a musketeer.

Then Lew broke the awkward stillness, rushing forward with a handkerchief that he pressed to Kate's cheek wound to stanch the bleeding.

Meanwhile Tybalt knelt beside the fallen form of Mercutio. He removed the dagger. He checked for a pulse. There was none. He closed the right eye. There was no way to close the hole that had been his left eye.

Then Tybalt stood, drew his sword, and rushed at the English boy. But he was grabbed from behind by three of his comrades. "Enough, Tybalt," said one. "It was a fair fight. We all saw that. Let him be."

Lew pressed the kerchief tight to Kate's wound. Then he hugged Kate, turned her around, and quickly led her away, waving to the musketeers in what he hoped was a friendly gesture. He had no idea what the proper etiquette was when you killed someone in a duel, and you were leaving his friends with the corpse.

Kate was on an emotional high. She felt no pain from the wound, not yet. Was that Will she had sensed in her head? That was impossible. But her fighting a duel with a musketeer, much less winning it, killing a man, probably a good man, friend to many, loved by many, that too was impossible. By all rights, she should be dead.

This was unreal. Life was unreal. Now you're here. And a moment later, you no longer exist. What was the point of it all?

She laughed like a madwoman as they crossed the bridge over the Seine to the Latin Quarter. Lew grabbed hold of her and squeezed her tight while she convulsed in laughter and relief and total confusion. She banged into the cart of a riverside bookseller. The cart toppled and she was buried in books, buried in the wisdom of the ages, without a clue of what it meant to be alive or dead.

31 ~ Brother by Blood

Paris, August 1580, age 16

Kate couldn't share her thoughts and feelings with Molly, whose emotions were in a different place now. Molly was still high from the ball and the possibility of follow-up visits and invitations from men who had shown an interest in her, including the son of a count.

But Kate could confide in Lew. He didn't say much, but he listened well, and he made no demands on her. He accepted her as she was, and he was always ready, without warning, to race her through the fields outside Paris by horseback or on foot.

Hearing what had happened and seeing her wound, Sir James was shocked and worried. He wasn't concerned about legal repercussions. The King's Musketeers were notorious for their duels. When musketeers were involved, the legal authorities didn't investigate or prosecute violations of the decree against duels. And a fair fight, presided over by seconds, was soon forgotten, even if it led to death, which was common.

He also wasn't worried about Kate's physical condition. The wound was shallow, barely breaking the skin. After a week, the scar could be easily disguised, but instead of trying to hide it, she used cosmetics to exaggerate it. And when going out in public, in addition to a new fake mustache and goatee, she wore a patch over her left eye, although the eye hadn't been damaged. That gave her a scary look, like a soldier with war wounds. People avoided eye contact with her, which made it easier for her to be convincing in the role of a man.

It was her mental state that troubled Sir James. He told her, "A fraction of an inch and you could have lost your eye, or you could have been killed,"

And Kate replied, "We are such stuff as dreams are made of."

"What's that?" he asked.

"A snippet of poetry I once read."

Before now, she had only read poetry when forced to by her governess. And when she did, she couldn't remember it the next day.

Sir James had heard that an epidemic of melancholy was sweeping through Europe, and he was afraid that Kate might have caught it and hence might be at risk of doing harm to herself. It had been suicidal to engage in that duel that she had so narrowly survived.

He suggested that she go on an extended tour of the surrounding countryside, on horseback, with Lew as bodyguard. She needed a change of scene to get her mind back to a good place. He urged Lew to do all he could to distract Kate from morbid thoughts. They should stay away from Paris for a couple months. That would be good for her, and it would also be time enough for tempers to cool, in case any of the musketeers were inclined toward revenge.

They went to the Chateaux of Chantilly, Monte-Cristo, Vincennes, Breteuil, Pierrefonds, Chambord, and Cheverny, and the Palace of Fontainebleau. They slept at inns or in open fields, depending on the weather and their inclination. Though still dressing as a man, Kate felt more feminine, submissive, and vulnerable than she had ever felt. She slept fully dressed and cuddled close to Lew, who held her tight.

When they returned in late August, the city was quiet. Everyone who could afford to had left for their country houses, to escape the heat. Kate and Lew went back to their old regimen, lazily exploring the city by day and returning in the evening to their favorite tavern, which was still crowded with students who couldn't afford to leave. Kate abandoned the eye patch, the artificial scar, and her sword. She would soon be a student, so she started acting like one, even though she no longer knew what she would study or why.

No musketeers showed up at the tavern. The pre-university chapter of Kate's life was over, except the basic questions—what is life? What is death? Does it matter if you live or die? Does it matter if you die today or tomorrow or tomorrow or tomorrow, for you will die—that is certain.

One night as they left the tavern and headed home, it was raining hard and the soil and filth of the unpaved road was a thick soup of muck, into which they sank half-way up their calves. With each slow step, their boots made a loud sucking noise. There were no streetlights. The houses around them were dark. It was after midnight. The wind and the rain would muffle any scream, and there was no one around to hear.

When they were half-way across, a two-horse carriage raced down the narrow unpaved street. They waved to get the attention of the driver, but the carriage kept coming. Maybe he didn't see them. Kate and Lew scrambled forward to get out of its path, until they were pressed against the wall of the nearest building. As the carriage went by, the splash and the wave of muck knocked them off their feet. At that same moment, a passenger leapt at Kate. Lew jumped in his way and caught him. The momentum of their collision landed them both in a deep puddle.

***

Lew didn't think. He operated by instinct and emotion. He had fist-fought and wrestled with boys his age many times. He could hold his own muscle-to-muscle, when the issue was a disagreement or a matter of establishing pecking order among buddies, when you held your punches, not wanting to seriously hurt your opponent and not expecting to be seriously hurt, when there were unwritten rules that both sides knew and respected. But this stranger wanted to maim or kill and didn't seem to care what happened to himself. This was fighting with no rules, which meant Lew couldn't anticipate what might happen next. The stranger kneed him in the balls. By reflex, Lew arched his back in pain at the very moment that the stranger slashed at his throat with a dagger, the blade of which, by chance glanced off Lew's Adam's apple, giving Lew a chance to headbutt in response. The stranger struck back with forehead to nose, cracking Lew's nose, with a mind-numbing pulse of pain, then choked him with his left hand, forcing his head into the muck, while plunging the dagger deep into Lew's shoulder.

The struggle was over in less than a minute. Lew couldn't move if he wanted to. He might already be dead, for all he knew. Maybe that was what death was—pain and the inability to move.

***

Confused and inebriated, Kate was slow to move, not realizing that a life-or-death struggle was going on ten feet away from her, in the mud.

Then she woke up as if someone new were looking through her eyes and could see through the darkness. A dagger was stuck in Lew's shoulder. Lew had shielded her, and now the attacker was holding Lew by the throat, strangling him.

Seeing Kate rise to her feet, the assailant let go of Lew and lunged at her, grabbing hold of her legs and pulling her down, then forcing her head into the liquid filth, and holding it under while she struggled to avoid drowning.

Lew saw Kate go under, and a surge of strength rushed through his body. In a rage, mindless, determined, he scrambled to his feet, tore the dagger out of his shoulder, fell on the attacker and drove the blade into his back again and again, forcefully and rapidly, until his fit of will was done, and he collapsed on top of his victim, unable to move at all.

Kate pulled Lew out of the mud to the steps of a nearby building. She cradled his head on her lap and told him. "Hold on, Lew. Hold on. I'm going to get help. We'll get you home. We'll get a doctor. We'll do everything for you. You're going to live, I promise you. We're going to ride again together."

"You can do anything, absolutely anything," he smiled.

"Of course, I can. I turned myself into a man. I turned myself into a musketeer. And, by God, I'm going to save you."

"And can you make me a gentleman?" he asked.

With a convulsive quiver, he died before she could answer.

He had shed his blood for her. He was her brother by blood.

For an hour, she sat there in the rain and the filth, with his head on her lap, brushing his hair and caressing his cheeks. When she had run out of tears, she propped his corpse on the steps and went home for help.

The coachman and cook fetched his body with their carriage. Then they went back again for the body of the assailant, and took it outside the city walls, and dumped it in the river downstream from the city.

The attacker was Tybalt. The dagger was the same dagger Kate had used to kill Mercutio.

32 ~ The Mourning After

August 1980, age 16

"Lew," Molly screamed, shaking when Gertie told her that Lew was dead. He had been her backup, her reality dream, the anchor of a life that could actually be hers, the father of her children, as opposed to these titled toys, these little girls' fantasies. He was gone. No one could ever fill that emptiness in her heart, in her dream of the future. It mattered not that he paid no attention to her as a woman. Sooner or later, he'd tire of chasing Kate, who didn't take him seriously, and she'd be there waiting, patient, loving, lovely. It had helped that he wasn't focused on her. That meant she could feel relaxed around him, not worrying about how she looked or what she said, being relaxed and natural. She liked the self she was around him. That's the self she wanted to be forever and ever.

Kate had fallen into a deep sleep after frantically telling her tale. She would sleep for more than twenty-four hours.

Sir James might have had them pack and leave for England immediately, but little Jimmie was feverish, pale, and coughing. They weren't going anywhere until his health improved. Children, especially infants, died all too often.

Now, before Molly could recover her equanimity, the son and heir of the Count of Tours arrived at their house. His carriage and driver were waiting in the street. He wanted to take Molly for a ride in the country, having stayed in the city through the heat of August expressly to spend time with her.

Numb, she joined him, though she paid no attention to what he had to say. She was preoccupied with the images the news of Lew's death had conjured.

Near a meadow, several miles from the city gates, the count's son began kissing her neck, her ear, her lips, oblivious to the fact that she was distracted and hadn't responded to anything he had said. She let him fondle her breasts. She let him lift her out of the carriage and stretch her out on the grass. Then she looked up, as he bent over to lie on top of her, and she realized that he didn't have an Adam's apple—he looked nothing at all like Lew. That infuriated her. She kicked him in the balls, tripped him, and pinned him down. Then she socked him hard with one fist and then another, as she imagined Lew fighting the attacker. Then she spit in his face and insisted on being driven home immediately.

She told no one, not even Kate, about that incident. Later, she heard a rumor that the count's son had two black eyes, from having been assaulted by thieves. She laughed when she heard that. She never saw him again, nor did she accept invitations from other men who had met her at the ball. She had had enough of egotistical snobs. She had had enough of France. Maybe in England there was someone else like Lew. There certainly wasn't here.

When Molly's depression continued for months, Sir James confronted her, "Why this prolonged grief? Lew was a fine boy. But enough is enough. Get over it. I'll not have you or Kate fall victim to the epidemic of melancholy that's spreading through Europe. You will be cheerful. I demand it."

Molly laughed and kissed him. Old men were so naive. They believed that the passage of time gave them wisdom, as if aging was a voluntary transaction, trading the deterioration of the body for understanding. But, in fact, people get nothing in return for their physical decline. It was a bad bargain.

"Paris is yours," he said.

"I don't want it," she replied.

***

Meanwhile, Kate found respite in her studies. Without objection, having no fight left in her, she followed Sir James' advice, stopping her fencing lessons and starting to attend lectures at the University. Without Lew as bodyguard, she went back to wearing eye-patch and false scar, and unlike all other students, she had her sword at her side at all times. She never returned to the tavern. She had no desire to fit in and fraternize with other students. She figured that her weird and scary look would keep her safe and allow her to pursue her studies with no distractions.

A month after Lew's death, she wrote to Will.

Dear Will,

Since last I wrote to you (was it two years ago?), I believe there's been a change in my personality—not that anyone here would notice it, wrapped up as they are in their own lives. Gertie and Jane are focused on the babies, Jimmie and Freddie. Jimmie is sick and failing, and Freddie seems to have the same ailment. Nature is cruel. We are so drawn to infants when they are so small and helpless. We bond to them quickly. And all too often they die. In self-defense, not from the illness but from the possible grief, I've kept my distance. I don't dare let myself feel too much for them. I never want to have children of my own.

I understand that Molly sent you a long letter a while back. Don't expect to hear from her again. She's no longer interested in corresponding with a country bumpkin in Stratford. She is now very much the young lady, not just physically, but also the way she thinks and dreams. She battered one suitor who played too loose with her, the heir of a count, no less. And others come calling. I can't keep track of them all. She no longer dons the clothes of a man, even in jest. And she has no interest in getting a university education.

As for me, with a ragged scar on my cheek—thanks to Gertie's skill with makeup—and a patch over my left eye, and a sword at my side, no one would doubt that I'm a man, and no one is going to challenge me on the street. If I wanted to, I could probably join the King's Musketeers. Instead, I choose to go to the University, where my fearsome look makes others shy away from me— just as I would wish.

I'm withdrawn, brooding. I read when I'm not at lectures: philosophy, history, literature, even religion. I need to make sense of life and death. Life isn't a game for me anymore, and I prefer to be alone with my thoughts.

Why this change in me? In brief, I fought a duel with a captain of the King's Musketeers and killed him. Yes, I survived. Yes, I killed a man. The shock of killing a man. The reality of death—that death is so close, always. The finality. That shook my make-believe little-girl world.

Then, in revenge, the man's friend, his second in the duel, ambushed me in the dark of night and would have murdered me if Lew hadn't intervened. Yes, the gangly, pimply stable boy you knew grappled hand-to-hand with a King's Musketeer and killed the attacker, saving my life. He died saving my life.

Lew loved me. He truly loved me. And I didn't love him back, and he knew that, but he died for me, and he was happy. I could see it in his eyes—he was actually happy to die for me, that's how much he loved me. I never imagined there could be a love that strong in one so young, so unschooled, a stable boy—on the surface someone not worth notice, but at his core as noble as any knight of the Roundtable. Love. True Love. And I didn't pay any attention to this man, this more than a man when he was at my side every day, selflessly serving me while I selfishly ignored him.

But that isn't why I'm writing to you. That is only the context.

I don't know what happened, but it happened once for sure and maybe twice. It makes no sense to me, but there are more things in heaven and earth than I ever dreamt of.

In the duel, I was overmatched, out classed, totally at the mercy of Mercutio, the musketeer. He was toying with me. I was tiring. He could have killed me whenever he felt like finishing me off. Then, suddenly, there was a foreign presence in my head. It was like someone else was looking through my eyes; someone else was controlling my muscles. I tossed my sword and my dagger in the air, like a juggler, like I had never done before. I caught the dagger in my right hand and the sword in my left. Then I threw the dagger with deadly accuracy.

And later, when I was ambushed and Lew saved me and died for me, I felt a glimmer of that same sensation. Someone else was in my head, seeing through my eyes. That woke me up, or otherwise I might have drowned in the mud.

I didn't hear voices like Joan of Arc. I didn't see a blinding flash of light like Paul on the road to Damascus. But I did think I had been touched by an angel, until I remembered that once, years ago when you and I bumped into one another and spoke, I had a feeling like that. That was the only time we spoke. I don't know if you felt what I did at the time, but to me it was as if I was inside your head, seeing through your eyes. It was totally weird. Inexplicable. That experience years ago with you was the closest I had come before to what I felt in that duel. But in the duel, you were in my head, and at school I was in yours.

I've been reading in history, philosophy, religion, and literature, and haven't seen a reference to anything like that. But it was real. It saved my life.

My best guess is that it has something to do with the soul. Maybe the soul can move from one body to another and then back again. Writing that down makes the idea seem even more crazy than when I first thought it. But maybe we're soulmates and this only happens with special pairs of people like us.

God! What a terrible idea. That I could be soulmates with someone I know very little about and don't even like.

Or maybe this is some special power—nothing to do with romantic love— that you and I have under special circumstances. Maybe we can get inside other people's heads, not just one another's. Maybe we were gifted with a special ability that lets us empathize with others, to get a deeper understanding of other people than is normal.

I do believe this is a matter of the soul. The living soul can move from one body to another. Our souls can do that. We can do that with one another.

That's it. That's what I needed to say—that I have this whacky superstitious belief that you have been inside my head and that I was inside of yours. And thank you, because if you hadn't done that, I would be dead.

We'll probably never see one another again, and if we do, we probably won't like one another. But the two of us have this strange connection with one another, this power that maybe no one else has. Isn't that special, glover boy?

So, I'll keep studying and reading, hoping to find a better explanation. And I'll keep playing my boy-girl identity game and maybe take on other identities, that being a way to feel like I'm inside the heads of others. I like that illusion. Why live just one life if you can live many?

Maybe I should become an actor and take on one identity after another. I had thought that here in France, where there's no law to prevent women from acting on the stage, I might try my hand as a player. But there's only one authorized theater troupe in all of Paris. There's more theater in Stratford than in Paris. But thank God, there are street performers—puppeteers and mimes and wandering troupes of gypsies. Maybe I'll join them, like Gertie did when she was younger than I am now, and spend my life pretending to be anyone other than me, whoever I may be. We are such stuff as dreams are made of.

Mine, never yours, truly,
Christopher Arden

***

Dear Christopher,

This is weird. There's no link between us. We barely knew one another in Stratford. And now you claim we're connected on at some primal level. Nonsense. Fantasy. By sheer coincidence I had fantasies similar to yours. This is much ado about nothing. People dream. Sometimes they have similar dreams. Don't jump to conclusions. The world is not that much out of joint.

Have a good life.

William Shakespeare

33 ~ True Glove

Soon after Kate had completed two years at the University, Little Jimmie died of a persistent fever. Even aggressive bleeding couldn't save him.

When the family limped home, the household all knew that Sir James and Gertie were living together as man and wife, but the local gentry either didn't know or didn't care. So long as they didn't have to meet Gertie and treat her as a social equal, it was no business of theirs who he shared his bed with.

Jane, Lucien, and their two-year-old son Freddie were treated as family members. They continued to tutor Molly in matters appropriate for a young lady and helped arrange opportunities for her, in the role of Sir James' orphan cousin and ward, to meet eligible young men. Molly had fully recovered from her gloom and was looking forward to playing the marriage game on English soil, with English suitors.

Kate abandoned the scar, the eye patch, and the sword, but she still wore the mustache and beard and dressed as a man, which gave her greater freedom of movement than women's clothes and also meant that she could go where she wanted when she pleased, without being accompanied by a chaperone or servant.

Neither Kate nor Molly contacted Will. Exchanging letters with him from far away had helped them sort out their thoughts and feelings. But they had been pen pals and nothing more, and they now considered themselves beyond such childishness, and socially superior to the son of a glover. Having been so intimate with him in letters, it would have been embarrassing to encounter him in the flesh, not knowing what he might expect, what liberties he might take, verbally or otherwise, that were out of the question considering their social distance. They knew from his letters that he was now working as a clerk for Stratford's one and only solicitor, six days a week, dawn to dusk. Although they lived just a few miles away from one another, the chance that they would see one another was slim, given the difference in their social standing. And even if they did meet by chance, they probably wouldn't recognize one another since now, at age eighteen, they bore little resemblance to their thirteen-year-old selves.

Kate spent most of her days reading—on sunny days in the flower garden, or at favorite spots in the woods, or even on the banks of the Avon River. But when theater troupes from London passed through Stratford, Kate, dressed as Kit, stayed close to the Guildhall, where they performed, and watched their rehearsals. She followed them about and helped when she could. And when smaller groups of half a dozen to a dozen players arrived, carrying all their costumes and props in a wagon or two and set up to do performances in a pasture near town, she volunteered as a bit player and sometimes as a mime, building on what she had learned from street players in Paris.

In such a pasture, on a summer-like day in early October, Kate spotted a young man, who didn't look like the Will she remembered, but who looked very much like she did now, except he had no facial hair, and she had her fake mustache and beard. That meant it was easier for her to recognize him than for him to recognize her. She had to admit that he was quite handsome, which was also an admission of how good she might look to women who looked at her in the guise of a man. He was alone, but with an edge, alert to the possibility of meeting someone new. A green cap with a feather added a flirtatious flair to his look. He idly chewed on a straw and didn't look in her direction. She guessed that his employer had sent him on an errand, that he had finished early and was about to treat himself to a show on this glorious sunny day, rather than hurry back to his desk in a dark corner of the law office. And if he should chance upon a kindred soul with kindred body in the audience, he was open to such an opportunity.

The leader of this group of players sought Kate out. She had filled in as a mime a couple of times, and now he needed not just her, whom he thought was a man, but another player as well, because a member of the troupe was ill. Kate smiled and pointed at Will as a likely candidate, which the leader quickly agreed, because for this skit their similarity of looks could work well.

Will agreed, not acknowledging that he knew Kate, if, in fact, he recognized her, which he might not have. He had never seen her with mustache and beard. For the skit, one of them would play a young woman and the other a young man. They flipped a coin. Kate would be the woman. So, she went into the wagon to *shave* and change into her costume. Will's street clothes would do for him.

When she came out, Will stared in disbelief. Kate guessed that he hadn't made the connection. He knew that the Kit he went to school with was really a woman. But he didn't know that she was his twin sister. And he didn't know that this was she. He may have heard that the Ardens were back, but it had been two years since they last exchanged letters, and their school days and their thirteen-year-old bodies were in the distant past. All he knew was that this strange boy now dressed as a girl was disturbingly attractive to him. She took impish delight in that realization.

The skit was to end with a kiss. She flirted with him both before and during the performance, savoring his discomfort, knowing that he was drawn to her, but also knowing that he thought she was a man, that he found his feelings disconcerting.

At the end of the skit, in the kiss, she looked him straight in the eye and slipped her tongue into his mouth. At first, he responded passionately with his own tongue. Then he did a double-take, remembering this was a man he was kissing, and he pulled away, abruptly.

The audience, believing that the woman was a man playing a woman found the kiss and the reaction hilarious. Will stomped away humiliated, which triggered another roar of laughter.

Kate caught up with him at the far side of the field, turned him around and kissed him again. Once again, at first, he returned the kiss, passionately. Then he pulled away and looked back in anger—mad at himself for his physical response, and mad at this strange man for tempting him this way.

"Glover boy," she whispered in his ear. "Do you not know me? Your old buddy Kit Kate. Yes, Kit from school and Kate from the letters. You need not pull away, you silly boy. You know damn well that I'm a woman."

His eyes lit up, he cradled her head in his hands, and he kissed her again with gusto.

This was the first real kiss that Kate had ever had. It was also the first time that she had enjoyed attracting a man. She was glad that he now knew who she was and that she was really a woman. She was very glad that he didn't know that they were twins because the thought of incest would have stopped him short, and she didn't want him to stop.

They continued to kiss, oblivious of the people in the audience a hundred feet away who thought this was a comic continuation of their theatrical performance. She stared at him as they kissed, amazed at his resemblance to her. They were the same height. They had the same blue eyes and black hair, the same longish face. Yes, she could believe that they were twins, and she found that titillating. She remembered the moment, years before, when for a few seconds she had seen the world through his eyes. She remembered, too, the moment in Paris at the duel, when she believed that he was in her mind and guiding her hands to save her life. Looking at him was like looking at herself directly through someone else's eyes, not reversed as in a mirror. She hardly knew this fellow, and yet they were linked at a primal level. They were meant to be together.

***

Someone in the audience who they didn't know, had known them when they were born—Flo Harrison, the midwife. To her eyes, this young man who played the part of a woman, looked too much like a woman to be a man playing a woman and looked far too much like Will Shakespeare to be anyone other than his twin, Katharine Arden. She had heard that Kate had gone to the Continent, and she had been pleased that the two of them would be kept apart during their mating years. But now it appeared that Kate had returned to Stratford; and like in the plot of an old romance, the twins separated at birth had found one another, and, not knowing they were twins, they were likely to fall in love with one another. She must stop this abomination, immediately.

She couldn't explain to anyone, much less Will and Kate themselves, how she knew that they were twins and how they got separated. That would mean admitting that she was responsible for the death of the Arden baby, for stealing one of Anne Shakespeare's twins, and for fooling Sir James into thinking that the Shakespeare girl was his own. But she had to find a way to stop the two of them from joining together in unholy lust.

The Lord works in mysterious ways. He must have guided her here to this performance so she would see the danger and act before they committed mortal sin.

She got the attention of the leader of the players. "Do you be seeing those players of yours, your local recruits for the mime? Do you not see what be going on? They be getting all too friendly with one another. Like the Puritans be saying, plays, all plays be unholy, leading to sin. Yes, women be not allowed to perform. But men dressing as women—that be leading to unnatural temptation. There be standing the two of them, in plain sight of the townspeople gathered here. They be kissing like only married folks should kiss in the privacy of their homes. And they be men—men kissing men like that, and not on stage as part of their act, which be bad enough. They be kissing like lovers. That be unnatural, unholy. That should not be allowed.

"I be of a mind to tell the vicar of this, and I wager he be telling the constable, and the constable be chasing you out of town. Break it up, I say. Do so now. And tell them you'll not allow such goings on in Stratford. There be respectable folks in this town who will not be standing for this."

34 ~ Anne Hath a Away

Stratford, October-November 1582, age 18

Flo's faith in the Lord was reconfirmed that very afternoon. In her capacity as midwife, she was summoned, confidentially, to see Anne Hathaway in Shottery, a town just over a mile to the west of Stratford. Anne had suspected she was pregnant, and Flo, with her infallible instinct, confirmed that she was indeed, and nearly three months gone. Soon that would be clear to everyone, and Anne had neither a husband nor a likely candidate for husband. The father, whoever he might be—and Anne wouldn't say—was not free to marry. Anne wanted Flo to end the pregnancy and was willing to pay handsomely for her to do it. But Flo offered her an alternative.

Here was Anne needing a husband fast. And there was Will, a handsome full-grown man, itching for sex and likely to mate with someone soon. And he had already taken a fancy to the one person he shouldn't mate with.

Of course, Flo didn't tell Anne about the twin issue. But she did describe this young man in the most glowing physical terms. And she had seen that very day, in the pasture where passing players performed, that he was so randy as to make a public display of his physical lust for a young woman he hardly knew. Natural as lust was for a young man, he had put on a shameful display. He was eighteen, old enough to marry, but young enough for a woman eight years older than him to mold him into a stable, reliable, and companionable husband. Will was naive enough and Anne world-wise enough to catch him while the catching was good.

Flo could have some friends of hers invite Will to the tavern and treat him to tankard after tankard of ale, in a spirit of camaraderie, making up reasons to celebrate, so he couldn't say no. Why should he say no to free ale? When he was drunk enough to need help walking, they could put him in a wagon, drive him to Anne's house, and put him in Anne's bed. In the morning, Anne's brothers could find him in bed with her, pretend to be scandalized, and insist that they marry.

Anne needn't have relations with the lad, unless she wanted to. He would be trapped. They could hurry up the wedding, getting a dispensation from the vicar to have the banns read just once instead of the usual three times. And in just a few weeks, before word got around that she was pregnant, they could be married.

Anne was desperate, and the plot sounded plausible. If it worked, she'd have a husband. If it didn't, Flo promised to make the pregnancy go away.

Not wanting to miss this opportunity, Flo put her plan into action that very day, and it worked just as the Lord had intended. The couple, accompanied by Anne's brothers as sponsors and witnesses, went before the vicar the very next day. Anne then gave him a course in sexual delight. And in three weeks, the happy couple moved into Will's father's house on Henley Street. That house was one of the largest in town, consisting of three adjacent houses that had been joined. The new couple had one of those three houses to themselves.

Anne's father, who had died the year before, had left Anne six pounds thirteen shillings and fourpence to be paid to her on the day of her marriage. So, the newlyweds had a nest egg. And Anne was skilled at brewing ale, on a small scale, in the home. With Will's wages as a clerk, and no expense for housing, they were set to live a quiet and comfortable life together.

Flo congratulated herself. Will was settled and under control. The chances of him ever mating with Kate were now nil.

Six months later, Flo helped with the birth of their first child — *Susannah*. Once again, Flo took charge and turned what could have been a source of marital discord, fretting over who might have been the real father, into a matter of personal pride. She informed Will, before he could ask, that the shortness of the pregnancy was due to his exceptional virility. And he believed her, since she was such an expert in birthing, and he knew nothing about such matters.

Now Flo could be confident that she had done the Lord's work thoroughly and permanently, and that this matter would never again be a source of concern.

***

The day after Kate met Will at the theater in the pasture, she returned there expecting to see him again. She went back every day for a week and stayed all day, either watching performances or reading. The weather was exceptionally good for autumn, and she was in good spirits, believing that the two of them had made a connection and that now her life would be very different than it had been before.

Finally, she asked around about him and learned that he had suddenly become betrothed to some woman eight years older than him and would soon be wed. Weird, she thought. She could have sworn that he lusted for her as much as she for him. This made no sense, or she was even more ignorant about men and their ways than she thought she was. Will and Anne had probably been having sex for some time. Maybe his tie and obligation to Anne Hathaway, and not the sexual ambiguity of being attracted to her when he thought she was a man, was the reason for Will's hesitation and confusion. In any case, their kissing, which to her had been life-changing, to him had only been a distraction from his real life. It was the amusement of a moment. It had no meaning and would lead to nothing.

It was time for her to move on and forget him. It was time to begin a new chapter of her life.

But that kissing had awakened curiosity and desire. Maybe it was time for her to play the part of a woman in the real world, to find some man she could enjoy, and to acquire a taste for such enjoyment. Maybe she should join Molly in her quest for a mate.

35 ~ Home Again

Stratford 1582-1583, ages 18 to 19

Kate and Molly were now physically mature, and their interests, their expectations, and their habits had changed. The Arden estate had been their entire world. There they had fought their make-believe battles and lived their make-believe lives. It was smaller to them now, and no longer alive with the magic of their minds. It was an abandoned theater. The structure evoked memories of what had been before, but it was no longer full of players and audience. It was empty, except for distant echoes of what had been.

Their dreams were now too big to fit there. Having lived in Paris, the estate was no longer enough for them. Probably all of England wasn't enough, though they hadn't seen the rest of England. They had never been to London, never been outside of Warwickshire aside from the carriage ride to and from the ships that had taken them to and from the Continent.

Before, Kate and Molly had been company enough for one another. Each could play many roles, live many different make-believe lives. School had been a place of learning and only that, with no social interaction with the boys around them, aside from Kate's one brief and momentous encounter with Will. They had had Lew and the challenge of learning how to act like boys, but now they no longer needed to act like boys, and Lew was dead, and no make-believe magic could bring him back.

In Paris, Kate and Molly had grown apart. Kate with her studies and Molly with her suitors had little in common. Pursuing their different dreams, they couldn't empathize with one another's ups and downs. They no longer confided in one another. Now that Kate was ready to try the courtship game, to play the role of a young woman who wants to mate, she turned to Molly for advice, and they rebuilt their bond with one another.

Kate confronted her father, "You treat Molly like a daughter. You always have, even when we didn't know that is the truth. Now it's important that other people know."

Molly added, "Yes, in Paris it was easy. We were English and rich. That was enough. No one knew us. No one expected pedigrees. Here, I'm a nobody. If people don't know that I'm your daughter, no one who is anyone will want to marry me."

"But if I publicly acknowledge you as my daughter, you'll be a bastard and that won't help your marriage prospects."

"Then marry my mother."

He laughed. "That would be worse. That would be a scandal, and still you'd be a bastard, born out of wedlock."

"Then God stand up for bastards," she shouted.

Kate suggested, "Make Molly your heir. Say she's an orphan cousin who you have welcomed into your home. Let the world know that she will have a substantial dowry and will be included in your will. That should be enough to attract the mercenary suitors she wants. Lord only knows why she wants them."

Sir James lit up. "Brilliant, my dear. Brilliant. So it shall be."

On his return, Sir James, too, had found his ancestral estate quiet and strange, quite different from what he remembered. He had never before felt the need to interact with the gentry of Warwickshire. He had preferred the company of his books, and in the rapidly changing religion-charged politics of the time, he had considered every social encounter as fraught with danger. He preferred being alone with his immediate family.

Now he enthusiastically took up the project of the girls' introduction to English courtship. He looked forward to people, noise, and activity as a distraction, a way to overcome the danger of melancholy in the wake of the death of Little Jimmie. He wanted crowds of happy people, evidence of the joy of life, and he had the perfect excuse for such a transformation—two beautiful and accomplished young ladies needed to be introduced to the gentry of Warwickshire. They would hold a ball, the biggest and best ball ever held in the county.

With the help of Jane and Simone, Sir James and Gertie planned the decoration and refurnishing of the mansion and instructed the servants to open up and restore previously unused rooms. The new cook, Antonio, was ordered to restock the larder and the wine cellar. It was time to entertain the gentry of the neighborhood on a scale that they had never seen before, for their home to become a center for hospitality and fellowship and courtship, as well. This could be the glorious beginning of a new stage in all their lives.

In anticipation, Molly gave Kate advice about men, "Remember, it isn't the hope of having sex with you that will draw men to you. It's the flirtation, the tease, the possibility of future delight—plus the dowry, of course. These men can buy sex any time they want it, any flavor of it, with a variety of partners. I hear that every tenth house in London is a bawdy house. And syphilis is rampant among the rich as well as among the poor. Remember that infamous Catherine de Medici? Her mother and father both died of syphilis when she was a few months old, or so it's rumored. So, get you a young man, preferably one who hasn't been to London, and keep him so well satisfied that he never feels the need for someone else."

"And how do you know all this?" asked Kate.

"I talk. I'm sociable. And the young ladies of Paris are far more open in their talk than we English, and far more willing to experiment with men, both before and after marriage. They freely admit what they want and what they fear. And when it comes to diseases of sex, they share what they know and who they suspect is infected, for mutual protection."

"And knowing that danger, women risk their health, their very lives for a few minutes of physical pleasure?"

"And men, too, take that risk. That's why some of them make a fuss about virginity."

"Then why does anyone have sex? It makes no sense to me."

"Children, of course, to make children. And for love, too."

"Love? Sticking that member into a woman is love?"

"I hear it can be, if both parties feel that way about one another."

"Nonsense. Love is madness."

"On the contrary. It's a blessing. It's the holy grail we all seek."

"You mean, knowing what you know now, you still believe fairy tales about chivalry and true love?"

"Of course, I believe, like I believe in Jesus."

"And did Jesus have sex? If romantic love is real and having children is important, why didn't he do it?"

"Maybe he did," said Molly.

"If he did, the *Gospels* would say so. The way parents and preachers indoctrinate us with those ideas, surely, they would add such scenes to the *Gospels* to make it all the more likely that we would do what they want us to do—pair up and procreate. But the *Good Book* says nothing of the kind."

"You forget *Genesis*," Molly reminded her. "Be fruitful and multiply."

"Math is not my strong point. Love—romantic love—is a myth to make marriage palatable to young women. Marriage is just a matter of property, a business contract. The father and the husband exchange property. The woman is part of the property and is expected to produce the heir who will get the property next. I'll have none of that. I'll never marry. But I'll play the game. I'll flirt and tease and get what fun I can from exposing suitors as fools. Let's enjoy that together, like the games we played in the old days."

36 ~ Unsuitable

Stratford, 1583. age 19

After dinner for fifty, the massive table was carried out and the dining room turned into a ball room. Hundreds of long thin strips of colored silk hung from the rafters. A chamber orchestra played. Every unmarried man and woman of marriageable age from every wealthy or noble household in Warwickshire and nearby counties attended. There had never been such an event in this corner of England.

Simone had dressed Kate and applied her makeup, but Kate herself had paid no attention to the little details of appearance that the other young ladies obsessed over in their last-minute preparations. While the other young ladies strove to be pleasant and alluring. Kate was short-tempered and often distracted. She danced but kept her distance from her partners and never looked them in the eye. Nonetheless, half a dozen men fought over her dance card. They found her insults clever and her personality unique and intriguing. She was a shrew, but a delightful shrew.

When introduced to the grandson of a duke, Kate told him, "Ah, I've never had a gander at a duck before."

When introduced to a graduate of Oxford, she said, "Ah, the brain of an ox." He was named Roland. She called him Orlando, the Italian equivalent. She considered him good-looking in an androgynous way. He was no taller than her and beardless. If Kate dressed as a man, with mustache and beard, but without scar or eye patch, he'd look far more feminine than she did.

He doggedly followed her when she tried to skip a dance. She turned on him and addressed him in Latin. He didn't understand her but tried to pretend that he did. So, she quoted in Latin from a salacious poem of Catullus that began, "Up your ass and in your mouth, Aurelius." He smiled as if this were love poetry. Then she switched to French, then to Italian, insulting him with the nastiest of expressions. He smiled and stared. He was puzzled by her words but was enthralled with her. Then she asked him in French, "How is it possible to talk to a man who has read nothing? Who has never had an original thought?" He smiled broadly, apparently delighted that she was paying attention to him.

Then she grabbed him by the hand and led him to the flower garden. She might as well get something out of this event. She wanted to know if kissing any man would be like kissing Will. She kissed Orlando long and hard. She slipped her tongue into his mouth. She felt nothing, absolutely nothing. Then she abruptly left him in the garden and went back to the dance floor where her next scheduled partner was delighted to see her.

Other persistent admirers included Horatio, Duncan, and Harry, all uneducated heirs of wealthy estates, and Falstaff who was portly and ten years older than she was. Falstaff frankly admitted that he wanted her father's money. She found his candor refreshing.

After the ball, Kate told Molly that she had kissed a man, but that it was disappointing, nothing at all like the one time she had kissed Will.

Molly replied, "Well maybe you aren't doing it right."

"There's a right way and a wrong way to kiss?"

"There's a right way and a wrong way to do everything."

"Then show me."

"What?"

Kate grabbed hold of her, pulled her close, and kissed her like she had kissed Orlando. Molly kissed back with enthusiasm, tongue playing with tongue.

Then Kate pulled away, "Nothing. Still nothing," she said, and went to bed.

When Sir James threw a second ball, two months later, Kate insisted on dressing as a man. Sir James was annoyed, but he figured that she had to get this out of her system and opposing her would just make her stubborn.

The cover story was that Kate was sick, and this was her cousin Christopher, who had gone to school in Stratford years before. A bevy of young ladies lingered in his vicinity and sought to catch his attention. One of them was so bold as to mention that her dance card had an opening for the first dance. Kate graciously took her hand and led her to the dance floor.

"And what's your name, fair lady?" asked Kate.

"Ophelia."

Kate started laughing.

"What's funny about my name, sir?"

"Has no one ever called you *Ophelia Genitalia*."

"What?"

"Get thee to a nunnery, fair lady."

"But I'm not a Catholic. I would never go to a nunnery."

"Good God, woman, have you no wit? That's irony. That was joking with opposites. By nunnery I meant whore house."

"Whore house?"

"Bawdy house. Sluttery. Have you never spoken of country matters? Have your tender ears never heard such words? A house of ill repute. A place where women rent their bodies. It's a noble profession, reputed to be the oldest in the world. Adam went to one when Eve had a headache."

"Headache? Why would Eve have a headache?"

Kate laughed again.

She danced with Rosalind, Cordelia, and Miranda, joking at their expense, complimenting them on the presumed beauty of their lips, their cheeks, their hair.

"Why presumed?" asked Rosalind.

"Because, of course, my dear, I have not yet seen them."

"You haven't seen my lips, my cheeks, my hair?"

"Your nethers, my dear. You lower lips, your lower cheeks, and your unsightly hair."

"Why, how could you say such things? How could you think such things?"

Kate laughed and gave her a quick kiss on the lips in the middle of the dance floor.

Rosalind blushed, "How dare you, sir?"

"Enough then, madame. As you like it," she answered with a bow, and left the dance floor.

37 ~ The Marriage Games

Stratford, 1583 - spring 1584, ages 19 to 20

After that second ball, Sir James invited the most ardent suitors to take up residence at the Arden Estate until the competition was settled. Orlando, Horatio, Duncan, Harry, and Falstaff all accepted the invitation and for more than a year were part of the household.

All of them were interested in Molly as well as Kate, and their presence made every day an adventure. Neither Kate nor Molly took these suitors seriously, treating them as fodder for their pranks.

Kate and Molly looked enough alike that with the help of cosmetics and clothing they could be mistaken for one another. Sometimes Kate would build a false bust out of cloth and would dress and wear her hair as Molly did. Other times Molly would strap her breasts tight and pretend to be Kate. One night, Molly showed favor to Orlando, and suggested that they meet after dinner for a private walk in the maze. There he met Kate, thinking she was Molly. When he tried for kisses, she accommodated him. No sooner was his ardor aroused, then along came the real Molly, who broke them up and chastised him for being unfaithful to her. Another time, Molly convinced a drunken Falstaff that she was Kate and lured him to bed. Then Kate, as arranged, found them, feigned a jealous rage, broke a chair on his head and chased him away. Another time, Kate donned her mustache, beard, scar, and eye patch and played the part of their over-protective and easily aggravated cousin, who threatened to challenge the suitors to duels. They all cowered and abjectly apologized for non-existent insults, to avoid having to fight this fearsome swordsman, reputed to have killed a captain of the King's Musketeers in a duel in Paris.

By Kate's twentieth birthday, both the suitors and the suited had grown weary. The suitors wanted a resolution. All five of them were willing to marry either of the Arden girls. It was up to the girls and their father who would be matched with whom. But they banded together and demanded an answer. They had lingered here far too long as it was, and this shouldn't prove a futile quest for all of them.

Every one of them was a good match. The jokes and humiliation that they had suffered had been in good fun, and they had become good friends with one another. It had been an amusing and unforgettable interlude, but they must get on with their lives. And it was only fair that two of the five suitors should win.

Sir James asked the girls to choose.

Kate suggested that the competition be decided by a foot race, like the mythical race of Atalanta. Molly didn't want to run and didn't want to choose either. Kate said that she would run for both of them. If any of the suitors beat her in the race, she would marry him. And whoever came in second among the suitors could marry Molly. Molly thought this was silly, but she would be content to marry any of these men who had been such good sports for so long and all of whom she now considered good friends.

Kate marked out a two-mile track around the vegetable garden, the flower garden, the maze, the orchard, and the house. The men were all content with the arrangement—there was no way that Kate dressed as she was now, in full womanly regalia, with farthingale and half a dozen heavy petticoats, would have any chance of beating any of them. The matter would soon be resolved. The only question was which two of the five would be fastest.

As the suitors mulled about, chatting with one another, assured that their long and pleasant residence here was about to end and that two of them would soon be proud and happy grooms, Kate informed them of another rule of the game. "You expect me to run dressed as a woman and you to all run dressed as men? That's patently unfair. Of course, all of society is unfair to women. But this is my fate and Molly's fate at stake here. And this is my father's estate, and he said I could make the rules. So, I insist we all start this race dressed the same. I'm sure that none of you courteous gentlemen would expect me to degrade myself by dressing like a man. So, it's only fair that you should all dress as women. Jane and Simone have costumes ready for you and will help you put them on."

Falstaff laughed, "But you couldn't possibly have an outfit that would fit my girth."

"Have no fear, dear John. Jane and Simone were up all night making alterations, and they have an outfit just your size."

"Outrageous," Orlando objected. "There's no way you'll get me to dress like a woman."

"Fine, dear sir. If you choose to withdraw from the competition, that will improve the odds for the remaining four."

"No. No," he protested. "I'm not a quitter. But there must be no audience other than your household. You must promise not to invite the neighbors and make a spectacle of this."

"Have no fear, my dear Orlando. I have no such plans. Now get ready and may the best two men win."

Once the men were dressed, all five of them insisted that they needed time to get used to this cumbersome clothing. They all tripped within their first few steps and needed help to get back on their feet. Three hours passed before they could all slowly and with great difficulty complete a practice walk around the course.

Sir James was betting on Orlando, who came in first in the practice walk. Gertrude was betting on Falstaff, figuring he'd come up with some trick to beat those younger and faster than he was. Molly was rooting for Duncan, Harry, and Horatio, who she liked a smidgen more than the other two, though she liked all of them.

Standing at the starting line, Sir James fired a musket.

Orlando got off to a fast start, with Horatio, Duncan, and Harry struggling to stay on their feet, and Falstaff stepping ever so slowly and carefully. Kate went nowhere. She stood at the starting line, watched the others struggle, and burst out in uncontrollable laughter. Horatio turned to see what the laughter was about, and tripped, falling into and knocking down Duncan who knocked down Harry.

Then Kate removed her skirt and petticoats and farthingale. Underneath she was wearing a man's doublet and breeches and hose. She then jogged past the bewildered suitors and around the track.

"You cheated," Orlando protested. "Why hold a race like this if you were going to cheat? I thought that you wanted the best man to win, and that you wanted to marry that best man."

Kate replied, "You think I want to marry a man who is fast of foot? What does that have to do with your fitness as a husband? No. Molly and I want men who think fast, and, clearly, that's not you, not any of you."

38 ~ Kiss Me, Kate

Stratford, spring 1584, Will and Kate 20 years old

There was a pause in courtship at the Arden estate. Word of the race and its humiliating finish had spread far and wide. It would be many a day before these suitors or any others sought the hands of these two shrews.

Kate was pleased, Molly less so, though she, too, would welcome a change, having tired of the marriage games. While Molly had liked all five suitors, she had loved none of them. Part of her still believed in true love and preferred to hold out a little longer, before settling for friendship, wealth, and comfort.

Kate showed a renewed interest in theater. She wanted to spend all day, every day with whatever troupe of players was performing in the Guildhall.

"You go alone to Stratford and mix with theater riffraff?" Sir James objected. "You an unmarried young lady, a lady of position and culture?"

"Me as Kit, not Kate. I go as a willful young man, out to learn what he can of the world."

"And how long will you continue this farce?"

"As long as I can."

"And marriage?"

"Perhaps someday. I'm in no hurry for that. That's part of the gift you've given me, father. I don't need to depend on a husband. And I don't need to play the part of a woman. I can do what I please when I please, like a man can. And when I wish, if I wish, I can turn into the ingenue, then the blushing bride, and then the mother. For now, I wish to be a man—a wealthy young gentleman who wants to dabble in the life of an actor, to see if he has talent and to see if that way of life suits his fancy. I won't join any particular troupe and travel. Rather, I'll attach myself, for a while, to each troupe that passes through town and make myself useful, filling in where they need me and where my talents and my looks qualify me. I'll play the role of a rich young gentleman, who wants to mix with the players on a lark."

Sir James, of course, supported Kate's new fantasy. Not only did he give his blessing to her theatrical adventures, he also invited more troupes from London to perform in Stratford and paid them a handsome subsidy for doing so.

In the guise of Kit, Kate became friendly with one troupe after another, helping where help was needed and serving as understudy for a multitude of minor parts.

And so, it came to pass that Kate and Will met again.

He came in the evening, soon after his work ended, an hour before the show was to start. Kate was sitting on the other side of the hall, eating bread and drinking from a tankard of ale. Their eyes connected, but neither moved, neither said a word.

The next evening when Will came back at the same time and sat in the same spot, he smiled at Kate and nodded. He knew very well who she was. She joined him.

Before she could say a word, Will blurted out, "I'm married. I have a daughter."

He was trembling. He was a loyal husband and father. He wouldn't flirt, much less do more with another woman. He was uncomfortable that she had been so bold as to come over and sit next to him. He closed his eyes and his lips moved slightly, quietly. Kate imagined he was saying to himself over and over again, "Lead me not into temptation."

"I heard about the marriage," Kate said. "It came remarkably soon after our encounter. Had you known the lady long?"

"No," he answered. "It chanced that we met that very afternoon."

"A lightning flash," Kate chuckled. "Love at first sight, or perhaps at first bite. Did she taste good, Will?"

He was too embarrassed to answer.

"And a miracle birth as well, I hear. Just six months of pregnancy and a healthy happy full-term baby. To what do you attribute such good fortune?"

He mumbled.

"What was that?"

"Virility," reluctantly replied. "That's what the midwife told me."

"Virility?" Kate broke out in laughter. "She told you virility was the reason? And you believed that?"

"And why not, Kit or Kate or whatever you're calling yourself now. Flo Harrison knows more about the making of babies and the birthing of babies than anyone else in Warwickshire. If she says it's so, it's so."

"Ah, the faith of the innocent."

"And what mean you by that?"

"You're as gullible as Joseph believing the Immaculate Conception."

"That's blasphemy."

"If you were a wealthy man and I a poor one, I would rejoice to have found such an easy mark."

"Why are you mocking me like this?"

"Nine months, Will. It takes nine months to take a babe to full term. It has always taken that long, and it always will. If a babe comes out a month before its time, sometimes, with luck, it will live. But three months early—never."

"Meaning?"

"The term of pregnancy has nothing to do with the virility of the father. You're not the father. Your fair innocent bride was three months gone before you came along. You've been had, my lad."

"Lied to?"

"Most certainly, by bride and midwife. I wager the midwife was paid handsomely to help pull that one off."

"No wonder," he said, finally putting together the pieces of the puzzle.

"No wonder what?"

"The free drinks at the tavern. Some men I didn't know suddenly got friendly to me and got me drunk and I woke up in Anne's bed."

"Then you weren't unfaithful to me," Kate concluded, brushing a loose hair out of his face and giving him a quick kiss.

"Unfaithful to you?"

"Yes, unfaithful to me, marrying another woman when we had connected as we did that day. But you were fooled. I forgive you." She gave him another quick kiss.

"Please don't," he protested. "People will talk."

"And what will they say? That a man kissed you on the cheek, perhaps a Frenchman who does that by way of greeting."

"Don't tempt me, please. I'll not be unfaithful to my wife."

"How could you be unfaithful to her? She tricked you into marriage. She cuckolded you before you even met her."

"Good God!"

"Yes, God's good, but not all women are. Certainly, your wife's not."

He stood suddenly and ran off.

The next day he appeared again at the same hour, this time with a black eye. He walked straight to Kate, took her hand, and led her out of the Guildhall. They walked along the river. They were beyond the last house before either of them said a word.

"You're right, you know," he finally said.

"Of course, I'm right. You'll find that I'm always right. At least, I hope you'll find that, because I hope we'll know one another long enough for me to prove that to you many times."

"Then you'll forgive me for not getting back to you after that one sweet moment we had together? You'll forgive me for being so naive as to let myself get roped into a rushed marriage with a stranger, and to believe that horseshit excuse, get saddled with another man's child and not even know it, though the whole town probably knew, like you did?"

She squeezed his hand.

"This will be a scandal, you know, the two of us being seen like this, and me married, for right or wrong."

"A scandal? For holding hands with a man and going for a walk with him?"

"If it becomes known that you're a woman, not a man, it's your reputation, not mine that I'm in fear for. From what you say, I'm already rumored to be the greatest fool in Stratford. But you, a beautiful unmarried woman, and gentry as well, shouldn't be seen alone with a married man."

"Yes, Will, you know I'm a woman. You feel it in your bones, I hope. But to everyone else in this town, I'm a man, an old friend of yours from our school days together. Fear not for my reputation. But let's go to the woods, maybe to the spot where you used to dally with Bridget. Let's steal some time together away from curious eyes and pick up where we left off before."

"But regardless of the fact that I was fooled and trapped, I'm a married man. I'm a father. And I'm an Englishman, not a Frenchman so such facts matter to me. And since I am not a king I can't divorce, so I'll never be able to marry you."

"You are quick, my Will, very quick. And better quick than dead. I'm not talking marriage. I don't wish to be your wife, your property. How could I? Before now, we've spoken twice. We've kissed, really kissed just once. Besides, I doubt I'll ever get married. But I see no reason why we shouldn't have fun together."

"Have you done this before, with others?" he asked hesitantly.

She slapped him on the cheek, a gentle slap that morphed into a caress.

They walked quickly, hand in hand, then sped up to a full run, all the way to the opening in the Forest of Arden where Will had years before carved Bridget's name on the trees.

There he held her close, looked into her eyes, and said, "Kiss me, Kate."

39 ~ Mustache Power

"So, you met Will again," Molly concluded, when she saw Kate sneak in through a back door with bits of leaves and twigs stuck to her hose and breeches. "And what did you do with him?"

"We kissed. We caressed. Fully clothed. Nothing more."

"With a married man, no less."

"Yes, technically married. And, yes, technically a man, though he still looks like a boy."

"Well, describe him to me, please. The last I saw him he was thirteen."

"He looks the same as I do when I'm dressed as a man, but without mustache and beard. The skin of his face is smooth and soft. There's nary a hair on his face, and I doubt there ever will be."

"So, when you're bearded and mustached, you look more like a man than he does?" Molly chuckled. "You should give him a mustache and beard like yours. That might improve his looks, and boost his confidence, too. And does he have an Adam's apple? Does he have one as good as the one Lew had?"

"That I don't know. He wears a ruff, so I haven't seen his neck."

"How can you take the measure of a man without seeing his neck?"

"Aren't you more interested in measuring what hangs between his legs?"

"That, too. What does he have there?"

"Now, Molly, you talk a good talk. But I wager that the only one of those you've seen was Lew's, years ago in the stable. All you know about male anatomy is secondhand."

"You're right that I'm a virgin where virginity counts. But my hands have explored the nether regions."

"And you never told me?"

"You never asked. In Paris we weren't the friends we'd been before or that we are now."

"So, what say you then? Should I let him have his way with me? Should I give my virginity to him, like a gift, like Bridget gave him her new-formed breasts? No way. Not worth the risk. If I got with child, it wouldn't just be the shame and what that would mean for my life. It would be the babe, who if it lived, would be deformed, because we're so close in blood. I don't want to give up Will. He means too much to me, even knowing him so little. So, I'm in a fix. He wants me that way. I see that on his face when he gets close, and I pull away. He says he hasn't done it with his wife for months. They stopped sleeping together even before he learned she tricked him into marriage with a babe that wasn't his. They grew apart before they ever really got together. He says she's bossy and controlling, that she acts more like a mother to him than a wife, ordering him about with no sign of affection. There's something about her manner and her tone of voice that drains the will from him and makes him do as she says."

"Will without a will," Molly noted. "What a sad sight that must be."

"So, I should make him feel welcome?"

"Yes, make him welcome. You needn't let him enter you. You needn't risk making a child. There are many ways to make a man happy, and for him to pleasure you as well. You have hands, lips, tongue. Be creative, Kate. A woman's not just a machine for making babies. Men and women are meant to join together in many ways. I'm sure of that, though I've only gone a short way down that path myself, not yet having found a partner I'd want to go farther with."

"But he might turn away from me if he finds out that he and I are twins. He might be repelled by me, because he was raised to believe that incest is a mortal sin."

"Well, he doesn't know, and there's no need for him to know, and there's no way he can find out if you don't tell him. Let the problems of the day be sufficient thereunto. *The Scripture* says that Adam knew Eve, and Eve knew Adam, and it was good. Knowledge is good, especially the knowledge that comes from living and loving."

That night Kate and Molly slept together in the same bed, in one another's arms, as they hadn't done in years.

***

For a week, Kate and Will got together every day, in the evening, after his work. On sunny days they went to the clearing in the woods.

When it rained, they went to the loft over the Guildhall where school was held during the day.

Kate felt very close to him, especially when they kissed, and their tongues touched. Several times, she imagined, for a split second, that she saw herself through his eyes; and he claimed he had the same impression. She felt connected to him as she had never been connected to anyone, even Molly. But she was content to kiss and hug, and occasionally let his hands wander. Knowing there were other options to try, as Molly had described, added zest to her experience with him. But she wasn't ready to venture far in that direction. There was no hurry. They had fallen into a comfortable rhythm. She would bring a basket of food, and they would share dinner together and chatter, before settling in for some serious cuddling and kissing.

As part of that routine, she'd take off his ruff, exposing the prominent Adam's apple that she would caress and kiss. That was one way in which their appearance differed. She wasn't ready to explore the other differences, being physically shy and inhibited, despite her bold candid talk about such matters.

She had Gertie make a false mustache and beard for Will. She showed him how to put them on. "Now we look like twins, identical twins," she dared to joke. "Seriously," she added, you look much better with hair on your face. Wear those all the time, even when you sleep at night. And don't tell Anne how you got them. Imagine how that will irk her."

When Anne saw him with beard and mustache, she didn't say a word about it. But she started treating him differently, taking him more seriously. She sometimes stroked his beard and smiled as she walked past him.

When Will was with Kate, he thought of nothing but the look, the feel, the taste of her. He was delighted and content, living in the moment. But sitting at his desk in the law office, copying one document after another, he felt frustrated and powerless. He couldn't get out of his marriage to Anne, and he was sure that sooner or later Kate would want marriage and children. He believed that that was what all women wanted. Since he couldn't give her that, sooner or later she would leave him for someone else who could.

One day, Kate didn't show up at their designated rendezvous spot. It had been a bad day for Will at the office. Because he forgot to blot the ink on a deed, it smeared, and he had to do it over. Then he spilt ink on the second version, so he had to redo it yet again. He needed Kate's comforting touch and words. Insecure and feeling sorry for himself, he wondered if she would show up the next day or the day after that, if he would ever see her again. He went to the tavern and had a few tankards of ale before heading home.

He woke up in the morning in bed with Anne.

When he saw Kate that evening, he told her about a dream he had had. "I was in the choir loft of a great cathedral; it was like the loft of Guildhall. There was an enormous organ, and the organist was a lovely young woman. It was you, Kate. We played it together. We made a joyful noise together. Then I woke and saw I was in bed with Anne. *Ah, Will,* she sighed, *I never knew you had it in you, and now you have it in me. Well done, my boy, well done. Uncommon good.*"

"Why are you telling me this?" asked Kate. "Are you and Anne back together again?"

"We were never together. We were barely on speaking terms until lately. I think it was the mustache and beard that changed her manner to me. She, of course, knows it's false. But I think that seeing me with it prompts her to think of me as a man, not a mere boy, as she always called me before."

"So, you did it with her?"

"I did, indeed."

Kate laughed, "What a terrible sin to covet your own wife, and to have your way with her."

"You aren't mad?"

"You think I should be? You think I should be jealous of a woman I know you hate. But I'm concerned. What if she gets with child from that drunken foolishness of yours? I presume you were drunk when you did it. How would you feel if she carried a child that was yours, truly yours? Would that change how you feel about me?"

"You think she could be with child from just doing it once? The odds are way against that."

"Your ignorance of human reproduction astounds me."

"I swear, Kate, it was you I made love to in the dream, not her."

"How romantic, my dear Will. You thought of me while fucking her. And nine months from today—not six months, nine—she'll have your child, a child that's really yours. She has you in her thrall. Whether you realize it or not, you belong to her now."

"No, Kate, it's you I love."

"And it's her you fuck."

"It's you I long for."

"But you got long enough for her."

"I'll be longer for you, I am sure."

"Nonsense. Your member gets no longer for one woman than another. More of your ignorance of anatomy."

"I'll leave her. You and I can run away together and start a new life."

"And live in poverty? What a wonderful imagination you have, my Will. Where there's a will there's a way. Enough. This must end here and now. The make-believe is over."

40 ~ Twins Run in the Family

Stratford, February 1585, age 20

Anne did, indeed, get pregnant, as did Gertie soon after.

Gertie explained to the girls, "You fall off a horse, you get back on again, as quick as you can. Lew be telling you that. Lew be knowing how to live and how to keep living. Would that he'd kept living longer, and Little Jimmie, too. But such be life. Crying over it don't change it. The only cure for death and dying be life and living. We lost us a child. We loved him dearly. And we be loving the next, too, God willing."

Nine months later, Anne, with the expert help of Flo, gave birth to twins. Will and she named them Hamnet or Hamlet and Judith, after their friend and neighbor the baker Hamnet Sadler and his wife Judith.

As she was cleaning up and packing up with the help of Will, Flo couldn't help but recall the earlier delivery of twins in this same Henley Street house. When Will expressed surprise at having twins, Flo remarked that it was no surprise to her. "Afterall, twins be running in your family."

"I don't know of any twins among the Hathaways."

"Your family, not hers. Twins be running in your family."

She was tired. This was the third birth of the day. Births came in bunches every February, the fruit of what was planted in May.

"What do you mean? There have been no Shakespeare twins as far back as anyone can remember."

"But you yourself, of course."

"Me?"

"I be birthing you and your sister meself." Then she suddenly stopped short, realizing her mistake.

"What? What did you say?"

"Nothing at all," she contradicted herself, not looking him in the eye, showing a sudden interest in scrubbing a blood spot on the floor. "That be a common expression—*twins run in the family*. But in your case, of course, that be not true. Like you say, your twins today be a surprise. Out of nowhere."

"Twins?" he asked sharply. "I was a twin?"

"My mistake, slip of the tongue."

"Slip indeed. I'll slip you." He grabbed her by her over-sized waist, pulled her to her feet and stared at her. "Look at me! Open your eyes. Look at me and tell me the truth!"

She shook without him shaking her. He didn't ask again. He just stared at her in anger. His eyes, not his lips asked for the truth over and over again.

"Lord have mercy on me," she muttered, under her breath. Maybe she was meant to tell him now. Maybe he had seen Kate again, and maybe it was the Lord's will that she let him know that Kate was his twin, so they not blunder into incest. Regardless of what delayed shame and even punishment might come down on her now, she must tell him, since the Lord now wanted her to.

Awkwardly, reluctantly, in broken sentences, she confirmed that he was born a twin, that the Arden baby born in the same house that same day came far too early and died. She didn't mention that she had dropped that one and it cracked its skull. There was no need for that detail. She portrayed herself as only thinking of others.

"It be the right thing. I be sure of that."

"What was the right thing?"

"The Lord God, He be inspiring me. There be this fine lady, frail and wanting a babe of her own, and not likely to have another. I be seeing enough of birth and death to know that for sure. And that poor lady after all her months of hoping and all her pain, would I be telling her that her babe was dead? And here be your mother, Mary, young and healthy and sure to be having more children and sure to struggle with the burden of twins. So, I be switching the live girl for the dead one. And no one knew, but me, until now."

"Did she live?"

"Lady Arden? No, she be dying the very next day. Too much blood lost in the birthing."

"Not the mother. The child. The baby. The twin you took away from her real mother. My sister."

"Surely, you be guessing by now. You be knowing her well, too well, if you ask me."

"Kate? You mean Kate, for God's sake? Kate Arden."

"That be her in the flesh. And you be lusting for her in the flesh. You not be fooling me. I be seeing what I be seeing."

"And she does not know?"

"Not she, not anyone but me, till now."

"Hell! Woman, how could you do that?"

"What be the harm? She be living in luxury, with a fine dowry, no doubt, to marry a wealthy man and live a good life. Would she be trading that for a life like yours, as ordinary folk, working hard day after day, just to live? I be giving her, no the Lord God, through me, be giving her a blessing."

"How dare you meddle in other people's lives like that? She is my sister, my twin, and neither of us ever knew. And we could well have mated, married."

"I be fearing that, and the Lord God, He be coming to me aid. Seeing the two of you making eyes and making lips and sure to be making other parts together as well, I be setting you up with Anne Hathaway."

"You did that? That was your idea? She didn't pay you to do it?"

"All my own, I be telling you, with the help of the Lord. Anne be needing a husband, and you be needing to be settled, married, safe from temptation to incest. And that be working well, I see. You be safely married to a fine woman and with three children. Now you be living a good life as lives go among us common folk."

"And you never told Kate about this? She has no idea she has a brother, much less a twin, and much less that I'm that twin?"

"No idea at all. She be such a fine lady now and likely to marry well, rich or titled or both. Far be it from me to be telling her that she be of common birth and blood and not worthy to marry some lord. And her father, I not be telling him his darling daughter be a changeling, not a true daughter, deserving of a dowry."

"But she should know."

"No need for that now that you be knowing. You be a god-fearing righteous man. No way you be fooling with the likes of Kate now, counter to God's law. She not be needing to know. You knowing be enough, I be thinking."

"But truth matters. At length, truth must out."

"Truth tooth. We be born with more teeth than we need and better to do away with one or two than suffer pain."

Will abruptly let her go, turned and walked out of the house. If he stayed, he might have hit or throttled this hateful woman who had meddled with his life and Kate's life, and now had told him something he would rather not know and couldn't unknow.

His anger continued to build as he walked down the street in the dark, toward the woods, and the clearing where he and Kate had met and kissed and been in love. And as he walked, he felt her presence and he realized he had felt her presence before, when Flo was confessing, as if she were in his head and seeing through his eyes and trying to make sense of what was said.

He loved her, not as a sister, but as man can and should love woman. Law and church be damned. No one knew but he and that foul witch who caused all this trouble, and she wasn't about to tell anyone else. If he told Kate, she'd never be able to think of him or feel about him the way he did her. So, he wouldn't tell her. Only if they mated, only if they had children would their incest have consequences. But they could and should be together, stay together, live and love together for the rest of their days. He would seek her out. She loved him. He knew that now. Their common blood was part of the bond that drew them to one another both physically and psychically. They were meant to be together. And they would find a way, so long as they had the will for it.

He lay down on his back in the clearing, despite the February cold, and stared up at the stars. *There are more things in heaven and earth than I ever dreamed of.*

41 ~ If You Incest

February 1585, age 20

Hours later, having been kept awake and warm by feverish thoughts and restless motion, Will walked from the woods to the Arden estate. He knew where the estate was, as did everyone in the region, but he had never been there himself. He knew he had to talk to Kate, but he had no idea how he would be able to. They hadn't spoken in nine months. For all he knew, she could be engaged to someone else by now.

He thought he would sit on the doorstep until dawn when the servants would be up. He would plead for someone to tell Kate that he was there and needed to talk to her.

He had decided that he'd tell her they were twins, knowing that the knowledge could drive her away from him, but knowing he must tell her the truth if they were to have any chance going forward together.

From a distance, he saw light in the windows above the main entrance. As he got closer, he realized the light was from not just one, but many candles, and a shadow was moving back and forth at an erratic pace. It was Kate. He knew it was Kate.

He threw pebbles at her window. She opened and saw him. She went out onto the balcony. He climbed a nearby tree, until he was even with her and could talk to her without shouting.

"So, what brings you here? What's happened?" she asked hesitantly.

"Twins," he replied.

"Anne had twins?" she guessed. "You're now the proud father of twins?"

"Yes. That and more."

"You seek out your former lover to tell her that your wife had twins?"

"And to tell you twins again."

"How twins again? What do you mean by that?"

"We—you and I—are twins."

"And what gave you that idea?"

"The midwife, Flo Harrison. She told me how we were born, and why no one knew but she. She swapped a live Shakespeare twin for a dead Arden baby, and no one was the wiser."

"Then I wasn't bought and sold?"

"You mean you knew already that we're twins?"

"Yes. But I thought I was sold. I figured it out on my own, the way we look, the same birthday."

"Then you knew all along?"

"Since we were thirteen. It was our thirteenth birthday that triggered my knowing."

"And you didn't tell me?"

"I thought that knowing would drive you away. Even then, I was drawn to you. And I thought that the sin of incest would drive you away from me."

"But your knowing didn't drive you from me? You wanted me then, and you still want me now?"

"Want you? Good God. I love you more than life. You are my life."

"As I love you, Kate. And the laws of man and God be damned. Nothing can keep us apart. And if we don't spawn children, what's the harm of it? But why are you up so late? You couldn't have known that I was coming. I didn't know that myself until an hour ago."

"You were in my head. You're still in my head. I don't know how else to describe the sensation. You're in my head or I'm in yours or both at once. Maybe we're one soul in two bodies."

The main door opened with a bang and out stepped Sir James, in loosely tied boots, with a wool mantle thrown over his nightshirt. He looked up at the stranger, whose legs were dangling nearly in his face and greeted him, "So now men grow on trees."

"And night is day, and all is right with the world," Will replied.

"The man is mad," Sir James chuckled. "Now help me understand—you, sir, were passing by in the middle of the night and decided to climb our tree. And Kate by chance was up and about and itching for conversation with a stranger from her balcony?"

"Will is no stranger, father. We've known one another for years."

"Ah, so Will is his name."

"Father, I would like you to meet the man I will marry—William de Vere of Oxford," Kate replied without hesitation. "That's William the True, my true William of Oxford, the town, not Oxford the university. He's a wool merchant."

"Ah, someone skilled at pulling wool over eyes." Sir James chuckled.

"I met him in Bruges and saw him in Paris. We've corresponded for years. I bribed your couriers to carry our messages. And now he's come all the way from Oxford to see me."

"You imp. You delightful imp. You carry on a romance right under my eyes, as if I would object. And here I worried you had no interest in men at all and would never marry, and who would you have to protect you when I'm gone?"

She assumed the *en garde* position, then made moves as if to slash and thrust.

Sir James laughed. "Yes, indeed. I shouldn't worry about protecting my musketeer. You can take care of yourself. But life is more fun shared, as I've learned full well with Gertie. I've wanted you to find your one-and-only as I've found mine. I've no doubt that Molly will find hers. She certainly wants to, and sooner or later will. But here you're outpacing Molly. You're a wonder, my darling. And you, sir, you who, I am sure, are soon to be my beloved son, get you down from there before you break your neck. Climb down. I'll let you in the door. You must be frozen. I'll have the servants make up a room for you. We'll make you full welcome and hope to enjoy your company and learn to know you well before you take my Kate and start your lives together."

42 ~ Double Identity

Kate, Will, and Sir James sat at the small table near the hearth in the banquet room.

"Welcome to Arden Manor, William de Vere of Oxford," Sir James shook Will's hand firmly and warmly. "So, you're a wool merchant?

"No, sir. Not exactly, sir," Will admitted.

Kate cringed and wrung her hands.

Sir James stared in disbelief. "Did I hear wrong?" he asked.

"No. You heard right, sir. That's what Kate said. But that's not actually true."

"Not a wool merchant?"

"And not William de Vere of Oxford. Kate was stretching the truth, sir. A bit, sir."

"A bit?"

"A lot, sir."

"Then who are you, actually?"

"Will Shakespeare."

"The son of the glover in Stratford? Our Arden cousin?"

"Yes, sir. The very one."

"You knew Kate at school. I remember her talking of you. When Kate was Kit. You know that. You knew that. You've known her for years, and I've never met you. Most interesting. And are you learning the glover trade with your father?"

"No, sir. That's not a life I would want. I'm not the kind of man who thinks with his hands and takes pride in what his hands do. I'm more bookish. So, I've found work with the solicitor."

"Nicholas Rowe?"

"Indeed, sir. The only one in Stratford. I help in the office and learn what I can when I can."

"Ah, Nicholas Rowe. I know him well. He drew up my will to my specifications, a most extraordinary will if I do say so myself. He's an excellent solicitor and a fine man. I would trust him with my life and the life of my daughters as well. He knows the law and respects the privacy and secrets of his clients."

"I have no complaints," said Will. "He treats me well."

"And you wish to marry my daughter?"

"Wish, yes," Will answered, looking Kate in the eye.

Kate's eyes flashed fear, then joy, then fear again.

After a pregnant pause, Will continued, "I love her with all my heart. But we can't marry."

Sir James was taken aback. "And why not, if you be her choice and she yours? Surely you don't think that I'd stand in your way."

Kate interrupted, "Will is already married."

"With three children," Will added

Sir James paused. "Well, I imagine that could be an impediment. But I'm sure you can find a way forward together with or without the sanction of church or state. My own irregular union with Gertie has been delightful. You won't let a wife and three children stop you, will you?"

"No, sir," Will answered. "I mean I wish that there was a solution, but I don't know of any."

Sir James chuckled. "Do you have so little imagination? Kate, what about you? What have you come up with? Aside from an improbable name for your young man. What are you plotting in that delightfully devious mind of yours?"

"Me? Devious?" Kate objected. "Father, you're the one with the imagination. It was you who thought to turn me into a boy so I could go to school."

"Brilliant!" Sir James lit up. "I knew you'd come up with something and here you have almost immediately. You are two people, Kate. Legally, you are two people. Thanks to the good work of that same Nicholas Rowe. You have identity and travel documents as Christopher Arden as well as Katharine Arden. A woman can't inherit in her own right, but only in escrow as her dowry for the man she will marry. And I feared that you might not ever marry. So, my will names Christopher Arden as my heir. Should you marry, Mr. Rowe will draw up a new will naming your husband. But if I were to die suddenly, you'd be provided for by this expedient. And Molly, too. Until Molly marries, Christopher Arden is her guardian, with control of her portion."

"But if someone were to challenge that?" asked Kate.

"Christopher Arden is very real in the eyes of the law and in the eyes of our neighbors, as well. He has been here many times, as many people can attest. He's our cousin, who lived with us for two years and went to school in Stratford and later traveled with us on the Continent and studied at the University of Paris. That same Christopher Arden scared suitors of my Kate and Molly by threatening to fight duels with them."

"And if Gertie has a son?" asked Kate.

"Then I'll draw up a new will and settle two thirds of the estate on you and Molly, by that same stratagem, and one third on the new Jimmie. If a girl, I'd provide for her as I have for Molly."

"And what of my wife?" asked Will.

"Pay her off, I'd say. I gather there's no love between you. I reckon she'd welcome the money and be as glad to be rid of you as you of her."

At that Gertie came stumbling in from the kitchen. Sir James rushed to her side, steadied her, and helped her to a chair.

"It be coming now," she said. "Now. Me water be broke. Fetch Flo quick. Send the coach for her."

When Flo arrived an hour later, she was shocked to see Kate and Will together, But she didn't say a word about past matters, not knowing what Kate, Will, and Sir James knew and didn't know. She went about her work as best she could, mumbling prayers under her breath. She hoped that the Lord God would protect her since she had always done her best to fulfill His will. If she had strayed, it was from ignorance, not from selfish ambition. God's will be done. Amen.

This time the birthing was a total disaster. The baby died. Gertie died soon after. And Sir James went mad with grief. For three days he raged, pacing rapidly, without sleep, without food, sometimes muttering and sometimes shouting a repeated litany of disconnected phrases.

Billicock sat on Billicock's Hill

Is man no more than this?
I am the thing itself, a poor bare-forked animal.
O cry you mercy.
Childe Roland to the dark tower came.
As flies are to wanton boys are we to the gods.
Let me not be mad sweet heaven. I would not be mad.
I am a man more sinned against than sinning.
For the rain it rains every day
Bless thy five wits.
That way, madness lies

Doctor Allworthy from Stratford attended him throughout, but Sir James refused his potions and his advice, and even refused to be bled.

Finally, on the third day, Sir James dropped dead as he wandered in the hedge maze, with both Kate and Molly following at his heels.

The doctor concluded, "Be it melancholy or stroke, the man be dead, that there be no disputing of."

Molly took charge of the funeral arrangements and managing the household.

Kate and Will made plans for the future and carried them out. If the myth of Christopher Arden was to be preserved together with the terms of the will, they needed to act quickly. Will dealt with the solicitor, his boss, introducing him to Kate in the guise of Christopher Arden, who then hired him as agent to sell the estate and everything in it. She took a large sum in cash and had him invest the rest to ensure a substantial secure income. She was generous to Jane, Lucien, Simone, the household servants, and others who worked on the estate. She wrote glowing recommendations. She gave cash to Will to pay off Anne Hathaway, together with the promise of a recurring subsidy. Anne was pleased with the windfall and made no fuss that her husband was running off and leaving her with three young children. She had found life with him as unbearable as he had found life with her. "Good riddance to you," she told him. He told his parents and siblings that he was off to London to make his fortune.

Kate immersed herself in the details of preparing for their upcoming travel. That helped distract her from thoughts of her father and Gertie and the second Little Jimmie—for it had been another son. Childbirth was dangerous. Everyone knew the danger and yet enough people were willing to take the risk for humanity to perpetuate itself. Kate found that unfathomable. She couldn't stand the anxiety, much less the grief of having a child.

PART THREE: The Rest of the Story

43 ~ Padua

Kate was weak and needed to take naps twice a day, on doctor's orders. So, it took two days for Bill to read her the whole manuscript.

When Bill got to the end, she was surprised, "Is that all?"

"That's all you told me. That's all I know."

"Yes. Yes, of course. I forgot that all you know is what I've said. It sounded so real, so right, as if you had been there and witnessed it. And, yes, I'm sure that to you that feels like an ending, with the parallel of the beginning and the ending, with Flo present at both times for birth and death. But there's more story to be told, much more."

"Then tell me what happened next, and then next."

"This body won't last that long," she sighed. "I wish I could trade it for a younger one."

"You underestimate yourself. You aren't like other people. You're amazing."

"But at the end of the day, it's the end of the day, for me as for anyone else. I'm human, and this human body I find myself in is all too frail."

"Tell me. Just talk. I'll record it. Let's capture all that we can."

"If you wish, I'll tell you what I can in the time I have left. But it won't be like the first part that you've written, all in order, this then that. It would take too long to tell it that way. I'll jump ahead to the most important moments, like a frog hopping from lily pad to lily pad."

"Start with the *lost years*."

"*Lost years*?"

"Seven years. 1585 to 1592. That's what scholars call that time. Yes, scholars. Hundreds of brilliant men and women have devoted their careers to understanding your plays and speculating about Will's life."

She stared at him blankly.

He prompted her, "When you left Stratford, where did you go?"

"Italy."

"Verona?"

"Never Verona."

"But *Two Gentlemen of Verona, Romeo and Juliet.*"

"That was Will's idea of a joke. Padua mainly. Venice, too. Never Verona. In Padua, we went to the university. The lectures were in Latin, which we both knew well. We could also handle Italian, thanks to tutors. Molly and I had learned the rudiments from Lucien, and Will was a quick study. We went to Venice as tourists. We couldn't resist the temptation. We wore masks and costumes in public. Padua was our home. Venice was our playground, where we practiced the basics of stagecraft.

"It began by accident, simply from the masks and costumes. Will, Molly, and I would roll dice to decide who would be man and who woman for an excursion to Venice. Seeing us dressed that way, passersby presumed we were a troupe of entertainers. So, first we mimicked street performances we had seen, miming and clowning. Later, we acted out skits we dreamed up on the spot or improvised from prompts shouted by the crowd. In return, passersby would leave us coins. We didn't need money, having the full wealth of Sir James' estate at our disposal. But it was gratifying that people wanted to pay for what we had to offer. Over time, we fell into the habit of going to the Rialto or to San Marco Square. By the time we left Italy, we had built a regular audience. They expected us on the ides of the month— the fifteenth of March, May, July and October, and the thirteenth of the other months. We went to the Rialto one month, and to San Marco Square the next. No other troupe would perform there when we were expected. Our draw was so strong that others didn't try to compete."

"What about you and Will? From what you said before, it sounded like the two of you fell in love at first sight, not just once, but several times."

"*Love at first sight* is a misnomer, as if love were born the moment a couple first met, as if it depended on chance or choice. Our love for one another was who we were. We were bound to one another from birth, from before birth. It took time for us to recognize that fact, but we had no choice. Romeo and Juliet, Anthony and Cleopatra, Othello and Desdemona. Their love was their life, and they knew that. They would live together or die together. That's the way it was with Will and me. We were soulmates. We were one. That was our destiny."

"So, what happened between you after you left Stratford, when you were in Padua where no one knew you, and no one knew that you were brother and sister? Did you forget about incest and follow your instincts, your mutual attraction?"

"Would that we could have. Molly and I had slept together in the same bed since we were little. We shared all our thoughts, all our fantasies. Of course we were curious. We wondered what it would be like to be with a man, to have sex like men and women do. We played make-believe. Sometimes she was the woman, sometimes I was. Often, we touched and rubbed ourselves and one another, discovering what felt good and what felt very good.

"In Padua, the three of us shared one room, one bed. At the university, word got around that the Englishman was living with two women. That wasn't a matter of scandal. Rather it was a matter of pride. Will was envied by his peers for that. He had a following. His words were listened to, as if he had discovered the secret of earthly bliss. In reality, among us, it was little more than flirtation. Hugging, cuddling, kissing, but with restraint.

"That's all there was among us, until one day when we were reading aloud and acting out a play that Will and I were writing. It was our first play, a variant of an Italian play about Romeo and Juliet. Romeo had a girlfriend named Rosaline when he met Juliet. She was Juliet's cousin. In that early version of ours, Romeo was attracted to both women and was unwilling to commit to either. He wanted to see them both together. He wished he could be with both of them at the same time, to know for sure which one he loved. The scene that Will, Molly and I acted out tested the limits of what was natural, the boundaries and the entanglements of love and lust. Rosaline and Juliet were both drawn to Romeo. He was drawn to both of them. And the women were drawn to one another as well.

"Rosaline overheard Romeo talking to Juliet on the balcony. Seeking jealous revenge, Rosaline dressed as a man, wore a mustache and accosted Juliet repeatedly on the street. Juliet showed curiosity, interest. The two of them exchanged looks, notes, sometimes a few words. They arranged to meet at an inn. Rosaline invited Romeo to rendezvous with her in the same room, at same inn, at the same time. That's the scene we acted out to decide the likely outcome. We wanted to know if that encounter would lead to anger and tragedy or to three-way lust and pleasure."

"So, what happened?"

"Lust, after a sort. Despite the temptation, Will and I kept our distance from one another. We were restrained by the notion of incest. But Will and Molly, me and Molly connected without limits. Hence Will and Molly became lovers, and, through Molly, Will and I became lovers by proxy, though technically chaste toward one another.

"After that, I said to Molly, *I don't want to be tempted by him. Take him for yourself. He's yours.*

"She replied, *But you love him.*

"*As do you*, I said. *You can't fool me on that account. You can have his body*, I told her. *I just want his soul.*

"Once I'd said that, I couldn't unsay it. I couldn't undo what was done. And I don't know that I would have if I could. Molly wanted children and I didn't. Far too often, women died of miscarriage or childbirth. And I preferred playing the role of a man, without the legal limitations of being a woman. I enjoyed being close to Will. He was literally my other half. Together we were one person. To kiss, to touch, to hold him brought me to life. But I had no need for or desire for him to enter me and satisfy himself in me. For that, he could turn to Molly. She gladly serviced him. She loved him that way, and I was happy they could pleasure one another. Thanks to Molly, Will's physical satisfaction wasn't my responsibility, it wasn't my duty as it would have been if I were his wife. Even if he could free himself from his legal wife, the woman who had tricked him into marriage, I didn't want him that way. I didn't want or need a conventional life."

"When and why did you leave Padua?" asked Bill.

"Five years later."

"1590? Not 1592?"

"Yes, I'm sure it was only five years. I remember it by Molly's pregnancies and miscarriages. We left after her third. She needed a change of scene, anything to lift her spirits, and Will and I were ready to try our luck in London.

"While in Padua, we had written drafts of half a dozen plays. We thought that two of them were polished enough to stage. Others we would return to and rewrite later.

"We had heard that theater was all the rage in London. We thought we had talent as writers. This was the time and London was the place for us. Never before had there been such an opportunity for spinners of tales."

They stopped the day's narrative there. Bill wanted to keep going, but Kate was tired, and the doctor had said she needed lots of sleep. Bill told her, "I'm afraid I have to put out the light."

"And then put out the light," she replied with a grin. "And parting is such sweet sorrow."

"Until the morrow," he answered.

"A hug," she requested. "I deserve a hug for all this."

Without hesitation, he leaned down and hugged her warmly. When he stood up again, her eyes were sparkling like the eyes of a young woman. Her look was direct and penetrating. He felt a warmth on his cheek, then on his neck, as if a hand were caressing him.

"Will," she addressed him. "It's been so long, too long. It's so good to see you."

Bill didn't know what to make of this. Was she seeing and talking to a ghost? To a figment of her imagination? She wasn't looking over his shoulder. Her eyes were fixed on his.

"I'm Bill, not Will," he gently corrected her. "Bill Greene. Remember. The reporter, the writer, the one who's turning your story into a book."

She smiled. "Would that we had met before. We might have had jolly times together."

Had she lost her mind? Was this the end of the story? Was she now so deranged that he wouldn't learn anything more from her? He tucked her in and gathered up his notes. Still smiling, she rubbed her cheek against his hand. He was surprised how good that felt. He hoped that tomorrow she'd be lucid again.

44 ~ London

The next morning, Kate asked, "Where were we?"

"London. You were about to go to London."

"And when were we?"

"1590 you said."

"After Molly's third miscarriage. Now I remember."

"So, what did the three of you look like as you entered London for the first time?"

"Two bearded and mustached young men and a buxom very womanly woman. All three the same height, the same blue eyes, the same black hair and light complexion. We dressed as ordinary people. We didn't want anyone to know we were heirs to a fortune, returning from years on the Continent.

"In England, where morals were a matter not of personal choice but rather of law, we couldn't live openly together like we had in Padua. I dressed as a man and lived in a rented house with Molly, as if she were my wife. Will took bachelor rooms nearby. Often, we all had dinner together at a tavern and then spent the evening together at our house.

"As in Padua, when Will and I were going to be together in public, I donned a style of mustache and beard very different from his, so as not to draw attention to our similarity. But when the two of us were learning about the theater business, getting to know and to be known by people with influence, we deliberately looked the same and acted the same, one person who could be in two places at the same time.

"For the fun of it, sometimes Will and I would both cross dress— he as a woman and me as a man. I suspect our random experiences dressed like that, our encounters with strangers on the street and in taverns enriched our understanding of life and the quality of our writing. If I were running a school for players, that would be part of the training.

"Imagine London when theater, real theater, secular theater was new and wildly popular. Not tied to religious cycles, not depicting religious themes, not staged just for the rich and well born. Stories about real people performed for real people, masses of people, thousands of them, sometimes tens of thousands, nearly every day, sometimes twice a day, at two, three, four, sometimes as many as half a dozen different theaters. The freshness, the newness, the enthusiasm.

"Imagine the actors rehearsing the next play and performing the present one on the same day. Imagine the demand for new plays and the scramble to write them and rewrite them over and over to meet the fickle demands of producer, director, performers, critics, and audiences. Teams of writers and rewriters, most of them nameless, like stagehands, scrambling to move words around, which the actors often forgot or chose to ignore, improvising on stage. And if the audience liked what a player improvised, the new lines or the new tom-foolery became part of the play the next time it was performed. Imagine working that way, living that way, writing that way.

"Imagine the challenges of writing for the stage of that place and time. Telling a story not with words on a page, but rather with actors on a stage. The audience knew little or nothing about the story. If they missed a line because they weren't paying attention or because of random noise in the theater— a cough, a sneeze, people talking— that line was gone, there was no way for them to know what was said. And likewise, if they didn't see what's happening on stage, because of obstacles like heads and hats in front of them and the angle of their view of the stage. We didn't just need to write. We needed to double and triple write. We needed to repeat everything that was important for following the story, but without being boring to those who did see and hear it. Part of that redundancy was in the action and didn't appear in the script, but rather was developed in rehearsals. The actions and interactions of the players, including their gestures and intonations, needed to give clues to people in the audience who couldn't hear or couldn't understand the words. Mistakes would happen. Players would forget lines and others would have to fill in the gaps and improvise to bring the story back on track. The rehearsals weren't just to learn the lines as written, but also to practice improvising, making fixes on the fly, and prompting one another without losing the attention of the audience and the illusion of the story as it unfolded. The troupe always included one or more clowns who could distract and entertain the audience when mistakes were made, so the show could go on.

"I went to performances every day. Sometimes I watched the same play done by the same players several times and the experience felt different every time because one or another of the players was particularly good or bad that day, and the players made different mistakes and came up with different fixes."

"That sounds like Hollywood in the early days," said Bill

"Hollywood?"

"Movies."

"Movies?"

"Stories acted out, like plays, only recorded rather than live. Images can be recorded just like sound can. The recordings can be replayed many times for large audiences. And writers are hired to write and rewrite many times, often namelessly, to meet ever-changing needs and tastes. In the early days, inventing a new form of entertainment and a new business based on new technology, it was often chaotic, having to quickly find solutions to problems no one had seen before."

"So, you understand this crazy world that Will and I lived in. Keep in mind that Will wanted to be both actor and writer. Imagine acting, rehearsing and writing different plays on the same day nearly every day. He felt that the acting gave him insights into what made scenes and characters succeed or fail. And working together, we were able to accomplish what otherwise would have been impossible.

"The writing was the part that mattered the most to him, though it paid the least, for underlings like us, who namelessly rewrote what others had written. But to him it was magic to see his ideas come to life on the stage, to hear his words spoken by others to audiences of thousands. I felt that high as well. It was like living more than one life, being more than a mere person. And I became addicted to the frantic pace of life, the daily scramble to meet deadlines.

"From the beginning we focused on character, not plot. There were plots galore in history and printed stories and in plays that had been done before. What mattered was what the situation looked like through the eyes of the characters. We tried to put ourselves in the skin of one character after another and see the world as they saw it. After we had talked it out between the two of us and bounced our ideas off Molly, after we had a handle on the characters and when the play was ready to be written, Will, or I, or sometimes both of us would hear the characters speak and see them act. We'd wake up in the middle of the night and write it down quickly before forgetting it. Sometimes it was like taking dictation. Sometimes I wasn't even fully awake, and it was like sleep-writing. Then we'd talk it over in the morning, and edit and polish, while Molly made fair copies, clear and flawless.

"Our first two years in London were *lost years*, just as *lost* as our years in Padua. We first wrote plays together in Padua, early drafts of four plays, *Two Gentleman*, *Comedy of Errors*, *Taming*, and *Romeo*, as well as notes for half a dozen more. But no one cared. No one would talk to us much less read our plays.

"Our first break came after Will got a non-paying job as a bit actor, with non-speaking parts, three different parts in the same play. He changed his clothes to go from guard to servant to person in a crowd. The playwright who was supposed to finish a script needed for a performance a week after that fell sick, and the usual backup writers were committed to other projects. Will volunteered, and they let him try while they looked for a real writer. The two of us started, then I continued while Will went back for performances. We finished in just three days, and Molly made three fair copies of the entire thing. She could take our scrawl with its crossings-out and scribbles on the side and turn out a manuscript that was a joy to behold. Hers was the only handwriting that anyone on the outside ever saw with the name Shakespeare attached to it. That first time, our breakthrough moment, I suspect that the director wasn't impressed so much with the quality of the writing or even the speed with which we delivered, as with the neat penmanship, which made it easier than usual for the players to learn their lines.

"So, we were called upon again and again to rewrite scenes that others had written and to make last minute changes. We were nameless, working much and earning little for it, learning the craft, getting to know people in the business, getting known by them. There was no time to write our own scripts, and no one would have looked at them if we had. Beggars we were, picking up scraps left by others until we solved the puzzle of how to succeed in such a world."

Bill suggested, "And by going through all that, the two of you learned the craft of playwriting, which led to your ultimate success."

"Yes, we learned to write quickly and well and to rewrite even more quickly, never clinging to any part of the script as if it mattered, ready to change anything as need be. But our success depended on our learning the business side of theater, and then buying our way in after *The Shrew* was stolen."

"Stolen?" asked Bill.

"Our play, *The Taming of the Shrew,* that we wrote in Padua. Molly had made a dozen fair copies and Will had handed them out here and there, trying to spark interest soon after we arrived in London before we knew how the business worked. Then one day, months later, we saw posters advertising the upcoming performance of *The Taming of the Shrew.* Even our title. And keeping our name for the Shrew herself— *Kate.* The pirate dared to name her *Kate,* but didn't give his own name, so we couldn't confront him. He was *Anonymous.* He stole the basic ideas, rewrote it, improved it, and got it staged, giving Will no credit as author, much less paying him for his work. Will tried to claim his rights but was laughed away. No one believed that he had written it, and no one would tell him who *Anonymous* was. But it wouldn't have mattered if they had. A writer didn't own his work. Anyone could perform it or print it and claim ownership.

"Will was depressed. I was angry. Will saw no way out. I found a solution.

"The competition among writers was cutthroat. The successful writers, the ones who got their names attached to plays were all friends with one another. Most of them went to college together. They rewrote old stories. They rewrote one another's plays. They collaborated, sometimes the one and sometimes another taking credit. How could we break in and make Will a named writer rather than one of the nameless mob of flunkies?

"It wasn't a matter of talent. It also wasn't a matter of knowing the right people and making sure they knew you. And it wasn't a matter of doing favors and expecting favors in return. All of that would help once you broke in. But to step into the spotlight, to be singled out from the mob, to become a known quantity, we'd need to do something else, and fortunately we were in a position to do so.

"Although no one knew it, we were wealthy. The big-name writers in the university clique all needed money and competed fiercely with one another for what money was to be had from this business. But we didn't need to be paid. I, in the guise of Will, first brought the matter up with a producer. I handed him a copy of *Gentlemen of Verona*, not a great play, but good enough. And I told him that rather than he pay me for it, I would pay him if he would produce it. And I named a price high enough that his eyes sparkled. All I asked was that the name William Shakespeare be on all the posters, be included in all messages about this play. He agreed before he even read the play.

"It wasn't a hit, but it wasn't a failure, either. And in a single transaction, we—Will and I—were on the inside rather than the outside. Soon after that, we paid for *A Comedy of Errors* to be produced. Then we got our revenge on *Anonymous*. We took his version of our *Taming of the Shrew* and improved on that and had it produced under the name *William Shakespeare*. We were in, totally in."

45 ~ Kit and Kit

The next morning, Kate was brighter and stronger. She had a caregiver help her into her wheelchair. Then she steered herself to the dining room for breakfast and back again. When Bill arrived, she was itching to get started. She wanted to talk about Christopher Marlowe.

"There was only one man I ever lusted for, aside from Will. That was Kit Marlowe. He was a fine figure of a man and would have been attractive as a woman as well, with the right makeup and proper attire. Marlowe's mustache, like Will's, was false. He was baby-faced, like Will and like you, too, Bill. In my day, I would have liked you, had you been in my day.

"Marlowe was very like Will in genius and imagination. But he wasn't my twin. That meant I couldn't get inside his head, and he couldn't get inside mine. That also meant that there were no barriers to our connecting and mating. And why shouldn't I mate with him? Molly had Will, and Will had Molly. I needed my someone. I was entitled to my someone. The thought of him, my lust for him helped inspire me as Will and I worked on what became *Romeo and Juliet*, which we pursued on our own, before we had a theater company who wanted it.

"Even before I met him, I was intrigued by Marlowe, for what I had heard of his conceit, his self-confidence. He had no doubt that he was the greatest writer in London, maybe the greatest writer in the world.

"Kit and Kit. Two of a kind, but not of a kind. Kit, cat, smelled a rat. What could have been, what would have been wasn't. I saw much of Marlowe, but not enough. We were together much, but not together enough. Will and I had heard tell of him when we were in Padua. There were rumors of his fame and success and talk of his genius from travelers who had been to London. That talk may have ignited Will's ambition to be a playwright. No. Will was born to write, Marlowe or no Marlowe.

"When Will and I first arrived in London, Marlowe was the number one playwright. His name was enough to draw an audience. At first, I didn't believe there really was such a person. I thought he was a myth invented by a theater company, that he was a marketing ploy. But a few months later, Will saw him in the flesh, coming out of a theater and swarmed by fans. Will tried to give him one of his scripts, but Marlowe looked straight through him, as if he didn't exist. Then Marlowe joined a group of friends. They threw their arms around one another's shoulders and went to a tavern, pushing aside a crowd of worshippers who struggled to see him up close, to touch him, as if his magic power might rub off on them.

"Marlowe was a Cambridge man, the acknowledged master of the London stage, known throughout the civilized world, And Will was a newcomer, a nobody, who hadn't gone to an English university, who knew no one, who didn't have a clue about London theater. But we were all the same age. Marlowe was born the same year as Will and I, two months before.

"Two years later, our leverage on the business side of theater was growing. Three plays with the name *William Shakespeare* had been produced and were successful. Audiences responded to our work. The name of Shakespeare made a play more in demand than one by Anonymous.

Instead of us wanting a chance to help Marlowe with his plays, to build our reputation by association with him, he came to us, to Will that is, wanting Will to collaborate with him, first on *Edward III*, and then for the three parts of *Henry VI*. For *Edward III*, Will didn't have enough clout to get credit for himself, but he was able to negotiate a compromise. Will paid the producer enough to make up for what was lost in receipts by not putting Marlowe's name on it, and paid Marlowe enough not to mind the omission. For the *Henry VI* plays, Marlowe got the playwright's fee, Will invested in the production so he got a percentage of the receipts, and the plays appeared under the sole name of *William Shakespeare*, regardless of how much Marlowe might contribute to the writing.

"I took the meetings with Marlowe, all of them, for consistency. He found it hard to believe that Will was able to do as much as we did as fast as we did, and that the manuscripts he delivered were always flawless, without crossings-out or notes in the margin. Early on, Marlowe exclaimed, *My God, how do you do it? How do you find the time? Do you ever sleep? How is it that all I see is fair copy, finished copy, with no corrections?* We didn't want to undermine that reputation by letting people know that there were two of us, three counting Molly, and that we were wealthy and were breaking into the business by money as well as by talent.

"For *Henry VI*, I did the research and sketched out the plot. I claimed precedence on matters of history by family connection, since Warwick, the *Kingmaker* in those plays, was an Arden, perhaps an ancestor, at least a cousin of ours. Whichever side in the Wars of the Roses Warwick backed won, and whoever he supported for king became king.

"The quality of Marlowe's writing was far less than his reputation had led me to believe. There were fine phrases and quotable quotes, but his *Tamerlane* plays were all bombast. The scenes were excuses for loud impassioned speeches. There was little interaction among characters. If you impressed the masses with set, costumes, and spectacle, there was no need for the speeches to be intelligible. His *Doctor Faustus*, a crowd favorite, was little more than a variant on an old religious mystery play, featuring the seven deadly sins. He could have done better with his *Massacre in Paris* if he had ever been to Paris.

"I admired his *Edward II*. That had potential. With that, Marlowe started the craze for history plays that Will and I would cash in on. We did *Edward III* and *Henry VI* in collaboration with Marlowe. Then, on our own, we did *Richard II*, *Richard III*, *Henry IV*, *Henry V*. The common mob liked to see the wealthy, the royal, the noble, the famous paraded on stage for their amusement. Marlowe did that well. But our plays were dramas, not just pageants. We showed real men, with all the faults and fears and feelings of men. These weren't godlike figures to be admired and envied from afar. Rather, they were fallible creatures, no better than the people in the audience. They reigned thanks to luck and greed and power politics.

"It was a shock when I saw Marlowe for the first time. This young man who already was deemed one of the greats not just of the stage, but of all of literature, was shorter than I was. If we were to wrestle, I could probably throw him and pin him. But he gave me a look like no one ever had before, not even Will. He looked at me like he could see through me, like he knew everything there was to be known about me. I guessed that he sensed I was a woman from my response to him, the looks we exchanged, the random touching, the hugs at greeting and parting. And he smiled at me, like he knew that I knew that he knew. To him, my disguise was transparent. He glanced at my cotton-stuffed codpiece with a look of irony. To him, it must have looked too large and obviously false. To him, I was woman and he wanted me. That's what I saw, that's what I felt, that's what I believed. Will looked at me with restraint when we were naked in bed together with Molly. Kit Marlowe looked at me with unbridled lust. I quivered in response and took a step back, and he smiled even more broadly, indulgently, patiently. He was in no hurry. He knew I knew he wanted me, and he knew that sooner or later he would have me. His air of confidence was magnetic. His unspoken prophecy was self-fulfilling, and he knew it. Our minds met, as we worked together. He toyed with me, knowing that he could have me whenever he wished, enjoying the power he had over me, without our ever exchanging a word about it. When he was ready, he'd take my body as it had never been taken before. I enjoyed the tension of mutual attraction whenever we were in the same room together. I knew I was his and enjoyed the thought of that. And I waited patiently for his inevitable summons.

"One day, after we hugged in greeting, he grabbed my codpiece and reached in. His face blanched suddenly. _Nothing?_ he asked in disbelief."

"_Nothing._" I smiled. The moment I had been waiting for had come.

"_You're a woman? Good God! A woman? You flirted with me so brazenly. You showed off that over-sized sack between your legs. And it's nothing? Well nothing will come of nothing. You're a damned woman._"

"Was he joking? I couldn't make sense of what was going on. I stroked his cheek and said flirtatiously, "_Many a man would be pleased by that discovery._"

"_But I am not such a man. Who the hell are you? You're not Will Shakespeare._"

"I'm Kate. Will's twin sister, Kate. Also known as Kit."

"Kit?"

"Kit and Kit. It's fitting that we be together."

"Damn you! Get you to a nunnery. I'll have nothing to do with you or your conniving brother. Do what you want with the plays. I'm through. This is over."

"The veins on his forehead stood out. He gulped down the ale in the tankard in front of him and stormed out of the room.

"Imagine my pain. I had thought that I loved this man and that he loved me. How could I have so grossly misunderstood?

"Later, I heard that he got stinking drunk that day and started a brawl in a tavern, and it got nasty and violent. He died from a knife through his right eye.

"Afterwards, when I thought about what had happened, I blamed myself for my stupidity. I had played the role of an androgynous male all too well. He believed me, and he believed that I was of a similar bent. He believed I had implicitly come to an understanding with him. He couldn't be open about his preference for men. Sodomy was a crime against the Queen, punishable by death. But so long as he didn't make a public display of it, he could live and love as he pleased. And in his world, that I was woefully ignorant of, this was how such matches were made. It took me months to get over the shock of his shock and the shock of his death. It was like the death of Lew all over again."

As Kate spoke, Bill saw both Kate and Marlowe, Kit and Kit. He didn't just hear the words. He saw the two of them as if they were performing their flirtatious farce in a play or as a movie recorded from a play performance. It was a comedy of errors. Each was lusting for the other, sensing the other's lust at the same time, through look and gesture inching closer to the moment of truth, only that truth was different from what either expected.

And a strange emotion lit that stage he imagined. He saw that scene, as the two of them stood close together, through a filter of jealousy. Unaccountably, he was jealous of Marlowe there with Kate, with a young Kate, in men's attire and with mustache and beard. Bill knew she was woman, a woman in heat, wanting beyond wanting this other man who Bill envied. And the thought went through Bill's mind that despite all reality, despite all probability of time and space this woman was destined for him; she was his soulmate. If he had been in a theater, he would have rushed onto the stage and punched Marlowe and kicked him, knocked him senseless and picked up Kate and carried her offstage into life, real life together, forever and ever. Amen.

As he went over his notes that night, after returning home, and he reorganized them as chapters, he realized that part of the story was about Kate and him as much as it was about Kate and Will. He felt he was a party to what was happening as well as a witness. Seeing her with Marlowe was like seeing the woman he loved with another man, seeing her tricked and seduced and humiliated by that other man. He wanted to intervene and take her for himself. She was his, and he was hers Anything else, any impediment was fantasy and delusion.

That way lies madness, he thought. Such a ridiculous idea. How could he let that creep into his writing? He would have to edit that out later. He would have to write dispassionately. He would have to edit himself out and include just Kate and Marlowe, Kate and Will, and stay as close to what happened as he could. He, Bill, wasn't there, couldn't have been there, was not himself a witness to this, was not a putative lover of that young woman then or this ninety-nine-year-old woman now. Stuff and nonsense. Begone. That was a dance of sprites and fairies conjured by Prospero, only to vanish suddenly.

When he returned to Kate's room the next morning, he saw her through different eyes. He found it easy, as he had found it impossible before, to see her as her former self, to look into her eyes and imagine the young woman she once had been, as tall as he, with blue eyes, black hair, with mustache and beard which she removed slowly like a striptease revealing her womanly, lovely face, like someone in a movie removing the face mask of an old woman to reveal the beautiful young woman beneath. He blinked, and she was an old lady. He blinked again, and she was young Kate. He tried not to look straight at her but rather to focus on her words and the notes he was writing about her words and the story he could and would turn those words into.

46 ~ Career

On the story went, every day for a week. Kate recounted their career and their lives, but not in chronological order, rather in a series of digressions, as one memory triggered another. Bill stopped her frequently when she talked too quickly for him to understand the context. He asked questions to fill in gaps and to satisfy his curiosity. He had no idea how this woman could know what she knew, but he had no doubt that the story she was telling was true, that this was a first-hand account of events that had taken place nearly four hundred years before. Every bit of information he could glean was unique, precious, irreplaceable. It would be a challenge to make coherent sense of it all, but the kind of challenge you run toward, not away from. He would tackle the hard work of editing and writing later. For now, he was just a scribe, a secretary for a frail and dying old woman with an amazing tale to tell in her final days. He went about this work coolly, calmly and professionally, keeping his distance, avoiding looking her in the eye, so as not to be distracted by thoughts of his attraction to her.

Each night, he had dinner with Kathy and took her to a movie, and made passionate love with her, erasing his mind of all thoughts of and feelings for Kate.

Kate explained what she thought was unique about her and Will's writing. "We understood that the popularity of a play could depend on the appeal and talent of the actors, on the spectacle, the set, the costumes, on the clowning sideshows, on the impressive effect of loud bombastic speeches boomed forth with a convincing voice, on the surprise of revelations and plot twists. Will and I could use all those tools like other playwrights did. But we wanted more than that. We believed that we didn't need to appeal to the lowest taste and the lowest understanding to get a full house.

"If a play provides more than basic entertainment, if there's a reward to be had for paying attention to the words rather than just the action, people will come back to see it again. If it's good enough, people will come back many times, catching and understanding more of the dialogue and enjoying the show more each time. And people will repeat memorable lines and describe scenes to their friends, spreading the word and drawing still more people. A great play could draw a much larger audience than an ordinary one because of all the people coming back for more."

Bill asked her why blank verse? Why would a largely uneducated audience want blank verse?

She explained that that wasn't for the audience. It was for the players, to make it easier for them to learn their lines, which was a challenge considering how quickly they needed to prepare for the next show and the next, in addition to the one they were performing at the time. And it was far easier to write blank verse than rhyming verse.

Bill asked about the *Sonnets*. Who were they addressed to? And who was the *Dark Lady?*

"I don't know what you mean by *Dark Lady*," she answered. "Maybe you mean the poems that refer to my black hair. Over the years, Will and I sometimes amused ourselves and one another by writing sonnets to one another. It was a break from the chore of writing three or more plays a year and rewriting and updating other plays, including those of others, as the theater company required. A few times, someone got hold of copies of our sonnets and sold them to printers who published them with no order and no explanation, as if they had been written by one person whose sexual preferences seemed to switch back and forth, sometimes writing to a man and sometimes to a woman with expressions of love."

"Why did Will stop acting halfway through his career?"

"You might better ask why did he keep acting for so long? It was a drain on his energy, and he was nowhere near as good at acting as at writing. No one would miss seeing him on the stage. The theater company didn't need him that way. He had kept doing it for years out of habit, expecting that routine discipline, not even imagining that he could stop. When he did stop, it was a relief. Finally freed from that daily tension, he wondered why he had ever done it, except as training for writing for the stage."

Bill asked if Will ever went back to Stratford-on-Avon before his retirement, at the end of his career.

"Will didn't want to go near Anne. He provided generously for her. He sent her enough money to live comfortably, in the manner to which she was accustomed. She had tricked and cheated him. He wasn't going to let her do that again. He knew that Susan, the first child, wasn't his. And although twins ran in his family, and he had been to bed with Anne around the time she got with child the second time, he suspected that the twins might not be his, either. Anne simply couldn't be trusted.

"It was only about ninety miles from London to Stratford. That was three days ride on horseback. It was far, but not too far. If he had wanted to see her and the children, he could have gone many times. It would have been easy when we first arrived in London and had no responsibilities. Then later, he could have gone when the theaters closed for Lent or due to the plague, and the plague came back again and again. But he chose not to. He felt a responsibility to send money for the upkeep of the children, at least of the twins, who might be his by blood. But he made no effort to see them, since that would have meant seeing Anne, and he loathed her.

"When his son Hamlet died, the news came as a shock. Death became real for him, as it had for me with Lew and later with Marlowe. Anne didn't let him know that Hamlet was ill. And then she discouraged him from going to the funeral. Her letter said that he had died of the plague, though they buried him in an ordinary grave. She wrote that Will shouldn't take the risk. I suspect it wasn't the plague at all but rather that she didn't want to see him, any more than he wanted to see her.

"He never knew Hamlet. We had left Stratford and started our *lost years* when the twins were only a few months old. He wanted to move on. He wanted for us to have a life together and a chance at greatness. But his neglect of his son, if Hamlet was his son, weighed on his conscience. I believe he thought that one day he would make up for that neglect. And then that son was dead, so there was no way to make up for it, ever.

In the play, in the indecision and hesitation of Hamlet and his complicated relationship with his father, Will was in part brooding over the relationship he had never had with his son. Hamlet's sense of responsibility toward his father echoed Will's sense of responsibility toward the son he had abandoned. And Hamlet's obsession with incest was in part Will working out his feelings toward me, since our incestuous love was the reason why Will had left his son. Likewise, Hamlet's relationship with Ophelia, both wanting her and pushing her away, reflected our relationship, that we always had to keep our distance from one another and couldn't simply do what we were born to do. That, too, reflected on the question of fatherhood, wanting to be a real father with the woman he truly loved."

"What about Will and Molly?" Bill asked. "Did they remain lovers after Padua, through all the years in London?"

"Molly had had three miscarriages, with all that physical pain and heartache, while we were in Padua. But still she and Will made the beast with two backs. And still we frolicked, the three of us together those years we were in Italy. Death was cruel but we laughed in its face. We wouldn't let the fear of death keep us from enjoying what life we had. The plague, accidents of chance and accidents of the enmity of men, miscarriages in the womb and miscarriages of justice. Laugh and live on. Enjoy. Enjoy while you can enjoy.

"And so we continued in London. But after a dozen miscarriages, Molly wearied of sex. I forget the year. It was after Hamlet the boy died, while Elizabeth was still queen. Molly wanted children but she finally conceded she never would. And the pain of repeated anticipation followed by disappointment and grief was too much. Affection yes. There was always deep affection among the three of us. But sex as between a man and a woman, that stopped between Molly and Will soon after Hamlet died. Losing a child in the womb, one you had never held, had never known, was bad. But losing a child you had raised and loved eleven years—that was unimaginable. Molly never wanted to have to go through grief like that.

"Will felt cursed. First all those miscarriages, then Hamlet, then estrangement from Molly. He said that he and I were cursed at birth, that our inevitable love for one another was the cause. It mattered not that we were technically chaste with one another. In our imaginations, we had sinned together many times since we had found one another and learned the secret of our birth. Lust ungratified was still lust. And it was the lust not the act that was the sin. Our bodies hadn't sinned, but our souls had willingly, repeatedly. We had felt it, we had lived it. The sin was part of our being, like Macbeth and his Lady before they killed the king, like Brutus before he murdered Caesar, Othello before Desdemona, Hamlet before his mother and Claudius. The guilt came before the commission, and regardless of whether the sin was actually carried out. The act itself was but the fleshing out of what they had already done repeatedly in their minds. Their sin was who they were, beyond choice and beyond redemption. It was as if God Himself had sinned in creating us and making us such that we could not help but love one another. We were God's original sin, and we must suffer for what He had done. That was our cross, our unbearable cross."

***

That night Kathy was busy, so Bill went home alone and went to bed early. He tossed and turned restlessly, unable to sleep. He sensed that Kate was nearing the end both of her story and of her life. She would never make it to her hundredth birthday, which was just a few days away. He would miss her and the world of Elizabethan London that she had opened for him, and the dream that life did not end with death, and that past and present were linked in intricate ways, with souls somehow switching from one body to another.

When sleep finally came, he found himself in a time and place with everyone connected to all information and to everyone else as well. In the dream, he took that capability for granted. Everyone had it. Everyone had his or her own computer and all those computers were connected.

He woke from that dream into another in which he thought about the first dream and realized that such a capability was physically impossible.

Then he woke again and remembered Hawthorne had imagined something like that more than a hundred years before in *The House of the Seven Gables*, written at a time when electric power was new and its promise loomed large and exciting, and capabilities that had been impossible since the dawn of time were suddenly becoming real through a flood of life-changing inventions made possible by electricity. Man was becoming more than what man had ever been before. So, why not such a leap forward now, one based on computing power, connecting first everyone in the present and then going a step beyond that and connecting the present to the past as well. What a brave new world that could be. And perhaps that could happen even in his lifetime.

If the time dimension could be connected, he could interact with people from the past as well as the present. In that case, the people in the past wouldn't remember encounters with people from the future because that would spawn anomalies, altering what happened in their time and leading to different futures. But if the people in the past forgot everything they heard from people in the future, such communication was feasible.

In that case, he'd be able to connect with Kate, the real Kate, the Kate who lived around 1600. He could learn what she was thinking and feeling, what she saw and heard and understood. He could share her experiences. Their minds could be connected. Their souls could touch. And even if the Kate here in the twentieth century were to die, as she certainly would soon, his connection with the real Kate, the Elizabethan Kate could continue.

In his dream, he laughed at himself for having such a science fiction utopian idea, but he wished for it all the same. In the present, he felt closely connected to Kate, to the ninety-nine-year-old Kate. He felt closer to her than to Kathy whom he loved dearly in the flesh, closer than he had felt about anyone before.

47 ~ Belated Seduction

Kate finished her tale the following morning.

"Under King James, when Will was well established, part owner of the theatre and the troupe, when he no longer had to act as well as write, my role changed. I no longer wrote, though I would read and critique, and we would read lines together aloud, he taking some parts and I others as we smoothed and polished. So, I was not the author, though I was a helper of *Lear, Macbeth, The Tempest* and others. And he sometimes would hire other playwrights, like Middleton and Fletcher, to collaborate with him, especially toward the end, when his powers were fading and he couldn't meet a deadline, and he didn't want to admit his weakness to me and beg me to rescue him. But even near the end of his writing days in London, he had his flashes of brilliance. *The Tempest* was my favorite.

"And I saw them all. I went to the theater every day and watched not just his but many others. He was addicted to writing. He needed to do it. It was who he was. I was addicted not to writing, but to the theater itself

"We still saw each other nearly every day and talked for an hour or more. Our casual talk was often laced with lines from our plays. That had become a game of ours, using a quote when it fit the thought of the moment, then laughing together if the line had been right, very right.

"But as he got older, his interests changed. He bought a big house in Stratford for his old wife. He invested in land near there. He spent a ridiculous sum to obtain the rights to a bogus coat of arms. That wasn't the Will I had known and loved. We drifted apart. We still met often, but out of habit, rather than desire. We'd sit together at a tavern and say little or nothing, certainly nothing of consequence.

"There was no special connection between us anymore, no flirtatious looks and touches, and no hint of secret intimacy. We would shake hands and hug when meeting or parting at a tavern, as any two men who were friends. That's what we were to one another—two men who were old friends. I always dressed as a man in those days. That felt natural to me, so I continued to do so after there was no need for me to pretend to be him in public to allow him to be in two places at the same time, doing double the work of an ordinary man.

"Molly kept her distance from him, not wanting to be tempted and wind up with another miscarriage. She and I still lived together and were still close, very close. The neighbors and the friends we had in common all knew us as a married couple, she the wife and me the husband. We had a good life together and shared everything and comforted one another in bed at night. But even with her support and closeness, something was missing from my life. I felt incomplete with Will at such a distance, with me never being in his mind and he never being in mine. The further I felt from him, the more I felt the need to be close to him, not just close as we were before, but physically close as well.

"As I neared the time when I could no longer bear a child, I was still a virgin in the literal sense of the word, and I began to regret my life choices. I wished I had had children and wished I had had physical intimacy with a man. I wanted the experience to know what it was. I, who had written so much about love, wanted to know what love was in its entirety, in the flesh as well as the imagination. I wanted it with him, with Will, who I had felt closer to than any other human being. And I wanted to bear a child, to raise a child, to feel that deep and fleshly bond as well, which is an essential part of life and living. But I couldn't have Will, the only man, aside from Marlowe, who I ever wanted that way. The very source of our more than natural closeness and attraction, the fact that we were brother and sister and that we were twins as well, ruled that out. Any offspring of ours would be deformed, doomed from birth to a life of misery and probably a short life.

"I couldn't do that. I wouldn't do that.

"And then the day came when the curse went away, the curse that was a promise, a recurring reminder that at my core I was a woman and could bear a child. I had passed the age of childbearing. Sometimes there would be a spotting, but never the full flow of blood that I had had every month since that first time in the schoolroom in Stratford. It was time. The end was as natural and unavoidable as the beginning had been. But it wasn't the end of my life or my longing. I was still a woman at my core, and at times when Will reached another peak of brilliance, writing in a way that made me see and feel the world as if it were newly created before my very eyes, I lusted for Will with all my soul and all my body as well.

"*The Tempest* was the tipping point. Not the performance, which was later. The writing, the first fresh conjunction of those words. It was magical. I was forty-five years old, beyond childbearing and hence, in my mind, beyond the prohibition and the curse of incest. To my mind, by getting rid of the one curse, I had gotten rid of the other as well. Nothing stood in the way of he and I finally making the beast with two backs.

"It wasn't romantic. Far from that. I got him drunk. He had a talent for impregnating women while he was intoxicated. He didn't know what was happening, and I didn't know what I was doing. There was no pleasure in it for either of us. Anyone seeing us would have considered my acrobatics a comedy of errors. But I went through with it. The deed was done, and I wondered why I had bothered to do it and would have been glad to forget it. I dressed him and myself and waited for him to wake up and be gone. He would have thought that we had fallen asleep together drunk, as we had sometimes in the past, and that, like before, nothing had happened between us. But I forgot the blood. I had been a virgin, and he saw the blood of my lost maidenhead on the bedding. Seeing that, he knew what we had done and fled without a word.

"When I knew I was pregnant, I told Will. He was horrified and insisted that I end it. I said that I would and sent him a note saying I had. I never saw Will after that.

"I named our son *Hamlet the Sequel, Seek* for short. Molly and I raised him together. Molly was ever vigilant, ever careful. She was up with him most of the night every night, for months. He was the child that Molly always wanted but couldn't have."

"And what about Will?" Bill asked.

"He lingered on in London for a while. He paid Fletcher to write three plays with him, terrible plays. And he made plans to return to Stratford. Living with Anne was to be his hair shirt, his self-punishment, his way of atoning for the sins of a lifetime, including his unwitting mating with me. He settled his financial affairs and extricated himself from his responsibilities to the theater company but procrastinated for nearly four years before finally making the move. Over that time, we didn't see one another, and he had no idea that we had a son."

"And did anything special happen on the last day that you remember?"

"I told you that before. And you wrote it. I remember clearly your reading it back to me. I was standing on the dock with Molly and Seek, ready to board a ship to France. Seek was six years old. It was my birthday and Will's birthday, April 23, our fifty-second birthday. I felt a pull toward Will. I tried to project myself to him, like I hadn't done in many a year. But he was dead, you tell me. And I woke up here in this old woman's body, nearly four hundred years later. That's the end of the story, a tale told by an idiot." She chuckled.

Epilogue

Bill was with Kate when she died the next morning.

As he looked into her eyes, a moment before they shut forever, Shakespeare's description of Cleopatra occurred to him. *Age cannot wither her, nor custom stale her infinite variety.*

Kathy was there beside him, hugging him and comforting him, as the doctor checked for a pulse and confirmed what they already knew. Then as orderlies and caregivers went about their accustomed business of dealing with the remains, Kathy led Bill to her office, shut and locked the door, pulled down the shade, and kissed away his tears. Soon they were on the rug making love like they had the day they met, with passion the like of which they hadn't felt since then. In their hunger for one another, they forgot about everything but the touch and taste of one another.

Afterwards, stretched out, physically and emotionally drained, Bill said, "It makes no sense. I have these notes, this incredible story. And yet it's as if it never happened, as if it were just a dream."

She flashed her eyes at him as she replied, "We are such stuff as dreams are made on."

He stared at her. Those eyes weren't Kathy's eyes. "Kate," he exclaimed.

She nodded and smiled.

"How is that possible?"

"There are more things in heaven and earth, Horatio."

"But if you're Kate, where's Kathy?"

She laughed, "I imagine she's waking up in my body on the dock about to sail to France. What fun she'll have figuring out life back then in the body of a fifty-two-year-old woman."

"But if that were possible, she'd be in danger. She knows nothing about that time. Whatever she'd say would sound like madness or even witchcraft. They burnt witches in that day."

Kate showed no sign of concern. "She has Molly. She has Seek. She's bright. She's educated. And she knows the future. She'll get along. I'm sure others have, many others."

"But I've never heard of such a thing."

"Because they've blended in and done it so well."

He laughed. This was the body of Kathy and the soul of Kate. What more could he wish for?

"Kiss me Kate," he ordered with authority.

And she did.

About the Author

Richard lives in Milford, CT, where he writes fiction full-time. He worked for DEC, the minicomputer company, as writer and Internet evangelist. He graduated from Yale, with a major in English, went to Yale grad school in Comparative Literature, and earned an MA in Comparative Literature from the U. of Mass. at Amherst. At Yale, he had creative writing courses with Robert Penn Warren and Joseph Heller.

His published works include: *Parallel Lives, Beyond the 4th Door, Nevermind,* and *Breeze* (published by All Things That Matter Press, *The Name of Hero* (historical novel), *Ethiopia Through Russian Eyes* (translation from Russian) *The Lizard of Oz* (satiric fantasy), and pioneering books about Internet business. His web site is seltzerbooks.com

Shakespeare's Twin Sister **and Richard's four previous novels** **(*Parallel Lives, Beyond the 4th Door, Nevermind,* and *Breeze*) can be** **read in any order. They are independent stories, with overlapping** **themes and styles. Each novel presents a different view of reality, a** **different way of trying to understand the mysteries of life.**

ALL THINGS THAT MATTER PRESS

FOR MORE INFORMATION ON TITLES AVAILABLE FROM
ALL THINGS THAT MATTER PRESS, GO TO
http://allthingsthatmatterpress.com
or contact us at
allthingsthatmatterpress@gmail.com

**If you enjoyed this book, please post a review on Amazon.com and
your favorite social media sites.
Thank you!**

www.ingramcontent.com/pod-product-compliance
Lightning Source LLC
Chambersburg PA
CBHW071432260626
47170CB00008B/2680